Street SWEEPER CHRONICLES

DISHONORABLE DEEDS

Anthony Hicks

EST. 2022

TOP of the LINE
PUBLISHING

Published By

TOP OF THE LINE PUBLISHING
Email: RaymarrLewis@TopoftheLinePublishingLLC.onmicrosoft.com

STREET SWEEPERS CHRONICLES DISHONORABLE DEEDS. Copyright © 2021 by Anthony Hicks and Keya M Myers

Cover Design by Lamar H.

<u>Dedication</u>

"To my daughter Kamanii and to my brother Rocky be in peace"

<u>Prologue</u>

Lying on her left side in the spoon position, Olivia stretched her right leg up until her knee kissed her chin, allowing deeper penetration.

"Yes! Right there, right there, right there!" Olivia whimpered in a muffled cry.

Feeling her partner on the brink of climaxing, her body quivered from the pounding she received as he lustfully whispered in her ear.

"That's how you want it?"

"Yes! Don't stop. Right there, right there, right there, right there, right there. Ohh god, I love you, Abdul!" She wailed in pleasure, spasming as orgasms shot through her body.

"Damn, that was the bomb." She heard Abdul say as he rose from the bed and exited the room. "You lucky you ain't wake the kids."

Basking in the bliss, Olivia laid there in all her glory as her mind raced and emotions began to surface. Then, just as she'd done so many times before, in an almost trance-like state, she began considering her life and all she had.

In these moments when Olivia reflected on her life, she always found her thoughts drifting from Abdul and the love he showered on her and their kids to the way he took responsibility for all of their well-being. It was these warm thoughts that usually gave rise to her darker, more pessimistic thoughts.

Generally comfortable with her life and the current state of their family, Olivia's cynical way of thinking had, on many occasions, created anxiety. This caused her to stress herself out, thinking about how vulnerable it all was. Even after watching Abdul do all he could to rid them of her check-ered past, preserve the unity of their family, and provide a sense of security, Olivia was still plagued by the nightmare that her past would destroy every-thing in her life today. She remained deep in these thoughts until the cries of a baby demanded her attention.

Olivia exited the bedroom, grabbed a robe, and stepped over cap guns, Legos, and other toys as she made the short trek across the hall. Minutes later, in search of a bottle, she carried their infant into the kitchen where a half-dressed Abdul stood at their kitchen table, covered in individual bags of cocaine.

"Somebody buying all that?"

"Yeah." He replied, grabbing a small handgun off the table and tucking it in the rear of his waistline.

"So you leaving before the kids go to school?"

"Yeah, I'm trying to make these drops before I go to work."

"Damn, how you know I was finished getting it in?" She asked, getting a bottle from the refrigerator. As she turned around to confront Abdul, she was interrupted by the sound of heavy knocks on the apartment door.

"Who the fuck is that?"

"I don't know, but we ain't done talking." She declared, storming off down the unlit hall, passing the first two bedrooms and then passing the last bedroom where her five and eight-year-olds slept. Olivia approached the apartment's front door and called out.
"Who is it? I said who..." Was all she managed to say before the door swung open only feet away from her.

Without looking to see who stood outside the apartment, Olivia, just making it past her son's room, spun on her heels to retreat down the hall. Just making it past her son's room.

"Gun!" Was all she heard before a piercing sensation of immense heat struck her back, knocking her forward.

"My baby." She cried out, but could not even hear her own words as a barrage of gunfire overwhelmed her ability to hear.

Facedown and all of a sudden feeling devoid of energy, the sensation in her back and legs quickly went from hot to cold, and Olivia, after vain at-tempts to lift her body off her child, felt as though the weight of the world was on her back. "Was this what it had come to?" Would everything end here? She thought, fighting to remain conscious. "Hell no!" She had Abdul, and one way or another, he would get them out of this. Sooner or later, he would be coming with guns blazing- but where was he now?

Gathering whatever little strength she had left, Olivia somehow managed to turn her head towards the kitchen. As she struggled to see through the dark soot and smoke clouded hallway, she noticed what she believed was her son's toy cap gun lying only a foot ahead of her. Just as the gunfire seemed to cease, her vision began to adjust, and she could vaguely make out an image of Abdul sprawled out on the floor at the end of the hall.

Chapter One

"Don't forget, I'ma need you to..."

"Pick you up in an hour." Omar cut off his girlfriend Tiffany before kissing her.

"Please don't have that shit in your car no more." She pulled away, climbing out of the jeep.

"I love you too."

"What she going to a clinic for anyway?" Omar's lil homie Black asked, getting into the front seat of the G-Wagon as Tiffany approached the front doors of the clinic.

"She think she pregnant."

"Really? More reason we need to get this bag today."

"Facts, You need to hit that nigga Twizzy Rollack and see what type of chicken he trying to spend.?"

"Already done. I busted it up with son so I could see where he at, if he outside on the block or at the Murder clubhouse."   "Nah, aint nobody trying to hit the projects and be in that crowded ass clubhouse today. It's always way too many niggas in there for me anyway. That shit like a death-trap."

"That aint where they at anyway." Black laughed, lighting a blunt as Omar maneuvered his white on black Benz in and out of traffic. "He in Jersey City on a block with a couple of his lil homies and the other two homies. I think one of them named Charley and the other one is something like Afghanistan or Taliban or something."

"Who?"

"The two brothers. They both west side, you gotta remember them. I think one of them Neighborhood and the other one Brim. They took our info when we sold them the handguns like a year ago, and they been getting at us ever since, trying to get us to link up with the homies out in Newark and Paterson."

"Oh, the dread head niggas that look like they Jamaican. Always on motorcycles and shit, Charley and Taliban."

"Yeah, that's them."

"What you think they trying to spend?"

"I don't know cause I don't remember the figures from before. I do remember Charley and Taliban spent something heavy cause they came with the money in a duffle bag and when we was leaving I was calling them cop heavy gang."

"Oh yeah. I remember the bag, and I remember you calling them that."

"If I aint mistaken." Black began passing Omar the blunt. "I think they both was somebody under they hoods too, that's why they was able to drop all that chicken like that."

"Yeah, they wasn't just copping for they self or for they block."

"They was copping for they sets."

"Kitty money. I hope that's how they coming today. What about Twizzy Rollack? What you think he trying to do?"

"I don't know. I'm looking for him to drop like six or seven, probably ten tops. You know I follow him on the gram and shit and based off his posts and everything it's looking like he out here getting that chicken. Plus, I heard something about him just moving up and getting some new status or something, so he might be trying to show time or anti up for his lil homies. If that's the case, you already know he could wind up dropping double the numbers I'm expecting."

"Damn."

"Yeah. It's real. Doing the math, you already know if shit go the way I'm thinking, we gon need to get some more shit out of storage before we can even think about going to New York to see niggas tonight."

"I'm saying, if shit close to what you think, and we get low like that we just gon have to shoot by my g-moms spot and pick up what I got left their cause I don't feel like going through all that shit in storage today."

"Hold up, bruh. You still got shit at your grandmother house?"

"Couple crates of shit in the basement but she don't go down there so it's good."

"You terrible," Black said with a laugh as Omar turned the vehicle up another street.

Arriving on the inner city block less than twenty minutes later, Omar, looking out the window at a bunch of homies spread out on the corner, made a left turn onto the tight one-way traffic block. Driving past the crowd, he stopped at the midpoint of the block and parked behind a burgundy Suburban. Then, upon exiting the vehicle, he and Black were greeted with signature handshakes from their three counterparts.

"What up, though? What's rolling, bruh?" Charley began addressing Omar. "If it's possible while they handling business over here, I wanted to step to the side or cross the street with you so we could bust it up about some personal shit. My bruh got my chicken, and he already knows what I want. Aint no money lost or nothing, I'm just trying to pick your brain about some shit that crossed my ears."

"Fuck all that, what's popping nigga? Let me see that work." Twizzy Rollack began sounding animated as Omar and Charley crossed the street.

"Come on bruh, kill all that loud shit," Taliban stated. "You gon draw unwanted attention, and aint nobody trying to go to jail."

"This the mother fucking Murder hood. You aint see all them goblins up the block? Police aint coming through here with no dumb shit."

"Aight. But we still don't need no heat with all this shit out here." Black added, opening the trunk of his SUV. "Welcome to the candy store. We got ten AKs, ten SIG Suar-two twenty-seven semi auto pistols, twelve Mac-tens, twelve Mac-elevens, twelve compact M.P.5-k's, four M-sixteens and four M-ninety's."

"Fuck everything else." Rollack cut in, grabbing the largest weapon he had seen. "How many of these you gon give me for nine?"

"What the fuck is that?"

"We call it the M-ninety. It's a stronger version of an M-16." Black told Taliban as he grabbed the assault rifle from Twizzy. "I see you got champagne taste with malt liquor money."

"Twizzy you aint even know what the fuck that was."

"It don't matter. I know it looks sexy as hell, so I need one."

"What the fuck is that under the barrel?"

"It's like a M-two-o-three small grenade launcher. This whole shit is like a modified, souped up M-sixteen with a grenade launcher on it. It's the gun Scarface had at the end of the movie."

"Okay, you wanna play rough." Twizzy Rollack mimicked Tony Montana before addressing Black. "Let me hear some prices."

"You said you got that nine right, that's all you can spend?"

"Hell no. You in the Murder hood talking to Twizzy Rollack, aint no limit on what I got."

If you got more than fourteen, we could work something out and give you a deal. Don't go crazy or nothing, we reasonable as fuck, but you gotta be realistic and let us know what other shit you was trying to get."

"You know I got homies in Newark, Paterson, Camden, Trenton and couple other spots that's trying to see you about getting some iron and shit, so how you wanna go about linking up with them?"

"I'm saying, long as they coming correct, I'ma have Black hit a couple of them when we ..."

"Whoa, hold up. Let me stop you for a second." Charley interrupted. "It's a reason I came across the street with you to chop it up about this. I know that's your lil homie, so you gon rock with him. But the homies out here that I'm trying to put you on with don't know son so they aint trying to fuck with him. Yeah, niggas don't know you either but they still trying to do something with you cause they know me. And me and Taliban and vouched for you."

After looking into the trunk full of assault weapons and doing a lil haggling to negotiate numbers, Rollack agreed on the details of a purchase.

"I got the money in my g-ride, so I'ma shoot up the block and pull the car down here."

"Now what's popping with y'all?"

"We trying to get some of everything," Taliban answered Black as he began removing small wads of money from the duffle bag thrown over his shoulder.

"This why I call you niggas cop heavy gang."

"Aint no need to waste time. I come through and unload the bag on you cause we here for the best shit you got."

"What's this, fourteen knots of all fifty dollar bills?" Black asked, flipping through the wads of money.

"Fifty, fifty dollar bills in each knot."

"That's like what, twenty-five hundred in each? So, this is like thirty-something racks?

"Thirty-five even." Taliban clarified, "I'm saying, I aint trying to go back and forth with you, but half of this chicken came from Brim, and the other half came from Neighborhood. Something like seven racks out of the Neighborhood half came straight from the homie Mill Hood in Newark. That said it'd be fucked up for me and Charley to leave here without three of them M-ninety's cause we both trying to get one and the homie Mill need one too."

"I don't know how I can argue with that." Black laughed, helping Taliban put the three assault rifles in the back of his Suburban before they negotiated the rest of their deal.

"I hope y'all got my shit ready." Twizzy Rollack said double parking a red Audi R8 Quattro and blocking in the rear of Omar's Benz truck.

"Took long enough nigga, you better have every dollar of that eighteen."

"Why the fuck wouldn't I?" Rollack challenged hopping out and joining Black and Taliban at the trunk.

"You telling me the homies you trying to plug me in with is willing to fuck with me even though they don't know me, but they won't fuck with my lil bruh strictly because they don't know him?"

"Come on, bruh, don't even try to make it sound like it's the same. You know you and your homie got completely different circumstances." Charley reminded. You aint originally from Jersey or the East Coast, period. So niggas in Jersey know that they shouldn't know you. But your homie is from Jersey, the same city I'm from, born and raised, and nobody knows him.

"I know him. That's my lil bruh."

"Personally, I aint saying he shouldn't be. I don't know son and I don't know if it's some shit wrong with him or not. All I do know is right or wrong niggas got they reasons they feel skeptical about him."

5

"And what's these reason?"

"I'm saying." Charley began slowly. "I aint into the gossip shit bruh. All I can tell you is on top of niggas not being able to find any stand up mother fuckers from son hood who can vouch for him, I heard niggas bring up and question a case he caught for a body he supposedly bailed out on a couple years ago. Long story short, it's being said that the circumstances surrounding that case were suspicious as hell."

"Now it sound like you trying to say he a rat."

Briefly laughing, Charley stepped closer to Omar, looking him in his eyes as he spoke.

"I don't know how much you know about me bruh, but I don't try to say shit. If I got a message for you, you gon get it. No subliminals. Dig me?"

"I was thinking." Rollack began. "You should keep like three of them Macs and throw me another one of them M-nineties cause when Hoffa come home he gon need one and aint nobody touching mine."

"Can't do that. No disrespect, but me and Omar don't even know this nigga Hoffa you talking about. Plus, the four M-nineties we had is gone."

"Hoffa my twin nigga."

"What up, what's good with Twizzy Hoffa anyway?" Taliban asked, redirecting the conversation from the rear driver side door of the Suburban. "I forgot your brother was still behind the wall."

"He's about to max out next month."

"He good, right?"

"Come on, bruh, that's my twin. I wouldn't be out here spending this chicken if that nigga needed anything." Rollack said, almost sounding insulted.

"What up, big bruh?"

"Y'all still handling business." Rollack's lil homies walked up greeting.

"Nah, we done. I want y'all to ride with me. We are about to go somewhere to test fire these ratchets. But first, let me introduce y'all to the homies." Rollack replied as someone began struggling to maneuver a Chevy around his double-parked Audi.

"Y'all got dope out here?" The old white man driving the Blazer interrupted the group.

"Nah, unc. That's all up the block. You rode right past it."

"All right then. Thank you, sweetie!" A white lady screamed from the passenger as their vehicle picked up speed.

"Like I was saying, Taliban and Black, these my lil homies right here." Twizzy introduced before continuing with an afterthought. "Black why the fuck you aint say nothing about selling me none of the things that shoot out the bottom of these M-nineties?"

"Cause they grenades. They like short range RPG's and we aint got none of them shits right now. We are looking, though. We come across them; I have you in mind.

"Rollack what the fuck is you trying to do with that anyway?" Taliban challenged as the earlier seen white Blazer approached again.

"I'm trying to blow something the fuck up. First nigga run around disrespecting the gang or the set I'ma ground zero his whole fucking block."

"It sounds..."

"Freeze!" The older white man demanded, jumping from the white Chevy.

"Hey! Hey! Don't try anything, you two." Added his female partner, training her glock nineteen on Charley and Omar. "Hands where I can see them! Now!"

"Aight, calm down."

"Wasn't y'all just trying to buy something a minute ago?" Taliban asked the guy wielding the service weapon as he cautiously approached the group of five men.

"Jersey City police department, narcotics division. We've received information about suspicious activity, and it appears you're currently involved in a transaction. We're just going to check you and these vehicles. I need all hands on top of the nearest car."

"Narcotics, requesting back up in the Greenville area. The current location is Grant Avenue, between Bergan and MLK Drive. The female stood in the street, reporting into her radio as the two groups of men complied with the orders.

"Two pigs can't lock all of us up."

"I'm working on it," Taliban whispered, looking over the top of the vehicle across the street to his brother.

Staring at each other, the two seemed to communicate through looks or, at the very least, had nonverbally agreed. After a positive head nod, in one fluid motion, Charley ducked behind the vehicle, drawing his weapon, and reached back over the car's trunk to fire at the female officer who stood in the street. With the first two slugs striking her midsection, she hit the ground hard before gaining her composure and dragging herself behind the safety of a parked car.

"Officer down! Officer down! Shots fired! Officer down! Shoot out in progress at the Greenville location!"

Standing behind the group of five men when the shots rang out and seeing his partner collapse surprised the male officer. Struggling to maintain an offensive position, he sidestepped to the right, vainly attempting to see where the men across the street had gone. But, briefly taking his eyes off the five men on his side of the street, he didn't see Taliban reaching until it was too late.

Taliban turned, pointing his weapon, and opened fire on the foolish cop, hitting him in the chest. Repeatedly struck center mass, the man stumbled backward, desperately trying to aim his weapon. Then, being hit with a third bullet, out of sheer response to the impact, the male officer squeezed his trigger, and one errant bullet struck Taliban's left shoulder blade, knocking him down.

"Come on, bruh!" Black yelled, grabbing Taliban's other arm as the faint whisper of sirens could be heard.

"I'm good!" Taliban yelled back, pulling away.

Putting the SUV in drive, Charley turned his head just in time to see his brother jump in the passenger seat.

"Took your scary ass long enough."

"Aight, go nigga!"

"You got hit?" Charley demanded, pulling the SUV away from the curb as his brother reached to the rear of the vehicle for something.

"I think it went in and out."

"You think?"

"Man, fuck all that and drive!" Taliban scolded his brother as he positioned the barrel of an assault rifle out his window.

"Don't even worry about this; I got the wheel," Charley said, looking back and forth from his brother to the road ahead.   Then, a police cruiser partially turned onto the block and stopped in the middle of the intersection, cutting them off as the officers hopped out with guns drawn, he warned.

"Hold on!"

Looking up to see what the concern was, Taliban jammed a half-loaded clip into the assault rifle as they approached the cruiser behind which the officers seemed to be positioned.

"Fuck!" Twizzy Rollack shouted at his two lil homies as his sedan pulled out between the two SUV's.

"Y'all aint get hit, right?"

"They're trying to block us in," Black confirmed, pulling his torso back into the vehicle after hanging out the window to look.

"It don't matter. That Suburban's gon smash right through it."

"Knew we should of just met them niggas at they clubhouse."

Opening fire on the approaching SUV, the two officers received a rapid burst of assault rifle fire in response. Seeing that the driver or gunman wouldn't stop, the officers tried to flee to safety just before the SUV smashed into their cruiser. Sadly, one of them wouldn't make it.

Trying to minimize the collision, Charley held his head down while steering the SUV, as it smashed and easily forced the cop car out of its way. Taliban also held his head down but somehow managed to look up just enough to see the officer on his side trying to duck and run for cover. Pulling the trigger, Taliban sent six spent projectiles into the back of the cowardly officer.

After the cruiser was pushed aside, the SUV completed its right turn, and Taliban glanced back at three more cop cars approaching the block from its left side. The speeding cruiser in front was trying to turn right off Martin Luther King Drive onto Grant Avenue when it collided with the Audi that was trying to follow the Suburban's right turn off the block.

Twizzy's Audi was knocked halfway onto the sidewalk. This caused the passenger side of his vehicle to knock loose the corner fire hydrant, sending a stream of water into the air. Seeing this, Omar stomped on his break with his whole body weight, desperately trying to stop his Benz truck. However, having no time, the front passenger side of his SUV rear-ended the back driver's side of the Audi, forcing him to a complete stop.

After a moment, Twizzy Rollack managed to pull his head from in between the two inflated airbags and heard numerous shouts of inaudible commands but only comprehended one.

"Freeze! Don't move!"

Chapter Two

In a small, dimly lit room, one of the interrogating officers sat behind a small wooden table across from a handcuffed detainee. The second interrogating officer stood at the head of the table.

"Mr. Brown, I don't think you understand the severity of what's happening." The first officer played it nice.

"One highly honored and decorated dead police officer, five other officers hospitalized getting serious treatment right now along with one of your boys. Another one of your fucking boys is dead right now. All cause you fucking hoodlums running around totting guns like you're some fucking warlord! But you sit here saying you don't know what the fuck is going on!"

"Nah, I don't."

The second, more seasoned Officer dropped a clear zip-lock property bag on the table and paced the floor behind the detainee before beginning his inquiry. He rested his hands on the detainee's shoulders from behind and then whispered in his ear.

"In that bag, along with other shit we dug out of your pockets, is your phone, and in that phone is the phone number or some type of social media shit you're going to use to reach out to the ass hole responsible for the death and injuries of my officers."

"I don't know what you're talking about."

"You know exactly what I'm talking about!" He almost yelled, slamming the prisoner's head down until his face smashed into the table.

"I'm telling you, man. I don't know what you're talking about."

"You know what the fuck I'm talking about."

"No, I don't." The detainee lied just as the phone in the bag began to ring. In one swift motion, the aggressive officer grabbed the bag and stormed out of the smoke-filled room.

Similar renditions of the same interrogation played out throughout the evening and early morning hours. Other than minor variations, depending on the detainee being questioned and previous information gained from his codefendants, an untrained eye could easily mistake this meticulous, tedious, time-consuming process for being moot, repetitive, and fruitless. Only one who had been through this process or seen it play out numerous times could see and identify the differences.

As subtle and unmeasurable as they were, these small differences meant everything. One of Twizzy Rollack's lil homies had died in the accident, and the other one was kept in the hospital because of his injuries, so only three men were interrogated. But one of them was different.

After being interrogated and booked, Rollack, Omar, and Black were sent to the Hudson County jail, where they were processed and placed on the maximum security tier. Arriving a little after five, they were all locked in different cells until the six o'clock count cleared, and everyone was let out of their cells for breakfast.

"Something ain't right." Twizzy Rollack complained as he put his food tray on the table and sat across from Omar.

"What do you mean?"

"I mean, why the fuck we just got here like an hour ago? We got bagged before lunchtime yesterday and were done at the hospital and shit at like two or three. The dick heads at the precinct ain't even start trying to hit me with their little questions until like five or six last night, and that was done way before midnight. So again, why the fuck we just got here?" Twizzy paused to taste his breakfast waffles. "I'm trying to figure out what the fuck was going on from one until five."

"I don't know, but you can't clock every minute like they were supposed to talk to everybody for the same amount of time."

"If niggas ain't have nothing extra to talk to them about, nobody shouldn't have been talking to them that long."

"What's gang banging?" Black greeted, sitting down.

"Oh shit, that's the hood!" An unknown inmate's outburst caused everybody to crowd around the TV to watch a news broadcast.

"I am Katty Lue with the eyewitness news team, reporting live from Jersey City, New Jersey's Liberty State Park. I'm standing in front of what some authorities believe is the charred remains of the vehicle used to flee the scene of yesterday's gunfight with Jersey City's finest. At this point, there is still considerable speculation about whether this is the vehicle used by the suspects. That explains why I'm currently here with Jersey City's fire department chief, trying to get an update.

"Well, at this time, we're not aware of too many details concerning the vehicle itself. The fire had been completely extinguished for about half an hour, but it was still smoldering, and judging from the damage I'd seen thus far, it was burning for the better part of the night. Despite our initial attempts to extinguish the fire, it continued to burn, at which point it became clear that gasoline or another flammable substance had been used to ensure that everything would burn. So we had to wait it out, and as of yet, we haven't been able to assess what's left of the vehicle entirely.

"Considering the obvious damage." The reporter paused, glancing over her shoulder at the still-smoldering SUV. "Do you think it's possible for any evidence to have survived?"

"Well, at this point, we're not even prepared to identify the vehicle used in yesterday's events positively. But if it is the vehicle, although relatively unlikely, the possibility for evidence to survive always remains."

"We all hope that's a very high possibility, chief. In a related matter, sources have informed the eyewitness news team that after speaking with the four captured gunmen, the Jersey City police department has accumulated enough substantial evidence to positively identify and potentially lead to the apprehension of the remaining cop killing suspects. On behalf of the Eyewitness News team, I'm Katty Lue.

The three codefendants went back to their table, and Rollack broke the silence.

"That's the shit I was just talking about. If the fuzz stopped trying to talk to me at twelve, what the fuck was going on from then until five?"

"What the fuck are you trying to say?" Omar challenged.

"I aint trying to say shit nigga. You know what time it is; you see what the fuck is going on."

"What's going on?"

"Bruh, you ain't stupid. You heard what the fuck they just said on the news, and you know from what I just told you that the fuzz stopped trying to talk to me before one this morning."

"I'm tired as hell, bruh. I don't know what time it was when they stopped asking me questions." Black chimed in, drawing a suspicious gaze from Rollack.

"I don't even know what time it was when they stopped talking to me. But it seems like you take the fact that they had us sitting in the precinct waiting for a couple of extra hours, and you put that with the shit the lil Asian bitch just said to come up with the idea that somebody ran their mouth."

"I knew you weren't as stupid as you were acting." Twizzy Rollack said, speaking down to Omar while looking back and forth from him to Black.

Then, before either could speak of the men, a correctional officer informed them that he was there to escort them downstairs. During the walk, the correctional officer informed the three that US Marshals were at the jail's intake area waiting to transport them to the FBI's New Jersey headquarters.

After barely a twenty-minute ride, the three exited the vehicle and were separately guided through doors before they each entered interrogation rooms. All of this was done solely to create the illusion that the three were treated equally and that the bureau was equally interested in interrogating them.

While two codefendants were interrogated, the third was led into a much nicer office.

A middle-aged white man sat behind a computer, typing away as two uniformed Marshals led the shackled man into the room.

"I don't know why y'all are bringing me up here." The prisoner protested, cautiously eyeing the room's comfortability. "I'm telling y'all, I don't know nothing."

"Calm down, Mr. Brown." The white man said, with his eyes still fixed on the computer screen. "Has anyone here asked you if you knew something?"

"Not yet, but I know how y'all play."

"If no one has asked you anything yet, then why jump to conclusions?"

Suspiciously eyeing the female name on the desk, 'Helen Holmes,' the prisoner hesitated before responding.

"Long as you know, I ain't got shit to say to y'all."

"To the contrary, I don't believe you're here to speak at all. If I remember correctly, I was told you were brought in to listen."

"Listen?"

"Yeah, listen." An attractive female declared, entering the office carrying a bag that seemed to stop time as she gracefully sashayed across the room. "I had you brought in."

"Yeah?"

"Yeah." She confirmed, standing behind the man on the computer.

"I don't know why you did that."

"I guess you need your computer?" The white man said, standing as everyone in the room ignored the prisoner.

"Yeah, I need my computer and the privacy of my office while I speak with him."

"You don't got shit you need to speak to me about." He declared, eyeing the female as he began to feel a sense of familiarity. "Not without my lawyer."

"Yeah, I do." She flatly replied, sitting down and pulling a foil-wrapped sandwich from the bag she had carried before directing her attention to the Marshals. "Remove his shackle belt, leave the cuffs and leg irons, and you guys can wait outside while I speak with him."

The Marshals complied and headed for the door. She greeted the prisoner. "How have you been?"

"Not too good. I don't see my lawyer in here."

"Your lawyer?" She paused, unwrapping her sandwich and taking a bite. "As in legal representation, legal counsel, or the person legally advising you on what is and isn't legally in your best interest?"

"Yeah, my lawyer."

"Excuse my manners. Are you hungry?" She asked, removing food

15

items from the bag and placing them on the desk in front of the prisoner. "They're bacon cheeseburgers. I remember how you liked them when you were a kid."

"Nah, I ain't hungry, and what the fuck make you think you know what I like?"

"Boy, you don't remember me?"

"Hell no. I gotta know you to remember you, and I don't know too many pigs. I mean cops or FBI agents."

"Funny." She feigned a chuckle, pulling her auburn dreads into a pony-tail, then typed commands into her computer before turning the monitor towards the prisoner. "That was me. In '97, I was about twenty-two and twenty-three, taking criminal psychology and criminal sociology courses three times a week. I had joined the bureau about eight months prior when the agent trained me, and I was assigned to the Abdul Myers case. From then until the end of two thousand, I was tasked with providing legal and psychological counsel for an eight-year-old version of you and your guard-ian." She paused, watching the prisoner jerk his head back, eyes darting from her to the younger image on the screen.

Then, glancing at the name on the desk again, his face drew a look of total disbelief.

"My hair was shorter then, and I was obviously a lot younger, but I dis-tinctively remember helping to ensure that you psychologically dealt with the loss of your mother and baby sister in a healthy way. I took the less active role of drafting and monitoring your treatment plan. I determined the type of treatment you needed, petitioned the bureau to finance it in exchange for your cooperation, selected your therapeutic psychiatrist, and even monitored your progress to ensure proper mental and emotional de-velopment.

"I don't know why the fuck I'm here, but I think you got me confused with somebody else or something."

"You can try to play stupid if you want and try to cling to the loyalty or dedication you're supposed to have for your friends. But I saw the look of recognition flash across your face a second ago, so pardon me for be-ing blunt, but we don't have much time. You don't have much time. Some severe charges are being levied against you right now. At the crime scene alone, there's more than enough evidence to take you off the streets for good. It wouldn't matter if you could afford to hire the best law firms in the country to fight your case; you will never walk the streets again like a free man. There's only one way out of your predicament." She paused to adjust her tone to a more somber one.

"I remember needing to console and comfort a fragile and grief-ridden eleven-year-old who was practically on the brink of emotional calamity just seconds before he was due to testify. You bear no resemblance to that young man. Seated before me, you are a man. Yet, I know that you remember the name Abdul Myers, his power and influence, and his seemingly nonexistent conscience. Needless to say, life in prison for you would be hell. Either you would stay in no-contact protective custody, never being able to physically touch another inmate for the rest of your life or try your luck in a population where you'd probably last a few days, maybe a week or so, before someone found out who you were, and a gang of inmates slaughtered you. Bad news for you is, even if you take me up on my offer and you make the only decision that could allow you to earn your freedom eventually, you will still have to go through prison population to make it all work."

"I'm lost."

"That's to be expected. You're surprised to see me, and you're putting the pieces together. I'm asking a lot of you, so you're internally debating what's best for you versus what's best for your persona, reputation, and the you that everybody in the street knows. But self-preservation is most important." She stopped to remove a clear bag from her desk drawer and pulled out a familiar cell phone before handing it to the prisoner. "Somebody was blowing your phone up, so I answered it, and I spoke with them enough for me to know that they're legitimately concerned about your well-being. Considering things and making decisions would be selfish until you talk with this person.

Chapter Three

Within days, the federal government made arrangements that appeared to be implementing a traditional divide-and-conquer tactic. Separating the four co-defendants and housing them differently, the bureau sought to promote discord and distrust and to destroy any confidence the codefendants may have had in each other.

When he was able to leave the hospital, Twizzy Rollack's lil homie was brought to the county jail. With Rollack housed on the max tier, his lil homie was recovering in the jail's infirmary from a crushed spleen, shattered leg, and other injuries he sustained in the accident. While Black was sent to Newark's County jail where he'd previously bailed out on a murder case, Omar, who was already wanted for violating parole when they caught this new case, was sent to Northern state prison to finish the rest of his sentence.

Located in the same jail, it was easy for Rollack and his lil homie to have other prisoners smuggle letters to each other so they could communicate. It was even easy for Twizzy Rollack to get his sister, Dutches, in touch with Omar or Omar's people so she could relay messages between the two, and they could stay in touch. That said, though, Black didn't have any family or a support team, so after the four had been separated, communication between Omar and Black was almost nonexistent. Omar's girl, Tiffany, had even told him to call her regularly so they could stay in touch, but Black barely picked up the phone.

Located in Newark, New Jersey's largest city, Northern State Prison was practically gang central. With approximately ninety percent of the prisons population being Blood, Crip, Latin King, MS thirteen, Trinidadio, DDP or Arian Brotherhood everyday was a blessing if a gang on gang conflict didn't occur.

Occupying what had to be some of New Jersey's most unattractive real estate, the complex sat on marshy swampland. Set in this locale, the area's slime somehow seemed to seep through and permeate the prison's interior, perniciously infecting everything within. Thereby, the land itself on which the prison sat encouraged desultory and unenthusiastic attitudes, bred duplicity, deceitfulness, and chicanery, and gave birth to disputatious and argumentative personalities in people who were supposed to be rehabilitating themselves.

Being in prison for a few weeks Omar had gone through the orientation, been introduced to and familiarized himself with most of the need to knows under different gangs and their respective sets or factions, made himself and his rank known to those it concerned, been moved into the cell with and become somewhat acquainted with Got Guns, a high ranking homie under the Neighborhood Bloods from Paterson New Jersey.

"What up, what's popping bruh?" Got Guns greeted entering the cell after night yard and stopping at the sink to wash his hands. "Why you aint come out to the yard? Don't tell me you been in here stressing all day."

"Nah, I needed to stay back in the cell by myself so I could bust this move today."

"Bust a move? Nigga you aint go out to morning or night yard. You been in this hot, tight ass cell stressing all day and you done missed out on a whole lot of cannabis niggas had floating around in the yard."

"I'm trying to tell you something." Omar began, pulling a zip lock bag from beneath his pillow and handing it to Got Guns.   "I didn't know what time it would come through, so I had to miss yard and stay in the cell all day waiting on the drop. But a lil while ago, my peoples just came through."

"Yeah, this smell like that stank too."

"Yeah, it's that good ol' sour." Omar continued to remove a small object from his waistline after covering the window of the cell door with a towel. "I got this lil phone too."

"Damn." Guns said, examining the contraband. "You got the sour and a E.T."

"A what?"

"A E.T. nigga. It's a code word for a cell phone. Remember the movie?" He joked, making a hand gesture. "E.T. phone home."

"Oh, aight."

"Damn bruh, if I had your paws I'd cut mine off."

"Nah nigga you the big homie. I'm just a big homie. It's a big ass difference." Omar joked back as he lit two joints and passed one to Guns. "From what I'm told, you're the real big homie. You got the jail under your set and everything."

"Come on bruh, you know aint no big I's and lil you's in this shit."

"Spoken like a big homie. I really wouldn't expect anything less coming from your mouth. You supposed to talk like a boss."

"Yeah, you can miss me with all that. You the one that just got down here and you already making it happen, doing what the fuck you want and busting all type of dope boy moves."

"Whoa, what's that hate, bruh?" Omar asked with a laugh, exhaling a cloud of smoke.

"Absolutely not. It's just that I been down here for a minute trying to get my lil sis Big Red to get this cop bitch in pocket so she could make her shake and bake for me. Then, out of nowhere you came and you already busting moves and shit."

Omar joked that the officer was too much of a cop to be making moves, prompting Guns to elaborate about her being bisexual and trying to get his homegirl, who was also bi, to bag her and take her down. He told Omar he knew his pretty ass lil sis Big Red could easily pull the cop bitch, turn her out and have her in pocket because he'd seen her use her petite thick Rihanna frame and sexual prowess to do it to both square and street niggas and bitches.

Got Guns said the problem was his lil sis was a cannon. Big Red was pretty as fuck and she was one of the flyest mother fuckers in the hood

21

so you would think she was about her bag but as soft and feminine as she looked she was the definition of ratchet. He said if he was trying to get somebody's head knocked off he could depend on Big Red to rock them to sleep herself or send one of her bitches at them but trying to get her to help him secure a bag wasn't a priority to her.

When Guns was done musing about his homegirl Omar chimed in that the cop bitch wasn't going to be trying to jeopardize her job for a couple pennies anyway.

"I wasn't trying to get her to move for no pennies nigga, if she picked up and delivered the work I was gon give her the bag."

"I'm saying fuck the cop bitch, I got somebody that'll bring it in."

"You serious?"

"I aint talking to waste my breath."

"You saying you wanna get to this chicken?"

"Absolutely. You got some seed money, I got a connect we can make this shit jump."

"The only problem might be the Murder homie Bullet and the Shine homie Lucky." Guns said before going on to tell Omar who the two men were.

He said the weed wave that'd been going around the jail was due to the two homies. Omar, having not met either of the two men and only seen them briefly in passing, couldn't understand the potential problem.

Guns told him they were the only homies getting money right now. Being that they'd been the only ones supplying the whole jail for a minute, of course, they wouldn't be happy about some competition coming into the picture.

"So you think us making moves might start something?"

"Aint no might?" Guns chuckled. "Hell yeah, that shit gon start something. Sets trip on each other for shit like that all the time. They been the only ones moving since I got here. Once you used to having something on lock, you aint willingly trying to give it to some new mother fuckers without kicking up and trying to fight for what you feel is yours."

"So what we gon do"?

"Them niggas acting like they wanna trip aint gon stop us from chasing the bag. If you get the mule to bring it in like you say, we're going to make it happen. Fuck who don't like it." Guns replied, barely considering the implications. "Them niggas act like it's a problem we can shoot fades all day. If it's bigger than that, they wanna take it there and do something else. We just gon have to start set tripping."

Just like that, the possibility that their proposed moves could cause friction between them and other Blood members was dismissed in pursuit of financial gain. With Guns practically financing the venture and Omar reaching out to Twizzy Rollack in Hudson County jail to secure a connect who could supply what was needed, Omar and Guns banded together, pooled their resources, and started with a meager two pounds of weed.

A week later, they had orders for almost ten pounds and a few hundred pills. At this rate, they quickly began to keep a nearly endless supply of narcotics funneling through hands, from one person to another, until it landed in the hands of Omar's connect at the jail who would bring it to him.

In a matter of days, the two had spent a thousand dollars on two pounds of cheap weed and another four hundred to get it in. They smoked one and put the other thirty-one ounces on the market for $100 each, completely undercutting the competition, making them $3,100 and netting them $1,700 in profit. Operating under these margins, they were able to easily undercut the competition, which had been selling ounces of the garbage weed for two hundred and fifty dollars.

With the opposition out of the way, Omar and Guns soon had half ounces of drow for three hundred dollars and half ounces of Sour going for almost double that. While ecstasy, molly, and other pills were brought in on occasion for the right price, in no time, they quickly began to regularly have coke and dope brought in because it sold for three times street value.

Once the drug flow was regular, they started getting cell phones smuggled into the jail by Omar's connect. These phones, however, were only sold to certain people, usually high-ranking gang members who had to communicate to somebody in the free world what type of phone it had to be and when and where it had to be delivered. Omar's connect would then pick up the phone from the designated drop-off and smuggle it to him.

In the mere weeks that it took for their products to take over the prison trade, the threat of physical retaliation for their takeover bound the two together before the threat ultimately seemed to become unlikely. It was during this time that the handling of these transactions began to change.

Less than three months after Omar arrived at Northern State Prison, and with Guns' mutual interest, they began to make small changes in their hustle. At this point, the quantity of narcotics they moved inside the prison drew so much attention that the two stopped directly arranging transactions. They began paying different individuals from other gangs as go-betweens, who were paid to arrange transactions with their respective gangs.

On the streets, minor aspects of this hustle slowly began to change as well. Guns baby mother Melissa, a Dominican and Trinidadian street savvy female, did most of the operations trafficking. Initially, when they received all their work from Twizzy Rollack's connect and shipped it out once a week, Melissa had agreed to pick up everything dropped off, package it, and deliver it all to Omar's connect in the prison. But as the amount of shipments increased from one to four, sometimes even five a week, she found herself exposed to more risk and responsible for an increasingly uncomfortable amount of illegal transactions. Feeling that she had taken most of the risk, she quickly grew agitated with her role.

Melissa, being hands-on in the scheme, was privy to their numbers and saw kinks in the profit margins. So, after a bit of footwork connecting a few dots and pushing the plan to Omar and Guns, it wasn't long before she had them buying their cocaine and dope from a connect they'd made through her. Melissa's moves saved them a considerable amount of money and brought them better profit margins, but because her connect had better work for a lower ticket, Twizzy Rollack's connect still saw the bulk of their money because, in prison, weed was the one drug everybody brought.

While things were going well financially, Omar had new concerns. It had been a little while since the last time Tiffany told him she'd heard from his lil homie Black. Since they usually spoke every couple of days, this was somewhat concerning. Tiffany did tell Omar that the last time she talked to Black, he hadn't sounded like himself. She said he'd told her that his homies in Essex County were suspicious of him and that he thought somebody there might even try to move on him.

All of that said, not hearing from Black worried Omar. He even thought about sending him cell phone number so they could speak directly regularly, but he'd decided against it after considering how one wrong word said over the phone could affect the things he was trying to do. Omar did however have Tiffany reach out to a few of Black's relatives all to no avail though. Unfortunately, even Black's mother was saying she hadn't heard from him.

With what might seem like a possible threat against Black looming, Omar was still enjoying the height of his almost street-like hustle. Omar seemed like he was beginning to relax as much as one possibly could, considering his circumstances. This was until he was woken one morning and told to prepare for court, after which he was transported to the federal building in downtown Newark, New Jersey.

Entering the prisoners' waiting room and approaching the gate to a holding cell, known as a bullpen, a glasses-wearing Omar walked in and past the only person inside the bullpen, Twizzy Rollack, who stood at the gate speaking to a suited man outside the cage.

"Damn, what's gang banging nigga? I almost aint recognize you with them glasses on." Twizzy commented on his specs, prompting Omar to walk back towards him, replying with a smirk.

"You know the shit bruh, I got the specs on so I can make sure I see all the bull shit these people in this courtroom about to try to throw at us. So don't start trying to hate on my Ralph Lauren frames nigga."

When the two were done saluting each other and making small talk, Rollack turned back to address the suited man outside the gate.

"Now tell him what you was just telling me."

"Alright. As your counsel, I wouldn't recommend divulging sensitive information..."

"Man this my fucking codefendant." Twizzy interrupted. "He's here, so it can't be him, right?"

"Well, uh, I didn't know he was one of your codefendants. And yes him being here should just about exclude him from being the person you need to worry about. I can't imagine a scenario under your circumstances where the government would put their asset in a holding cell with his codefendant." He paused, rubbing his forehead, and adjusted his large bifocals before beginning slowly. "To put it in laymen terms, the federal government under rule three colon eleven dash one has proffered or given the defense teams notice that they're petitioning, even before indictment, to move for a rule thirty-five motion or five-k one application."

"Tell him what that means."

"One of your codefendants is in contact with the federal government and made them aware of the fact that they're willing to cooperate."

"Somebody telling." Rollack eagerly clarified.

"Who?"

"Come on, bruh, stop playing stupid."

"I'm for real."

Omar, it's only four of us. Me and my lil bruh aint telling. So if it aint you, it gotta be Black."

"How the fuck you coming bruh?" Omar cut in. "You can't just come at me like 'oh shit, I think your lil bruh telling."

"Fuck you mean how I'm coming? Somebody is telling, and it's only four of us. It aint me, it aint you, and it aint my lil homie."

"How do you know that?"

Insulted by the challenge, Twizzy Rollack looked at Omar with disdain in his eyes and tried to smile. "My lil bruh aint telling nothing. I raised that nigga. I know that shit aint in him."

"So why he aint here?"

"Aint we been in contact, sending messages back and forth through Dutches this whole fucking time?" He asked rhetorically. "You know why the fuck my lil nigga aint here. He in the county with me but they still got him on the medical tier cause he fucked up from the accident and stuck in a wheelchair. That's the only reason my lil nigga aint here."

"Nah. That's why you think he aint here."

"That's what I know." Twizzy declared before turning back to the lawyer. "Tell him the rest."

"There were two search warrants executed this morning. The first incident occurred in downtown Jersey City, within one of the housing projects, and the second was apparently in Jersey City's neighboring city of Hoboken. The details of this are just now beginning to come in, so unfortunately, I don't know the exact addresses, any details, or the results from the searches at this point. Furthermore, the correlation between these searches and the five-k one downward departure sentencing application is entirely unclear. But two things are crystal clear. First of all, the local police who executed these warrants had to have been highly confident that the searches would produce something substantial. Otherwise, I can hardly imagine the local P.D. violating protocol and going over the F.B.I. 's head to execute searches while the feds are still investigating or prosecuting.

"Aight."

"Secondly, to be brief, five-k one is a sentencing guideline that the feds started using to keep members of the mafia like Sammy the Bull, who'd turned into rats out of prison after they'd told on crimes they'd participated in or had knowledge of. Once this application is accepted, the person is no longer a codefendant of their codefendants. They're no longer defendants against the state or federal government. When the five-k one application goes through, the person cooperating is either considered an informant or a government asset, depending on the quantity and quality of information they are willing to provide.

"Damn."

"In theory, this person could have already been released and be on the streets under federal protection waiting to testify against you. Or even currently attempting to infiltrate you even further as an ongoing government asset in an ongoing investigation."

"How the fuck you don't know the addresses to the spots they searched?" Omar rhetorically asked, pulling the designer frames from his face.

Imagining the worst, he walked away from Rollack and the lawyer, allowing them to conclude their conversation as he paced the bullpen in deep thought.

"What's good with you nigga, you aight?" Rollack asked jokingly after his lawyer left the gate. "Don't be coming at my lawyer like that either, bruh; only I can talk to him like that. Dig me?"

"Yeah I'm aight, he just through me off with that shit he said about the search in Hoboken."

"Hoboken? He said they hit a project's apartment, too. That shit could be the Rollack headquarters in the projects and you worried about some spot up in Hoboken?"

"My g-moms live up in Hoboken. That's where we was coming from when we came to see y'all to make the sales." Omar almost mumbled, placing his hands on the gate as if to brace himself. Then, shaking his head, he continued. "I bred that nigga Black. It's hard to jump the gun and wrap my head around it."

"Man fuck all that. I can see the way you moving like you got some other shit on your mind or something. I don't know if you questioning something, like whether or not that nigga Black done said some shit about wherever y'all came from or whatever happened before y'all came to see us. But you already know what time it is, bruh. Just like everybody else, I heard the rumors about your lil homie, the same rumors you and Charley probably was talking about before the police burned down on us. You bred son, so it's hard. But it's the burden of command."

"It hurt when you gotta whack a nigga you love."

"I get it. But if you don't label that nigga dog food, I can't send word for the wolves to get at him and he gon keep talking till he put us away forever."

"I don't believe this shit." Omar declared, putting his glasses back on.

"Believe it? Nigga this real, it don't get no realer. You need to stop playing and label that nigga. So I can send word for some homies to deal with him." Rollack completed staring into the lenses of Omar's glasses.

"I don't know if I believe it enough to label him without seeing some paperwork. What, you gon get some homies in Essex County to pop off on him or something?"

"Pop off on him, give him some knife work. Shit if we can get him a bail I can get niggas to bail him out and knock his shit off or do whatever is necessary to shut him the fuck up."

"Lunch!" A U.S. Marshal interrupted the placing of wrapped sandwiches and juices on the bullpens' gate.

"Damn, its lunchtime already?" Omar complained, grabbing his lunch.

"Yeah, we aint seeing the judge or nothing today. My lawyer said it was a status conference. We should be going back to the county jail as soon as they finish doing our paperwork."

"Aww shit." Omar began lowering his voice as the Marshalls exited the door that led to the holding room. "I brought some shit up here for you, but I don't know how you gon get it."

"What you got for me?"

"Some of that good ol sour and a E.T. The only thing is these lil jacks old and small as hell so they aint no smart phones or nothing and they don't send or get pictures. But I got all that shit tucked and put away, so I don't know how you gon get it anyway."

"I'm saying, it's gon be aight. You aint going back to Northern state today." Rollack replied with an excited smirk. "Don't even worry about it, today just like any other day when you come from state prison to go to court, your ass is going back to the county jail with me for the night. The state boys will come to get you first thing in the morning and bring you back to Northern State.

"I heard."

"Now what's banging with this connect situation? Why you just cut my man off? What, you got a better supplier or something?"

"I'm saying, the nigga you had me copping from is still getting all my weed and pill money."

"Weed and pills bring in the coins, but niggas is trying to get to that bag."

"You counting shit like it's coins going in your pocket or something bruh."

"The nigga my sis getting that shit for you from named Paydro. Son don't just fuck with anybody and even if he do fuck with you he aint no couple grams or couple ounces type of nigga. He aint used to moving if it aint for that bag. While coins is money, that shit from weed and pills is like pocket change to Paydro and that aint enough for a nigga like him to get out of bed. He aint gon keep moving for it. The only reason he been moving is cause I'm involved and me and him is like the closest niggas can get to being family without coming out the same twat."

"You sound like this shit gon effect you or something though."

"I'm saying, when I first told Dutches to get at son and get some shit for you from Paydro the nigga hit me on the side with like a finder's fee just for bringing him business and then he kept hitting me every time sis copped something for you."

"Really?"

"Even though you aint know what was going on, it really was like we was down with each other on that shit cause every time you spent some money with him, he threw some shit my way and for a nigga in our position you already know a couple racks make a world of difference."

"So what you saying?"

"You know my set Murder in Jersey is ran like the nigga Tony ran his family on the Soprano's show, except its two bosses or OG's instead of one that control the whole state."

"Why you telling me all this?"

"Just hear me out for a minute. My big homie C-Green from Newark got north Jersey and this nigga named Nut from Lakewood got south Jersey under my set for the state. C- Green out in Kentucky finishing a sixty-month stretch, so Nut got the whole set statewide right now. Aint no real animosity or nothing between C-Green and Nut, but they stay out each other way for the most part cause they in competition for the same throne."

"Politics."

"Exactly. Now, I'm Captain under C-Green and Nut got two Captains under him, this nigga named Raw from Atlantic City and the dark skinned bald headed nigga Bullet from Lakewood that's down Northern state with you right now."

"Where you going with all this?"

"I got a whole lot of say under my set in jail and on the street. But it is a limit." Rollack paused to drink his juice. "You know everybody know we co-d's in this crazy ass case. So as soon as I told Dutches to get some work from the nigga Paydro, my homie Nut reached out to me on behalf of the nigga Bullet cause him and the Shine homie Lucky was talking like they wanted to set trip on you and your man Guns."

"Set Trip?"

"I'm saying them niggas know we co-d's, so they wasn't talking about trying to move on you. They did want some smoke with your man Guns, though."

"They don't know Got Guns somebody under that Neighborhood shit. Them niggas tripping on him would of started a dumb ass war and not for nothing, but your homies might've been on the losing end cause them Neighborhood niggas deep ass fuck down Northern."

"Don't get it twisted, they like the biggest set in the state. But that shit aint got nothing to do with whether or not niggas was gon pop him and it aint got shit to do with who would win a war." Rollack clarified. "Bullet pushed the issue to the nigga Nut and gave him the impression that he wanted to move cause you came through on some bullshit and stopped what him and the nigga Lucky had going on."

"Really?"

"He never told me how you fucked up his hustle, but Nut said he made it sound like a homie from New York just came to Northern on some bull-shit like 'fuck everybody and whatever the homies that's from Jersey might be doing. I don't respect none of these niggas enough to bust it up with them, let them know what I'm doing or see where they at. I'm just going for mine.'"

"All that?"

"Facts. I vouched for you to the nigga Nut, told him it sounded like Bul-

let was on some dramatic shit. And I told him the same way he was probably eating off whatever Bullet and Lucky was doing, I was eating off what
you was doing so he could tell Bullet to kill that tripping shit. The thing is,
now I'm not seeing anything from what you're doing anymore, and I don't
lie to my homies. So I'm letting you know if it come up again, I gotta keep
it a band with them."

"I heard, but I aint wetting that shit. I head a money target that I wanted to reach when I first started getting to it down Northern and now that
I done hit the target I'm about to leave this jail shit alone. Them niggas
feeling some type of way and wanting to trip is the last thing on my mind."
Omar smiled as he hesitated. "All this jail shit is coins, I got my peoples
on the streets eyeballing a couple spots we can open up shop in cause I'm
trying to get that bag you was talking about. Dig me?"

Omar went on telling Rollack that he'd come across a connect who
supposedly had pure coke and dope for damn near nothing and wanted a
distributor in Jersey but would only supply him if he could move weight.
He said as hard as it would be for anybody to set some shit up on the streets
from jail it'd be ten times harder for him to do it in a state that he not from.

"You serious?"

"Hell yeah, I'm serious. I don't know how you're feeling, bruh, but the
odds are we are about to face some time. Whether we getting time or not, I
gotta jump on every opportunity that come my way."

"It's a lot of shit that come with that."

Omar told Rollack all he had to do was connect the dots, draw up the
plays, put the right niggas in position and quarterback the moves cause
work move itself. He said his man, Young Du, had just come home. He
was a Brim homie from California, but Omar said he'd caught his case in
Jersey and was paroled here. Let Omar tell it; he already had him out there
looking at a couple nondescript blocks and checking different areas to put
trap houses in.

"I'ma have him overseeing whatever I do and making moves I would if
I was there. The thing is, I know he gon need somebody with him to help
monitor the day to day bullshit on the blocks and help him put a couple
boots on the ground that's familiar enough with the area to back him up."

"Back him up?"

"Yeah. If I'm putting together a team of hustlers, I need them to have some type of muscle around. In case they run into some problems or hit a road bump or two."

Pausing to consider the proposition, Rollack slowly began with a chuckle. "I guess this is where Rollack comes in. If you're trying to get to that chicken, it's definitely gon to be some type of problem in the process.

"This is why I need somebody familiar with the environment. I aint trying to have a million niggas trapping for me and shit. I just wanna get a couple trap houses and supply mother fuckers."

"You trying to supply the state?"

"Hell no. That would get us another case. I think it'd be better to supply the homies."

"That sounds like a plan. You bringing the nigga Got Guns in on this?"

"I briefly chopped it up with son about it. I had Tiffany mention it to Black, too, to see what he thought about it. But me and you both already know why I'm bringing it to you. Them Neighborhood niggas do got some numbers throughout the state but from what I'm hearing they only strong in two or three cities."

"Jersey City, Atlantic City, and Lakewood," Rollack confirmed. "That's like they three headquarters."

"I don't know if I'm hearing it right, but it sounds like the rest of the state belongs to your set, my set, Brim, Teck, and G-Shine. Plus, Guns is on his way out there to the streets, and I'm not trying to have him help me build something that he can go home and compete with or even try to take from me.

"It sounds good. I mean, my brother Twizzy Hoffa is already out there making noise in Paterson and Newark. I could easily get him to put a team of hitters together." Twizzy Rollack's evil mind began to work as he shook his head approvingly.

"What you thinking about?"

"Mother fuckers I already got on the streets that can make it easy to pull this off. On top of my twin, I got my man High Five out there. He about that chicken. He aint no real gunner, but he'll let his cannon go. Plus, he's from Camden, so I know he could run or oversee anything in south Jersey if you're trying to do something on that level."

"Hell yeah, we want the state."

"Aight, but if I'm gon be involved in any type of way, you can't discuss this or nothing I'm involved with, with that nigga Black, that nigga Guns or nobody else for that matter."

"Guns? I know how you feel about Black already, and I get that. But you specifically put his name with Guns as if it's some shit you know that I don't that put them in the same category or something."

"Aint nothing. I don't know son and I really aint into dragging niggas names through the dirt off speculation." He paused to consider his words. "All I can say is if what niggas is saying is true them Neighborhood niggas should of labeled son a long time ago."

"Yeah?"

"Yeah. That's all I can say." Rollack flatly said he was finished with his juice before standing to discard the carton. "If I'm in, I'm in. I aint got no problem putting up some chicken too. But you can't just cut me off when you get comfortable, start thinking you know the terrain, and start feeling like you don't need me and my homies anymore."

"I get what you saying you emotional ass nigga. I aint gon be trying to cut you the fuck off anyway. But a couple dollars don't make us equal partners when I already got more than a bird and a half of cane on consignment and I'm in the process of paying for damn near half a bird of smack just to start up."

I'm not saying we're equal; you've got the connect and more skin in the game. But I aint your flunky either, bruh. I know the wave you ridding in Northern got your pockets feeling heavy, but if I crew up a couple hitters, Murder, Teck and Shine homies to make the move happen, we closer to equal than you think."

"I got you."

"And if you putting up the weight you say and it's the quality you say it is I can get my paws on some smack to stretch out whatever dope you get cause you don't really wanna put nothing too raw on these streets or bodies will start dropping like crazy."

"That might be a nice amount of smack. You sure you can handle that, get your hands on the seed money you talking about and keep juggling your lawyer fees?"

"Oh, the lawyer getting paid," Rollack smirked, thinking about how easy it would be for him to get a substantial amount of dope and how much he wanted to reveal about exactly how he was able to do so. "I told you the nigga Paydro like family. Even though my pockets aren't like yours right now, I'm good for the smack, and Hoffa has already been scraping up this chicken to pay off this loan for me. But I could use that money to flip first."

"Loan?"

"Yeah. I done ran through like half the Murder kitty, so Hoffa and my sis Dutches went to the Neighborhood home girl and got a loan for me."

"From who?" Omar sounded concerned.

"Damn bruh. The old head home girl, the Brim nigga Taliban baby mother. I think she owns a store or something. Got a big boy white Range Rover. If I aint mistaken, I think she somebody under that Neighborhood shit too."

"Samantha. She owns a salon and a mechanic shop or something.

"Yeah, yeah. That's her, so you know her, right?"

"Nah, I never met the bitch. I just heard about her." Omar quickly replied, thinking if he'd already said too much before shifting the conversation. I'm saying, you didn't even know her name until I said it, and she threw you a loan?

"Nah, it wasn't that simple. Dutches and Hoffa know her and her son, Baby Taliban. Since Hoffa been home he went through her hood checking for her to see if she knew something about the niggas Taliban and Charley. She ducked bruh for a minute, then she popped up in his hood, they chopped it up and she reminded Hoffa that them niggas got low for a reason. So niggas shouldn't be asking questions about them or looking for them right now."

"That makes sense."

"She said she aint in touch with them and don't know where they at. Bruh said she was coming like she aint even wanna say they names." Rollack hesitated before continuing with an afterthought. "Aint you originally from California before you moved to New York? I think she's from somewhere out in Cali, too."

"Yeah, I was born in Inglewood. I heard something about her being from there, too, but I'm not sure. Even if she were from the area, I wouldn't know her from out there, though. My pops' mother adopted me. We left Inglewood, and she brought me to the east coast when I was like eight."

. . . .

In a dark remote cell in a Northern state prison, Got Guns sat on a toilet puffing away on a joint as his cell door swung open and numerous men ran in, swinging and kicking on him.

Chapter Four

In mere days, the conversation between Omar and Twizzy Rollack avalanched from a meager idea, turning the plan into something tangible. From the confines of his cell, Rollack sent messages out that resulted in Black being stabbed up, brutally assaulted, and hospitalized in Essex County jail. He also managed to scramble together a team of hustlers who would put action to his and Omar's word, and by this team opening shop on a handful of street corners throughout the state, they appeared to be doing exactly what they'd envisioned.

When Omar's man, Young Du, in possession of the coke and dope, met with Twizzy Hoffa, Rollack arranged for Hoffa, Young Du, and High Five to work in unison managing the daily operations on the streets. As an immediate result, the shop was open and fully operational on one small, unknown street in Newark, two in Paterson, and one in Camden. They also had two trap houses in Newark and another one in Camden. For two niggas in jail, while meager, this alone gave their enterprise a small but decent foothold in the state's drug trade.

While the state was small compared to most others, it did house two of the largest cities in the country, and it could boast of its burgeoning metropolitan districts, one of which happened to be the tourist destination Atlantic City. With more than twenty counties, most of the states' street crime occurred in less than a dozen cities. These cities, Jersey City, Newark, Irvington, Elizabeth, Paterson, New Brunswick, Trenton, Asbury, Lakewood, Camden, and Atlantic City, saw the bulk of the state's drug money.

That said, it was a tiny but shrewd and notable move for Hoffa, Young Du, and High Five to target Newark, Paterson, and Camden as the first cities they flooded with their work. But even with all this new money flowing in, they were still subject to the aggressively cutthroat underworld of street politics.

While the study influx of drug money made things appear copacetic, one firmly in touch with the pulse of the street could hear the silent threat of a retaliatory war lingering. In circles, it was being whispered that Got Guns wasn't assaulted by somebody neutral or even a rival gang. Everybody was hearing about him getting tripped on by homies from other sets.

That wasn't the worst of it, though. The homies went back and forth, tripping on each other all the time. But there were rules regarding how it was done and what could and couldn't happen, especially when big homies were involved. The real fucked up thing about what had happened with Guns was he was somebody under Neighborhood, and the homies who ambushed him moved on him while he was taking a shit and put feet on him and holes in him.

After showing that he could still put up an honorable fight even when being ambushed in a compromising position, an unconscious Got Guns was gurney from his cell where his lungs had been punctured due to multiple stab wounds.

Aside from the unbeknownst fumes of the brewing set war and the minor problems of any growing drug operation, business was looking just about as good mid-spring as anyone could have hoped for. This was until the first signs of a scorching hot killer summer began to show.

Inside a corner bodega on Nineteenth Street and River Road of Camden High, Five opened a soft drink and took a refreshing sip as he stood in line at the counter behind a light-skinned, dread-locked, lollypop-sucking Amazon. With his eyes fixed on her ass High Five observed her text something into her cell before reaching back and struggling to stuff the large iPhone into the rear pocket of her already too-tight jeans. Then, spinning around, she caught him off guard.

"Why you ain't try to help me?"

"I'm saying I can help you put something back there." He smirked.

"Ain't your name High Five?"

"Yeah. What's up, Ma? Do we know each other?"

"Nah, not yet. My name is Reda, like the gun. Beretta. I've just been hearing a lot about you. She said, flashing a flirtatiously cunning smile, grabbed her cigar from the counter, and headed for the door. "I'm in a rush right now, but I'm gon see you again."

"I'm saying..." He tried to rebuttal, following her to the door before the Spanish store clerk began to protest in his native language.

"Damn." High Five sounded insulted, returning to the counter to pay. "I wasn't going nowhere with your punk ass dollar."

Exiting the store, High Five looked to his left and then to his right, scanning River Road before turning around to gaze up and down Nineteenth Street. Puzzled by the Amazon's apparent disappearance, he watched a familiar SUV traveling east on River Road pull up to the corner in front of the store at his right. After looking up Nineteenth Street, High Five turned around to watch the dark-skinned driver climb from the SUV and find his way around the vehicle to greet him.

"High Five. What's up, what's up? What's popping, big bruh?"

"Same shit Dre. You ain't just see that thick ass redbone?"

"Thick redbone?" He repeated with a negative head shake. "Nah, I must have missed that."

"You got that money?"

"Yeah, it's in the G-ride."

"You the only one out here?" High Five began, just as the piercing screech of breaking tires redirected their attention toward the left at a minivan turning off of River Road onto Nineteenth Street. "Ain't no problems or nothing, right?"

"Nah, it's just early as hell. Niggas up the block in the trap house." Dre barely managed to answer before a thunderous roar of gunfire exploded to their right.

Diving for cover behind the rear passenger side of Dre's SUV, they were sheltered from the onslaught of fire when High Five drew a small pistol from his waistline.

"That ain't gon be enough," Dre warned as the approaching vehicle traveling west on River Road made a retreating right turn northward up Nineteenth Street. Quickly reaching into his SUV, Dre grabbed a TEC-9 and ran into the street, firing at the vehicle.

Standing now from his ducking position, High Five watched Dre for a second before instinctively turning his head to look back down Nineteenth Street, where he saw the minivan that had distracted them before the gunfire erupted, quickly reversing in his direction with an apparent gunman hanging from the sliding door. Finding cover now behind the front hood of Dre's SUV, High Five tried in vain to call after Dre until the minivan became visible from his current position.

"Get that nigga!" A feminine monotone barked, prompting the gunman to hop from the sliding door in pursuit of Dre as the minivan came to a stop in the middle of the intersection.

Grasping what he thought was his best opportunity, High Five first took aim at a second gunman who was now apparently prepared to offer cover fire after taking the position at the sliding door. Pulling his trigger just as the first gunman opened fire, High Five continued to squeeze until his target fell.

Then, rightly anticipating the barrage of fire he'd receive from the second gunman, he again found himself ducking behind the SUV, desperately trying to avoid the spent projectiles tearing through the frame of the vehicle. With distant wails of sirens faintly audible in the backdrop of the gunfire, High Five immediately realized that the slugs now hitting the SUV, giving him cover and hitting the storefront at his left, had swiftly gone from targeted to seemingly random. At once, he thought he understood exactly what this meant. They are trying to retreat.

High Five's adrenaline-infused tunnel vision didn't allow him to register the sounds coming from behind him as he stood to fire his weapon at his adversary. But watching his target fall from the sliding door of the fleeing van, he felt the burn of a projectile striking his back before he heard the bang of it being fired.

Being hit in the back by what felt like piercing nails, High Five was knocked forward onto the SUV's hood, where he immediately rolled left, falling hard back down against the sidewalk. Scurrying backward for cover, he stopped at the rear of the vehicle, where he heard close movement. Eyes darting left around the rear of the car, he watched his first target struggling to stand before he pointed his weapon to end these attempts with the pull of his trigger. Unfortunately, with the next two squeezes, he discovered his gun was empty just as he began comprehending what he'd been hearing.

"Freeze!"

"Don't move!"

Chapter Five

After a disastrous Friday ended with High Five's arrest for his role in the Camden gunfight, the weekend closed even worse with a Sunday raid, resulting in multiple arrests and the closing of one of their Newark trap houses. If things couldn't be worse, the morning Hoffa got up to visit his brother, he glanced at his phone and got the news that High Five had died in the hospital the night before. Being that his previous incarceration was due to a wiretap, Hoffa never spoke about illegal activities over the phone.

That said, these visits between the brothers were Hoffa's only opportunity to keep Rollack updated on the details of what was going on in the streets. Walking into the Hudson County jails, a non-contact visiting hall, Rollack sat at a booth looking at Hoffa, a near mirror image of himself, on the opposite side of the plexiglass, and spoke flamboyantly.

"What's popping nigga?"

"You know the shit ain't nothing new, it's just heating up out here."

"Yeah, that's what I'm hearing. Help me understand how that shit happened at the spot in Newark?" Rollack asked, getting straight to the point.

"From what I'm hearing, it wasn't anything out of the norm or suspicious. It was a nice amount of traffic, but that's expected at the top of the month."

"Sounds like you are drawing it up to chance. What they got six or seven niggas, like three of them was trapping for us, and you calling it a chance?" Rollack hesitated, gathering his wits and measuring his tone. "They get a lot of work?"

"A lil more than a fifth of cane and an eighth of smack, but the main casualty was the homies. I told you it was four different homies in there copping shit from us. Two Teck homies, a Shine homie, and the Brim nigga Stacks all got caught up in there."

"Damn, Stacks got caught up in there too? Did the nigga Young Du ever sit down and talk with Stacks about us supplying them Brim niggas?"

"They spoke about the shit; I was there when they chopped it up and everything. But Stacks couldn't make it happen. If we are trying to make one deal to supply a lot of them Brim niggas the call would have to come from Stacks big homie Run from Newark, and you already know that nigga different. Real antisocial. He runs a tight lil ship with they set, and he doesn't fuck with niggas like that unless he knows them and done did shit with them." Hoffa paused to rub his chin. "That wasn't the first time Stacks came through to get some weight, though. He got some light shit before, and this time he spent a lil more chicken, so we know it's some Brim niggas that wanna buy our work. The problem is that Run and Taliban share the throne under Brim, and everybody knows that Taliban was a lot more hands-on. With him missing right now, it might be a lil too much for the nigga Run, and that can take some getting used to."

"You should have had Young Du push for Stacks to at least plug us in with the South Jersey Brim niggas in like Camden, Atlantic City, and Trenton since that's the main cities them Brim niggas getting money at anyway."

"I got the vibes from Stacks that Run just ain't used to running the whole state, so he on some bullshit right now. Then you gotta remember, Taliban and Run both got double OG under that shit. The nigga Young Du is only an OG, but he's from out in Cali."

"Yeah? The nigga Omar ain't even tell me his man was an OG."

"Well, he is, and that changes a lot. Run got the state, and by rights, he should be able to out-rank Young Du if it came down to it, but just being from Cali might give Young Du a lot of sway with them Brim niggas. If I were in Run's shoes, I wouldn't be trying to do shit with Young Du that

44

could validate who the fuck he is."

"You're right."

"You know they grow up banging before they teenagers, so the nigga Young Du could have been banging a whole lot longer than Run. Plus, his father and his family are supposed to be somebody under that Brim shit. None of them Brim niggas on the street seem to know son except for what they heard about him, but from what I see, all them mother fuckers respect that nigga. If you think about it, Run might not wanna plug us in as the main supplier for them 'cause it's hard to do that without cosigning Young Du."

If he does that, Young Du could get enough of they set support and notoriety or whatever he needs to validate him pulling rank on Run and taking control of they set on the streets.

"Absolutely."

"So all in all, you saying we may miss out on money cause this nigga Run ego tripping?" Rollack shook his head in disbelief. "Fucking politics. I still don't know how you think that raid was coincidental. You're smart as hell, but you sometimes miss the big picture. All those niggas you said got bagged are some bodies under they sets. We just set up shop and started to get to the chicken, and they all got bagged at our trap house. How do you think that looks to the streets?"

"The streets, fuck the streets. I'ma bust it up with the Brim and the Shine homies and make sure them niggas that got bagged at the trap house is good. But fuck the streets, we got the streets."

Rollack found Hoffa's arrogance concerning the hustle they'd just started humorous, and he wanted to laugh because he knew their arrogance was a trait they shared. Still, fears of the possibilities made the moment too serious.

"What about the law? We got them, too. Cause that shit could be a lot bigger than that punk-ass drug bust. Right now, them mother fucking people could be in an office somewhere trying to link together connections from the niggas they cuffed to the niggas that's still out there or some other crazy shit. You do know they are trying to link niggas together just by proving they got the same work, right?"

"Cool out, bruh, you all paranoid and shit. Like you thinking a lil too much." Hoffa chuckled. "Everything ain't under a fucking fed investigation and we don't got the same shit they pushing at our trap houses. Anybody copping weight from us through a trap house is getting a good seven, maybe even an eight. And that shit is still way better than what's out here in these streets, but it ain't shit compared to our nine that we are pushing on our blocks. I'm out this bitch making money, not competition."

"I hear you, but we are still in a fucked up position. The work they took has got to be replaced, but I can't lean on Omar for it because he's already working on putting something together so that some money can be set aside for the homies who got bagged at the trap house. Then we ain't even break even with Paydro yet, so I don't wanna push up on him right now."

"Want me to chop it up with the nigga Paydro?"

"Nah, I'ma get Dutches to scream at him. Paydro might take a minute to give it to her, but he ain't telling his baby mother no. You stay low and be ready to go scoop that shit up when she get it cause you know she ain't trying to be just sitting on no work. You already know when you get it, use it as cut for the other shit we still got, so we can try to get back where we were at."

"Aight, I'ma handle that. What's good with you, though? How you holding up?"

"I'm living. You already know I'm feeling some way about the shit with High Five and the homie out in Camden. It's like the hits keep coming; I'm still fucked up over my lil bruh dying in the car when we got bagged on this case."

"Damn, BIP to the homies."

"Yeah, BIP to them."

"I'm saying, you know, I'm out here gunning at whoever was behind that shit with High Five and Dre. But other than getting word from Poppy in the corner store that High Five was in there chasing some redbone bitch right before the shit popped off, I ain't got nothing else to go off of."

"It's the Neighborhood niggas. How the fuck did I figure that out from in here, and you don't know?" Rollack scolded his twin before giving him the play-by-play of events in Northern State Prison concerning Omar, Got Guns, Bullet, and Lucky that led up to Guns being tripped on.

"So Bullet and Lucky got the nigga Guns popped?"

"And Guns probably made the call for that shit to trickle out there to the streets."

"I know Guns; I think him and the nigga Mill from Newark are like the only two Neighborhood homies directly under Charley. They both double OG's."

"I figure either the nigga Guns made the call for that jail shit to spill out to the streets, or one of his lil homies said, 'fuck that, I'm tripping cause these niggas moved on, big bruh.'"

"Or whoever running they set on the streets made the call."

"That's a possibility. I'm saying, with Charley still on the move if I had to take a guess, I'd say Samantha or the nigga Mill running they shit right now."

"Nah, I think the nigga Mill in a halfway house," Hoffa remembered. "He with the gun smoke, but he just did a dime. He is barely getting pussy right now; I don't see him pushing the issue for a war knowing parole be monitoring shit like that, and if it led back to him in any way, he is going right back in a cage for some dumb shit."

"So who next in command under that Neighborhood shit?"

"Crazy as it sounds, being that the nigga Got Guns is still locked up, I think the pretty redbone gay bitch with the dreads might be next in line."

"You talking about the bitch Reda?"

"Yeah, that's her name, Reda. That shit is short for Big Red. I know she's close to the top over there, but I don't see her or the bitch Samantha green lighting no tripping shit like that. So as stupid as it sounds, the nigga Mill might just be the one pulling the strings."

"I don't know about Samantha, but I always heard the pretty bitch Big Red is like a hundred percent goon."

"That's what they say."

"I don't need you out there gunning at nobody, however. If something happens to you and we both wind up behind this wall, you already know we'll be dead to the streets and everybody who acts like they love us right now."

"Out of sight, out of mind."

"Me and the nigga Omar trying to do a lot more than we doing right now, but we gotta be strong first. I've been thinking about us bringing your homie Psycho from Newark in, but strictly on some muscle shit cause we gotta limit his involvement. You already know he a lil different."

"Different? That nigga a certified nut. It's always good to have a cannon

47

on the squad, though, as long as we keep him on a leash. We just have to make sure he keep that nut ass nigga Itchy-Ru and the rest of they family away from everything we doing cause them greasy ass Green mother fuckers is way too extra. You already know they'll have us all on the radar of the major crimes and homicide squad.

Rollack told his twin that because he was under Psycho's brother C-Green, he'd already reached out to him to bounce his idea about bringing Psycho on board off his head. The Greens were probably the biggest family in the state. In North Jersey, you couldn't have been too deep in the streets if you hadn't known or even heard of Itchy-Ru, the most known cousin, or any of his family. It was like a million of them Green mother fuckers, and everybody knew Itchy and the rest of them for one thing, action.

That said, C-Green knew that when Rollack got at him about his idea, he was just making sure Itchy and the rest of his fucked up family would stay out of their business. C-Green told Rollack that besides their father Ponzi it wasn't many people in they family who fucked with Psycho so they wouldn't have to worry about Itchy or the Greens getting involved in they shit or bringing them unnecessary heat.

"So I'ma chop it up with the nigga. Get him a lil team of hitters, work it out for him to breeze through the traps, and keep a couple of hitters in the traps that see the most action. But if you are trying to add niggas to the team, you might wanna think about bringing my homie Ski from Paterson in too."

"What do you mean?"

"I mean, if you are trying to do more numbers like right now and make the team stronger, it ain't too many niggas that's more beneficial to bring on board than the nigga Ski. You already know he gets to the big bag, got a crazy wave, his lil trap network, and if it gets thick and pops off, he gon let his shit go."

"Damn, I ain't even think about son. I did put a lil work in with the homie before, too, so I know he about that life. The only thing is, he probably got his lil shit going on out there."

"That's facts. Far as I know, he moving a couple bricks here and there, but he got a bullshit connect otherwise, with Ski hustle, he'd be on top of the state right now."

Rubbing his chin, Rollack grinned in agreement.

"It's a go if you can get him to stop moving his shit. I'ma hit the nigga Omar later on so I can run the numbers by him and keep him up to date on what's going on. Still, I already know he just wants us to be supplying the homies all across the fucking state, so bringing Ski to the table only makes sense because he knows how to get our shit in everybody's hands."

"What's good with the homie, Omar?"

"He living. Them pigs on his heels down Northern, so they just put him in a cell with some weird mother fucker. He doesn't feel comfortable pulling his phone out around the nigga, so besides texting, we don't chop it up too often right now."

"Nah?"

"Hell no. The police down there already knew he was somebody under this Blood shit. Plus, his name is still in the news, and shit because our case is still fresh, so when the nigga Guns got popped and shipped out, the police down Northern used the fact that they had shared a cell before to throw Omar in I.P.C as soon as he got back from the court trip."

"Damn. Involuntary protective custody."

"Yeah, they said some shit about monitoring a possible threat against him for his protection. But they did that gay shit so they could take him out of population and throw him somewhere they could limit his movement and watch him. Cause son was getting that chicken down there."

"Speaking of money, I just brought your funny ass lawyer a payment." Hoffa declared, then continued before Rollack could chime in. "I ain't smelling that dude."

"Fuck you mean you ain't smelling him? Dude, just beat a couple of bodies for niggas. I know; he is like one of the hottest lawyers in the state right now."

"It ain't nothing specific that makes me feel like this. I just don't see that nigga trying to defend shit. He doesn't give off the vibes of a mother fucker that's trying to find alibis, exculpatory evidence, shit to fuck up the government witnesses' credibility, the question of the evidence, and anything else that's beneficial to his client. You mother fuckers ain't even indicted yet, and the few times I talked to that nigga, he was talking about plea bargains and shit."

"I'm saying, bruh, that might be the best he can do in this case, being that we already know the nigga Black cooperating and working with the people."

"Whoa, whoa. We think he is cooperating."

"Man, that nigga telling."

"I ain't seen no paperwork yet."

"So what you saying?"

"I'm saying, I don't know why you even think one of your codefendants telling when you know like I do that the police still got a fucked up description of Taliban and Charley." Hoffa hesitated before finishing. "You lost your lil homie the day y'all got bagged, B.I.P. to him. A cop got killed in the same altercation, and four or five other pigs got fucked up badly. I know it's still four of y'all, you, your lil nigga Dough, Omar, and Black, that's locked up, but unless the ballistics and shit show that y'all guns the ones that did all that shit, them pussies gon make anybody looking for a plea deal say something about the shooters that got away."

Chapter Six

After the visit with his twin brother, Hoffa reached out to Ski and Psycho before he went through their hoods and left them both a lil less than an ounce of coke and dope for them to have sampled before he came back to meet with them a few days later. To Hoffa's surprise, they were both calling, hitting him on all his social media platforms and practically putting up the bat signal for him to get in touch with them. Knowing they were pleased with the quality of the product, Hoffa told them about the few blocks they already had worked on and the two trap houses they now had left, and he sold them based on their bigger vision of supplying the homies throughout the state.

As should have been predicted, when Ski and Psycho heard that Twizzy Rollack and the Piru homie Omar that he'd gotten locked up with, whom neither of them knew, were the middlemen to the connect and the brains behind the vision, they were both a little hesitant. In the past, they had both known and done all types of shit with Rollack on different levels, so even with him being locked up for a high-profile case, their hesitancy wasn't due to him. They both believed that they knew Rollack was good. They were unsure of his man Omar.

Omar was an unknown nigga to them, and despite having a good connect, with the best product seen in over a decade and the cheapest prices on the east coast, without already having Twizzy Rollack on board fucking with him and thereby lending him credibility in Jersey neither of them would even be thinking about fucking with him. All that said, though, Ski and Psycho's response to Hoffa's pitch instantly changed when they got into the numbers, telling them how little they needed to back off all the weight they sold and how many points they'd see for every bird that got moved by them or through the traps. This wasn't even counting whatever premiums they could make off the top based on the differences between wherever they set their personal sales prices and what they needed to bring back to the table.

After hearing the figures and knowing the quality of the work, more and more Ski and Psycho both began to overlook what now seemed like their trivial and irrelevant concerns until they eventually said fuck it.

Once they were both on board, Hoffa introduced Ski and Psycho to Young Du and awkwardly told them in Young Du's presence that just like he was the voice of his twin Rollack, Young Du was there on behalf of the homie Omar. That said, his word should hold the same weight as Hoffa's. With that out of the way, Hoffa and Young Du began showing them the lil homies they already had trapping for them and the lil foundation they'd started to lay down.

Being different and having different strengths, Ski and Psycho dived in and contributed to the whole of the team in various ways. When Ski got some work in his hands, he brought in a few new lil homies to trap for them, moved around a few others already trapping for them, and opened two new trap houses, one in Jersey City and the second in Paterson.

Psycho, being more prone to action, regularly began showing his face on the blocks they had worked on and brought in and inserted trusted homies of his on these blocks as paid gunners. Even though no shots had been fired at them, at anybody who trapped for them or on any of the blocks they had worked on since the hit on Dre and High Five in Camden, Psycho, known for being over dramatic, paranoid, and even a lil schizo convinced Hoffa that the threat of some kickback from the Neighborhood homies tripping on Murder and Shine as well as any other niggas just trying to move on them out of greed or hate was much more serious than it seemed.

Because of that, he convinced Hoffa that they needed more shooters on deck. Knowing that Psycho had a flare for drama, Hoffa told himself this was exactly what they had brought Psycho on board for and reluctantly gave in to what he said they needed.

With business on the agenda, Young Du, Twizzy Hoffa, and Ski arrived in Newark to assess the volatility of their growing drug enterprise. Following Psycho through the carnage-ridden streets of New Jersey's largest city, the foursome visited the inner-city area where their products were sold. They also stopped on a few blocks that belonged to the state's largest and strongest Blood sets to spread the word to the leaders of those sets that they wanted to schedule a leadership meeting.

After checking the blocks where their work was sold and spreading the word about their desire to meet, Young Du, Hoffa, and Psycho all left their vehicles and climbed into Ski's SUV en route to Paterson to check out one of Ski's new trap houses.

Turning left from Madison Avenue onto a narrow one-way Twenty-first street where broke-down contemporary townhouses and chipped-up red-brick apartment buildings lined both sides of the street, Ski parked his suburban, and the men filed out. Once they entered a nearby building, climbed the steps to the third floor, and walked into the apartment that Ski had opened as a trap house, they all greeted the familiar lil homies trapping for them inside.

Then, with Ski preoccupied with a conversation, Psycho made note that Twizzy Hoffa and Young Du's eyes were drawn to the gun hanging from the neck of the lil homie sitting on the couch. So, taking the initiative, Psycho made small talk by introducing the lil homie he'd stationed at the trap house a few days ago as a paid gunner.

"Hoffa and Young Du, this my lil homie M Dot from Newark." He paused as Hoffa appeared to answer a phone call. "Him and my lil homie Slugs was co-d's on some shit out in B-More, did a lil fed time, they both been out about a year now. Anyway, Slugs is a cannon, so I got him ridding around with me like he my sidekick, and y'all had this nigga M Dot hustling hand to hand out the trap in Newark. Work moves itself so anybody can trap, but every nigga that traps aint ready to use his cannon. That was wasting talent. Luckily, he wasn't there when the police kicked the door in and raided. Now, being that I bred the nigga, I know he more of a trigger man than a trap star, so I brought him here to watch the door and hold this shit down."

"What up, what's popping with y'all?"

"What's good with you? Are you sure you know how to handle that?" Young Du jokingly challenged, drawing a laugh from everybody just as...

POP! POP!

What sounded like gunfire was heard outside, causing one of the lil homies to run and look out the window.

"That aint nothing but kids playing with firecrackers."

"Even if it wasn't." Psycho began to scold the lil homie. "Them mother fucking guns you niggas got in here aint got shit to do with nothing going on outside. Y'all keeping a couple cannons in here for one reason, to make sure don't nobody come to that door or come in this trap acting stupid."

"I wish a nigga would."

"I don't know; I still aint sure if you know what you are doing with that." Young Du continued to joke.

"Come on, bruh, I been pulling triggers since I was a lil nigga. I'm surprised you aint never heard my name on these streets from all the work I put in for this Teck gang. You are Teck, right?"

"Nah, I'm Brim."

"That's the Brim homie, Young Du." Psycho volunteered.

"Not the big homie in Trenton state maximum security, right?"

"Yeah, that's me." He said with a laugh.

"Yeah? So you under the Brim nigga triple OG Du Wrong? Aint he like your..."

"Come on, man." Young Du quickly interrupted. "If you know that much, you know everything you need to know. Don't start showering me with questions and shit like you a groupie or you are wearing a wire or something."

"Oh, nah, nah." M Dot began as Psycho shot him a disappointing look. "Pardon me, big bruh. I wasn't trying to come like that. I just heard a lot about you and the homie."

"I'm saying you good, just cool out with the questions and shit. For a lil Teck nigga you seem real interested in Brim."

"Nah, I did a lil Fed bid, and everywhere they had me, I always seemed to wind up jailing with some Brim niggas. The last spot I was in, I was in a cell with this Brim nigga from Cali, and he was writing you down Trenton.

54

I think he lost touch with you for a minute when they shipped you out of state, but he started writing to you again when you were in Pennsylvania. M Dot hesitated before an afterthought. "If I remember right, I think I saw a couple of pictures he had of you when you had your dreads and shit."

"Oh naw, the homie had me confused with somebody else if he thought he had a picture of me." Young Du wasted no time discrediting the story. "I got bagged and convicted for a body cause a couple of mother fuckers looked at a few pictures and pointed me out. So I don't do the picture thing, bruh."

"I jailed with a lot of Brim, Piru, Neighborhood, and other west side homies during my bid, and you already know that being that Du Wrong is one of the big homies that came from Cali and helped us get Blood right over here in Jersey and being that he got his own shit over here and everything them niggas talk about him like he a god or something. With you being..."

"It's official." Hoffa cut in, ending his phone call. "The Neighborhood bitch Samantha's son Baby Taliban just got bagged for that shooting in Camden, and the word came back that the two lil niggas that High Five wacked when they tried to move on him, and Dre was under the nigga Got Guns."

"Aight."

"Most likely, it was Guns or one of them lil dirty niggas under him that made the call."

"So when are we moving out?"

"Right now, we aint moving shit but narcotics." Hoffa tried to sound as if he agreed with his own words as he answered Young Du's question. "We gon get right, finish putting the word out that we are calling a leadership meeting. At the meeting, we gon let niggas know we are sweetening up our numbers, and we gon say whatever we gotta say to ensure the homies that the fiasco that happened at the Newark trap house aint gon happen again. I guarantee you that by the time we leave the meeting, Blood as a whole gon be committed to dealing with anybody who was involved with that dumb shit that happened in Camden. At the end of the day, we all Blood and niggas aint sign up to be out here just knocking each other shit off for no reason. We got the numbers, we got the streets, we supposed to be getting this fucking money."

"No disrespect, Hoffa, but this aint the time to be diplomatic. Them niggas already popped off, words can't fix what they did. It's the top of the summer, hotter than a sauna, and it's quiet as fuck outside for one reason. The streets are waiting."

"Waiting for what?" Psycho challenged Young Du and surprisingly got Ski to answer his question.

"The appropriate response."

"And what's that?"

"Tripping."

"Set tripping? Why it's always mother fuckers that aint known for knocking heads off advocating knocking heads off. I don't you niggas ready for shit to go there."

"They asking for it." Ski shot back.

"You niggas know everybody on this side aint under one set, right? We got mother fuckers under damn near every east coast set in Jersey trapping for us, so if it goes there, it'll be a war, and wars are hard to stop once they start."

"I'm saying, I can dig it if niggas don't wanna get their hands dirty..."

"Come on with the bullshit, bruh. My last name is Greene. Gunsmoke is all I know." Psycho spoke directly to Young Du. "At the same time, I know it's like a couple thousand Neighborhood niggas in the state. They got the numbers, but most of them are kids, and it's only a couple of them mother fuckers throughout the whole state that's worth mentioning. Our side against them won't be set tripping. It'll be like Blood as a whole, slaughtering everything repping Neighborhood." Psycho paused for emphasis. "If you, by yourself, could go out and whack the top niggas statewide under Neighborhood throughout the rest of the summer, assuming you was built like that, the feds would have you, every nigga under your set statewide that they think they got some type of status, along with me and everybody else in this room looking at life for some dumb shit."

"You niggas talking about the streets waiting."

"Yeah." Psycho cut right back in, interrupting Twizzy Hoffa. "You said that shit like you don't know they are watching and talking too. We supposed to be getting money over here. Them lil dirty niggas living on borrowed time. They know it, and we know even the police know them niggas are marks, they living targets. Them niggas running around on borrowed time, call them the walking dead." Psycho completed, evoking quietness throughout the room.   Be it his name, the fact that he was a lil off, or his reputation for regularly blacking out for no reason at all, but anytime Psycho spoke at length like this about one topic and sounded utterly rational, it seemed like the air left the room. It didn't always happen, but anytime Psycho did go on a diatribe like this, people tended to get quiet as if they were in awe that someone who always seemed to be on the verge of craziness could make so much sense. In rare moments like these, Psycho's words and demeanor seem to contradict his true personality.

Outside, minutes later, thinking of the possible implications of what he had just heard, Young Du sat in the rear, behind Psycho, as Ski started the vehicle. Maintaining a poker face, he internally debated whether he was overthinking things or if something said in the apartment could inadvertently have adverse effects on his plans. He quietly considered these things until the vehicle, pulling away from the curb, was abruptly knocked forward.

With everyone looking back to identify the culprit, Ski jumped from behind the steering wheel, feet hitting the paved street and approaching his suburban's rear.

"Damn, ma." This was the only protest he gave the female driver of the sedan that had rammed his SUV before he saw the tip of a barrel come out of her rear window and felt it before he could fully grasp what was happening.

POP! POP! POP!

The first three shots rang out in quick succession, and with Young Du and Twizzy Hoffa trying to duck for cover, Psycho stretched his body across the center console and driver seat and pointed his weapon toward the rear out the still-open door to try and return fire. Initially caught off guard, the other two in the Suburban sprang into action while a gusty Psycho, who now stuck his head out the door to target his shots, was completely unaware of his actual danger. Luckily, Hoffa identified the threat to his homie, and without aiming, he thrust his gun out his window, indiscriminately firing forward on an approaching minivan.

Meanwhile, Young Du began shooting out his window at a second gunman, opening fire on him as he walked up on the SUV from the rear. Catching the man off guard with an unexpected outpouring of return shots, Young Du struck him and made him stumble. Drawing his second weapon,

Young Du opened his door and hopped out of the Suburban to finish the would-be assailant. Hoffa, still unloading his gun, unwittingly dared to stretch his arm further out the window in search of a better shooting position and paid a price for that mistake when a projectile pierced his triceps, loosening the grip he held on his weapon.   With the rear vehicle starting to back away, Psycho, without really thinking, leaped from the SUV and picked up the fallen gun while still shooting as he ran to Ski's body.

Turning around, Young Du found cover behind the passenger side of the front hood, trained his weapons on the minivan, and moments later watched the driver slump forward onto the steering wheel. Then, drunk off adrenaline and believing the momentum of the gun battle had shifted, Young Du stood and boldly walked towards the minivan as he unleashed a barrage of shots. He closed the space between them as he walked them down, firing on both the gunman in the passenger seat and the one seated behind the driver. The gun he shot at the latter man emptied just as the target fell limp. Now, rounding the front of the minivan as he fired on the passenger, who now had his full attention, Young Du was struck at the base of his right shoulder before following shots from the still-living driver hit him center mass, lifting him from his feet.

Jumping from the vehicle with a quick barrage of gunfire, Hoffa threw Young Du's arm around his neck and hoisted him up to his feet as Psycho saw to it that all the occupants of the minivan were dead.

"I'm good! I'm good!" Young Du assuredly ripped his shirt from its collar to reveal a Kevlar vest, then reached for his shoulder. "Damn. One missed the vest."

Making their way to the Suburban, Young Du sat behind the steering wheel and deflated its airbag before shifting gears, prompting Psycho to jump into the passenger seat just as the vehicle began to reverse. Picking up speed, the rear of the SUV approached the intersection where Twenty-first Street met Madison Avenue just as a responding police car came into sight, trying to make the left turn onto Twenty-first Street.

Crashing into the sedan as Young Du twisted the steering wheel right, the Suburban forced the cruiser's passenger side onto the sidewalk, smacking into a street pole. Quickly putting the vehicle in drive, Young Du completed the left turn and accelerated in the direction the cruiser had come from.

"All them niggas dead!" Psycho barked aggressively, gesturing with his weapon to match his monotone. "From they big homies down to the pups."

"Say less." Hoffa chimed in, applying pressure to Ski's wounds.

"What!?"

"I said, say less. We already know what the response to this shit is."

"This aint the time for none of that shit."

Surprised at how Psycho and Young Du had seemingly swiped views since their exchange in the apartment, Hoffa looked at the rearview mirror to see the driver's face as he questioned him.

"What do you mean?"

"I mean, I'm trying to drive. That shit just happened two minutes ago. I'm lost, don't got no idea where the fuck we at, but I'm looking for anything that look like the turnpike so I can get us the fuck out the area and y'all wanna go back and forth with each other about how we gon retaliate to this shit."

"Fuck that shit you are talking about, bruh; you lucky you in this g-ride with us, and you aint get left back there with them Neighborhood niggas."

"Psycho, shut the fuck up. Young Du, you should have just said something if you lost."

"Fuck all this hoe shit dog!" Psycho cut in as Hoffa tried to give Young Du directions. "Them niggas Neighborhood so they west side Bloods and this nigga Young Du Brim so he west side too"

"What the fuck are you trying to say?"

"Don't forget five minutes ago when we were in the trap house, he was the one ready to trip on them when you and I talked about sticking to the script." Hoffa reminded as Ski groaned in pain.

"Aight. Fuck all this dumb shit. Get my homie to the hospital."

Following Ski's directions to make a right turn, Young Du dubiously looked at Psycho with new regard. Surprised at how quickly the man could flip on him for no real reason, Young Du knew he had truly earned and lived up to his name.

Chapter Seven

While everybody else was licking their wounds, Psycho was on the prowl. He couldn't believe the Neighborhood homies had ambushed them like that, but he was determined to pay them back. Immediately after they got blitzed in Paterson, once Ski was at the hospital, Psycho got the dirty guns they'd used in the shooting and brought them to his father's shop.

It was common knowledge in the right circles that part of the way the Green family was able to do so much of the bull shit they did without all of them being buried under jails was because Psycho's father, Ponzi, owned a pawn shop. This shop gave them the cover to get and get rid of all kinds of guns and fence-hot merchandise.

In the back of the shop, Psycho ran into his cousins D Green and Wee-Wee. As he swapped out the guns and gun parts for clean ones, he told his cousins about what had just happened, but he made sure to keep the details brief. Besides his pops, Wee-Wee was the only other person with his last name that he rocked with. Psycho fucked with his lil cousin Wee-Wee, but he couldn't go in depth talking to him because the older cousin D-Green was there, and he was a creep.

D- Green worked at the pawn shop, and he wasn't the aight kind of creep. You had to watch out the corner of your eye, but you could still hold your nose and fuck with him to get something accomplished. Nah, if you were looking for that, then you were looking for D-Green's older brother, Itchy-Ru. While mother fuckers in the streets respected or revered Itchy for being calculated and manipulative D-Green was avoided for being sneaky, shifty, and devious. Where Itchy was relentless and unforgiving, D-Green was ruthless and vindictive. They were both dangerous, but while everybody knew Itchy for being grimy, his brother D-Green was slimy—a certified creep.

At the shop, Psycho couldn't go into detail about everything that'd happened and his plans for get back like he wanted to because he couldn't talk around D-Green. Just from the few details, Psycho told them that D-Green was already talking crazy and acting like he wanted to ride for his lil cousin. Pyscho knew most of the family didn't fuck with him, though, so he couldn't trust anything D-Green had to say.

Just hours after the ambush, once the word of what happened got out, Psycho's lil homie Slugs, along with a Shine homie, caught up with a Neighborhood homie and put a couple of bullets in his face. Later that night, his other lil homies, Trey-Eight and A.K., pulled up on a well-known Neighborhood homie and knocked his head off. This only made Psycho wanna spill some Neighborhood blood with his own hands.

To make matters worse, somebody unknown to him had just streamed the killing of a high-ranking Neighborhood homie named Alpo on Facebook Live. Why the fuck should everybody else keep having all the fun? Psycho couldn't wait to move on them niggas. The same night he ran into D-Green and Wee-Wee at his pops pawn shop, Wee-Wee, the only cousin he fucked with, reached out to him saying he had the drop on a key Neighborhood nigga.

Part of the reason Wee-Wee and Psycho clicked was because they were both almost treated like outcasts by the rest of the family. The Greens were distant from Wee-Wee because while he was for his family, he was Blood and didn't put the Green family before his set. Pyscho's issue with the family went a lot deeper than that, though.

Psycho had a mother different from his brothers. Back when they were kids, it'd been rumored that something happened between his mother and his brothers that provoked him to try and stab his older brothers. At the time, the whole Green family knew what had happened between Psycho's mother and his brothers. But being dysfunctional, the family ignored the specifics, acted like he'd just flipped out for no reason, labeled him Psycho, and cut him off.

Wee-Wee was a lil off, too, though. Like most of the Greens, he was with all the bull shit, had been desensitized to all the violent, sadistic, and brutal shit they did, and put no filter on any of it. One of the minor vices that Wee-Wee and Psycho were known for sharing was that they both tried to bring their pit bulls, Rock and Cocaine, everywhere.

As Wee-Wee and his dog got in the car, Psycho looked in his rearview mirror at Rock, already trying to hump the backseat, and remembered why he hadn't brought his dog Cocaine with him. Wee-Wee's dog, Rock, was Cocaine's father, and he had a threatening look that pit bull owners wanted. But Rock was like a professional breeder dog; all he wanted to do was fuck and hump. Wherever Wee-Wee took him, Rock would find another dog, a person's body part, a piece of furniture, or something else to hump on. That being the case, Psycho didn't bring Cocaine because he didn't want her father trying to slide inside her.

When they got to the business at hand, Wee-Wee told Psycho that after he'd left the pawn shop earlier, D-Green told him he'd been serious about ridding on some Neighborhood niggas for his lil cousin. Neither of them believed he was serious but Wee-Wee said he'd given him all types of information about where they could find a Neighborhood homies baby mother he used to fuck.

Psycho didn't wanna waste time hunting down and killing just another random Neighborhood homie, so this news didn't excite him until Wee-Wee went on to say that he knew the Neighborhood homie in question, could vouch that the nigga was stupid in love with his baby mother and that he was under the Neighborhood big homie Mill. That was enough to get Psycho's attention, but he was in when Wee-Wee told him if they snatched the bitch up, he knew the Neighborhood nigga would do anything, even help them find some of his big homies to get her back. This was right up Psycho's alley.

Their timing couldn't have been better. Just as they pulled up at her house to snatch her, she and her baby's father were in the doorway kissing. When the cousins hopped out, guns were drawn. The female cried and pleaded, and her baby's father swore up and down on his set, making threats about what he would do to them, but he and his baby's mother both wound up knocked out and hogtied in the back of Psycho's car.

A lil later, feeling a hot, steady squirt of liquid slap across his face, the Neighborhood homie awoke on a floor looking up at the ceiling. Realizing he was still naked, hog-tied, and had tape over his mouth, he turned his head to look around and spotted Rock standing over his baby mother's naked, motionless body.

"Finally, you woke." Psycho stood over him, taunting.

The Neighborhood homie tried to yell, but it all came out muffled through the tape.

"I don't know if you are trying to yell at us or get your baby's mother's attention," Wee-Wee said, entering the room smoking a PCP-laced blunt, carrying a jar of some spread and couch pillows. "How the fuck you think we supposed to hear you when it's tape over your mouth. If you are trying to call that bitch it's even worse. Even if it weren't taped over your mouth, she wouldn't hear you. That bitch is higher than a light bill right now nigga. She aint trying to hear shit nobody got to say."

The Neighborhood homie couldn't believe his ears. His baby's mother didn't get high. Looking at the dog drooling as he paced around her, the Neighborhood homie fidgeted around until he sat up and recognized a syringe lying beside his baby mother's body.

"This shit real simple dog." He heard Psycho's voice, but all his attention was on Rock as he sniffed the naked legs.   "We aint gon threaten you, we aint gon hit you or none of that goofy shit, but if you don't give us what the fuck we want, something real fucked up, like tragically fucked up, is gon happen in here real fast."

"I want you to tell us where the fuck we can find that Neighborhood nigga Mill."

The Neighborhood homie looked up, mumbling, as Wee-Wee passed Psycho the PCP-laced blunt and walked over to where the man's baby mother lay. Rock backed away as Wee-Wee rolled her onto her back so he could pour the contents of the jar all over her pussy and put a belt around her ankles before lifting it to pull her legs up in the air. Before Wee-Wee was done, Rock eagerly dove his nose in, sniffling between her legs before flicking his tongue out, lapping her whole pussy with licks of his tongue.

His baby mother was so high that she let out a deep moan and began to gyrate her hips a lil. The Neighborhood homie closed his eyes tight as tears ran down his face. He didn't wanna see it, but he could still hear the loud smacking sound of licks. A few minutes later, Wee-Wee shooed Rock away so he could roll the female onto her stomach, stuffing couch pillows under her midsection to prop her up onto her knees a little.

"You gon let this shit happen?" Psycho taunted, making the man open his eyes just as Rock came back for more, sniffing her ass.

When she was finally on her stomach with her ass hiked up in the dog-gy-style position, Rock's nose went right between her cheeks before pulling it out, abruptly standing on his hind legs and resting his front paws on her back. The Neighborhood homie screamed through the tape on his mouth as he could see the pink of the dog's penis slide from its foreskin in search of a wet hole.

Chapter Eight

After the wounds had been treated, the following days seemed to flow somewhat blurry. Across the street from a popular sports bar on a corner in a residential section of Jersey City called Five Corners because it was a wide intersection where five instead of four street corners met, Psycho left his lil homies M Dot, A.K., Slugs, and Trey Eight in his Jeep Cherokee as he got out to talk with his older cousin Itchy-Ru. It was the opening night of the NBA finals, and rain poured from the sky. This was the perfect type of night for Psycho and his goons to be out putting in work, which is exactly what they were doing before Psycho got the call to meet Itchy on this corner.

"What's popping, bruh?"

"I'm scheming slime, you know the shit."

"Why you got me meeting you on this corner?"

"Yall out here tripping on them Neighborhood niggas, right?"

"If that's what you wanna call it."

"Well, I got a proposition for you." Itchy paused, passing Psycho a blunt of weed that was wet from being dipped in PCP. "Most of the niggas who lead that shit in Jersey City is in that bar right now."

"Aight, so why are you helping me?" Psycho asked, highly suspicious of the most devious man he knew.

"The Neighborhood nigga Freak is in the way of some shit I'm trying to do. I need him dead immediately. Me and the family is off duty tonight, letting the streets rest, letting mother fuckers get a couple of dollars and shit like that. But then, I got the drop on where Freak and a couple of his homies were at, so I hit you up thinking you and your lil vultures could probably get here before I could put together a team of shooters to handle this shit. Why not put it in your hands and let y'all handle Freak and a couple of his homies? I get him handled, and I helped my lil cousin. Two birds, one stone."

Psycho knew that when Twizzy Hoffa first brought him on board, the only condition was that he couldn't involve his family in anything they were doing. This involved his family. Getting Wee-Wee to help him with a hit or two and even speaking about an incident in front of D-Green was one thing, but this was completely different. Itchy Ru was the most evil, manipulative mother fucker in the world. Because of that, Psycho knew if he executed a hit based on his intel, it was no way to separate Itchy-Ru and the Green family from the other shit he was doing.

Psycho didn't buy Itchy's reason for giving him the kill, but he didn't have time to do the math, and he couldn't pass on an opportunity like this. A few days had passed since the blitz at their trap house, and Psycho hadn't had a chance to touch Mill or any of the big Neighborhood niggas he wanted.

While the Neighborhood nigga Psycho and Wee-Wee kidnapped led them straight to a few other Neighborhood homies resulting in their deaths, he hadn't been able to tell them shit about Mill before he and his baby mother were put out of their misery. As far as Psycho knew, Freak was one of the movers and shakers under Neighborhood.

Looking up at the falling rain, Psycho took in the ambiance. PCP made him think in crazy ways. As the rain poured on his head, Psycho looked around and thought that the scenery looked like the end of a gangster movie, and at that moment, he decided it was time for Freaks movie to end. He had to die.

By the time the game was over and crowds started to funnel out of the bar, Psycho had M Dot, Slugs, Trey Eight, and A.K. each positioned on the two adjacent, adjoining, and diagonal corners, acquiring their targets but waiting on his signal to fire.

From the driver seat of his Jeep, Psycho watched the crowd growing, and when he spotted Freak with a few of his homies, he hopped out shooting. Freak, another Neighborhood homie, and a bystander were the only fatalities of this episode.

About a week after the shooting, Twizzy Hoffa, Young Du, and Psycho met in Ski's Hospital room.

This was the first time the four men had all been together since they were blitzed in Paterson, so they sat around updating each other on where things stood.

They had all heard about different shootings on reputable Neighborhood homies in the days after they were ambushed, so the attention of the room naturally went to Psycho, whose eyes lit up as he got animated, reliving highlights of his favorite shootings.

"The streets know them niggas blitzed us in Paterson. So I'm riding around trying to get high, looking for the hot shit."

"Hold, hold. What's the hot shit?"

"PCP," Hoffa answered Young Du's question before Psycho could. "Everybody in this nigga family inhales PCP like its air. He usually tells you about putting in work; his story starts with smoking water. We say that when he high on that shit, the demon is in him."

"So was the demon in you when you rode on them niggas?"

"Absolutely. But I couldn't find a dipped cigarette, so I settled for the angel dust. Anyway, I burn down on them niggas trap, it's like three of them outside, so I pull up on them like 'what up, what's popping, I'm looking for the hot shit.' Of course, I'm trying to feel out if they Neighborhood or not, and these stupid mother fuckers replied right back, talking about 'what's rolling' and a bunch of other Neighborhood lingo. So I drew and squeezed on them."

"All three of them?"

"All three of them."

"I heard about the shit. One nigga died right there, one died at the hospital, and I think they said the last nigga look like he gon make it."

"What happened with the lil rapping nigga that was in the car with his bitch?" Ski asked, sitting up in his bed.

"Oh, that was the day before yesterday. Lil Fly Neighborhood nigga, I

69

think his name was Swag or some dumb shit like that. Lil social media celebrity got a whole lot of pussy, the bitches loved him, and the streets were talking bout him like he was a cannon. But the streets were wrong cause any nigga that's bout this life, live for the gun smoke or call they self a cannon wouldn't have let me get the drop on them as easy as I did."

"You had the demon in you?"

"Why wouldn't I? The way this pretty nigga been tweeting and posting shit on Facebook live, I was running around like a madman trying to find him so I could knock his head off."

"How you caught him?"

"My mother fucking cousin Wee-Wee hit me like 'bruh this lil nigga been coming crazy like he with the smoke or something. I'm gon do you a solid and give you the drop on him, but for the family, you gotta make it impossible for this fuck boy celebrity ass nigga to have an open casket funeral."

"Come on, bruh; you know your family aint supposed to be involved in none of the shit we doing." Psycho heard Ski chime in, and he shook his head, acknowledging his concerns.

Before continuing his story, Psycho thought that if Wee-Wee helped him get the drop on somebody, it was an issue, and he wasn't going to tell them how he'd got the drop on Freak.

"The lil rapping nigga was crazy for running his mouth the way he was and not being ready when I pulled up on him," Psycho said before narrating the story. "I aint in my g-ride; I'm in a jeep leaving the dust spot with the lil homies Slugs, A.K., Trey Eight, and M Dot, and we just out cruising looking for some action, and out of nowhere, I spot the nigga Swag g-ride. I followed the nigga, and after a minute, he saw me and took off flying. Mind you, this pretty nigga in a Beemer, if he knew what he was doing, he was supposed to leave me. It's a lil hard to keep up, but this fuck boy pulls up at an intersection and stops at a red light. I guess he thinking I'm playing with him and I aint gon finish him cause it's broad day in a public place."

"Your lil homies was there for the whole shit?"

"Yeah. It's a couple of Murder and Shine homies out here tripping on these Neighborhood niggas, but these are my lil homies. They the ones responsible for the bulk of the Neighborhood niggas heads that's getting knocked off."

"It aint no coincidence that all that nigga lil homies besides M Dot is named after guns and shit."

"They're all shooters," Psycho said, returning the spotlight from Hoffa. "Anyway, though, I hop out and run up on the Neighborhood nigga, and he is sitting there smirking, trying to talk to me with some bitch sitting in his passenger seat. I drew the cannons on him, and he threw his hands in the air, still trying to talk."

"So what happened?"

"I put like five in his face."

"And two in the bitch face?" Young Du asked.

"Wrong time, wrong place."

Psycho went on for some time, telling them story after story until Young Du went on his phone and sent everybody a link to the video of the nigga Alpo getting killed on Facebook Live.

"Tell us about this shit."

"Oh, Nah, that wasn't my work. That nigga still had half his mother fucking face on. He was a rat, too; whoever got him should have knocked the rest of that shit off. Don't leave nothing for a nigga like that family to have an open casket."

"It was Alpo and his man, Boss, right?"

"Alpo and Boss was heavy as fuck in these streets." Ski thought out loud. "Them niggas supplied a lil bit of everybody. I'm surprised niggas got to them."

"Somebody put the hammer on them before I could."

"They were the only two that got whacked, but in the video, you can see it was like four bitches that got shot in the process. Said they both ate the cheese and told on niggas before."

"They did eat the cheese; I saw the paperwork. Them niggas been telling."

Psycho told them for years niggas had been saying Alpo and Boss were rats, but they'd been paying off Itchy-Ru and the Green family for protection.

"Only reason they aint been get they heads blew off is cause them niggas get that bag and they aint got a problem paying they weight in gold."

After the laughs and stories were told, Young Du told the room he'd visited his man Omar, who had heard about the run-in they had in Paterson and was concerned about everybody. Twizzy Hoffa said that Twizzy Rollack was equally concerned about the four men. He also said that his brother began suggesting that maybe he should consider delegating his oversight of the blocks and distribution responsibilities and taking the leash off Psycho so he could handle whatever was going on with the Neighborhood homies.

Rollack suggested all this so his brother could be less involved and less hands-on and if the incidents that had already taken place resulted in all-out set tripping. They never wanted to make peace. Having a rapport with the Neighborhood leadership, Hoffa could argue that his hands were clean while trying to squash the war.

Hoffa had expected Psycho to agree with this suggestion but didn't expect anybody else to. It was a lil surprising when Young Du told him he should think about listening to his brother and falling back. Even more surprising, though, was Ski, still hospitalized, agreeing with the suggestion and sounding eager to get back on the streets, making the possibility of Hoffa taking on a less active role sound like a minor detail.

From that point on, with Ski still bedridden, Hoffa introduced Young Du to more heavy hitters throughout the state to increase the clientele. He also designated Psycho as the unofficial leader of their retaliation efforts.

One week turned into another, and with leaders of different Blood sets spreading the word that Ski and some nigga named Young Du were calling for a leadership meeting, the pressure was building. With Ski still out of commission, Young Du tried to hit the ground running by meeting up, trying to make deals, and even giving out free samples to different mother fuckers that Hoffa had put him in touch with.

But the more people Young Du chopped it up with, the more he realized that not being from Jersey or knowing the movers and shakers made things much more difficult than he'd anticipated.

Of course, everybody knew that most of the people they were trying to supply would be cautious about copping from somebody none of them knew. Nobody was naive enough to think that it would just be a walk in the park for Young Du. But it wasn't exactly like Young Du was just some unknown nigga off the streets, either.

Though the people he was meeting with didn't know him personally, pretty much all of them who had been living this life long enough had heard his name before and knew he had to be somebody who had put it down for the gang and was well connected because they all knew he was from

California and was an O.G. That being the case, Hoffa, Ski, and Young Du assumed that because they had the best shit niggas would give Young Du a chance, but as much as he tried, shit kept moving slowly.

Their sales hadn't fallen off, trap houses still had new walk-ins, and they were still supplying everybody on the streets who'd ever touched any of their work. But their clientele wasn't growing the way it should have been. The buzz about their work wasn't constantly bringing in new money the way it should have been, and Young Du attributed all of this to the idea that because niggas didn't know him, most of the real movers and shakers were uncomfortable dealing with him.

While Ski sat on the sideline, he gave Young Du a couple of amateur sales strategies he could employ to get at some homies. Ski told him he could approach whoever was at the top of each set with a proposition. Because of their time in the game, Ski told him big homies wouldn't waste his time, they knew a good deal when they heard it, and they knew how to conduct business minus the bull shit. He said the downside of approaching the set leaders was that their wisdom made them cautious of new business.

Ski told him he could reach out to their underlings, who were typically so ambitious to do almost anything to help them move up the status ladder that they were easier to connect with. Or he could skip the levels of bureaucracy, go straight to the streets, and directly give work to every reckless lil homie he could find occupying street corners, trapping hand to hand.

With the big homies being hard to deal with due to the unfamiliarity and all the unnecessary risks that would come with directly supplying the foot soldiers, Young Du was instead meeting and dealing with many of the underbosses. However, as beneficial as they could be, these dealings were sometimes failures.

Since they started getting money, they'd been trying to sit down with the leaders of the state's biggest and strongest Blood sets, like Brim, Piru, Neighborhood, Murder, Teck, and G-Shine. The first three, being west-side sets and originating in California, almost dwarfed the other sets because they were made up of smaller subsets called branches.

Naturally, they were supplying a lot of Teck and Murder homies because a couple of them were Teck or Murder. But they weren't attracting much new business from homies under the other big sets. With Neighborhood, of course, being off the table due to the tripping and them having no strong relationships with any of the leadership from any of the other sets, Young Du walked into a boxing gym in Paterson to meet with three low-ranking Brim homies.

At this point, they'd given up on sitting down with Run, but because his lil homie Stacks had dealings with them before his arrest, Young Du felt good about the meeting with Stacks' underlings. The three men were lieutenants of different branches under Stacks, and after wasting Young Du's time with greetings and small talk of their sets politics, they confirmed that Young Du was the real deal. But before they could agree to do business, they demanded he end the tripping against Neighborhood. Young Du told them that couldn't happen because the blood had already been shed, and they flat-out ended the meeting.

When that was done, without fully considering precisely what had gone wrong or what might need to be changed for the next pitch, Young Du reached out and arranged to meet with Psycho's cousin Wee-Wee.

Just reaching out to Wee-Wee or any of Psycho's family to discuss any business, Young Du had to ignore everything he'd heard about their family. But Wee-Wee was Piru, and although he wasn't one of the leaders of the set, he did have enough status to make calls authorizing deals on behalf of his lil homies.

Young Du believed that with a foot in the door, Wee-Wee could eventually open up Piru to their business. Less than five minutes into the meeting, though, Young Du had realized that it was likely a lost cause.

Wee-Wee had Young Du meet him at a Mob Piru trap house. Loud music could be heard outside the Jersey City apartment, and PCP could be smelt. Inside, the tiny railroad apartment looked more like a teenager's clubhouse than a drug dealer's trap house.

A fiend opened the door before taking a seat on the arm of a couch where a lil homie slept. Another lil homie sat at a small table across from Wee-Wee, and a young female halfway under the table had her face buried in his lap. Rock panted behind her, his tail wagging. Young Du could see they weren't really about money, but as Wee-Wee moved his gun and a jar of PCP off the cluttered table and shooed Rock away, he sat his small duffle bag on the table and emptied its contents.

Minutes after Young Du had entered the apartment, as he and Wee-Wee discussed prices for different amounts of product, the female on her knees crawled out from under the table once the lil homie had finished in her mouth. Wiping the drool from her cheek, she fondled Young Du and grabbed his crotch, offering to suck his dick despite not knowing him or even exchanging a word with him. It took Wee-Wee barking on her...

"Fuck you doing!" For her to get up pouting.

"Damn." She sounded annoyed. "I thought he wanted his dick sucked; I'm just trying to be nice."

"Find something to do with your mother fucking self before I make you put Rock in your mouth."

As she grabbed a bottle of water from the table and drank it, Wee-Wee told Young Du not to mind her. He said she stayed at the trap house, exchanging sexual favors to feed her addiction until the drug took its toll on her looks, at which point they'd trade her in for the next new thing.

With the games out of the way, the man who'd opened the door dipped the tip of his finger in Young Du's sack of coke before placing that finger in his mouth and twisting his face up in approval, lightly nibbling on his now numb tongue.

"Damn nephew, I ain't taste shit like that since the mid-eighties."

With drool still on her face, the female who tried to give Young Du fellatio eagerly helped the man open the bag of dope as Young Du marveled at how young and pretty the light-skinned girl looked. She couldn't have been older than twenty, and while her clothes were dingy, she was pretty and youthful. Her light complexion still shined, and her hair was almost perfectly wrapped around her small head in a doobie wrap.

"Pretty young thing, ain't she?" Wee-Wee asked, noticing Young Du's stare.

"Yeah."

"That's only cause she just started fucking with dope."

"It's only been a couple of days." She wined, causing Wee-Wee and his lil homie to laugh.

"This bitch ain't left this trap house since the end of the winter, and she is talking about it only been a couple of days."

The second the bag of dope was opened, a repugnant chemical odor filled the air, and both the fiends squinted their eyes, fumbling with their syringe and spoon setups as they prepared their fix.

"Mmmm, Mmm! I can tell you off the top you can't put anything like this on the streets. Or mother fuckers aint gon know how to act."

"Somebody gon O.D. every day." The man said, finishing the female's train of thought. Once the two injected the poison into their veins, their highs immediately came down. "Shiittt. If I knew I was gon O.D. and die..." He began as the female sucked on her thumb and twisted her earlobe between her fingers. "This would be the horse I wanna ride through the pearly gates on right here."

"How much work you brought with you?" Wee-Wee asked.

"It's only like fifty grams of each, something small. I already told you the numbers; now you see it's good. I figured ya'll would buy this lil shit today and I'd be waiting to hear from ya'll to re-up in the next few days."

"Come here bitch!" Wee-Wee demanded, smacking the female's ass real hard, which prompted her to go to her knees, crawl under the table over between his legs, unzip his pants and bury her face in his lap.

Running his fingers through her hair as he pushed her head down hard, Wee-Wee spoke across the table to Young Du as if he wasn't being sucked beneath the table.

"I'm saying, niggas ain't have no chicken out to be buying no work today. I thought you were coming to chop it up with us and show us what you are working with. On the flip side, though, you brought the work here; I know it's good, so you minds well leave it here, and I'll make sure you get..."

"Oh naw, I ain't have no plans on leaving niggas with that much work on some consignment shit."

"You just said it was something small; now you are coming like you don't trust niggas or something."

"It ain't even about trust."

"That's exactly what it's about." Wee-Wee's lil homie broke his silence from the other end of the table. "Ain t nobody here gon rob you for a couple of thousand dollars' worth of shit, bruh."

"Oh, I ain't worrying about nobody trying to rob me."

"So act like that then nigga. Act like you know what mother fucking time it is, keep it pushing, and tomorrow or the next day, I'll get with you to give you what's yours off of this, and we'll be able to put some of our money in your pocket for some more work."

Though the request completely blindsided him, Young Du didn't feel played or like he'd been robbed when he left the work. While him and Wee-

Wee didn't know each other personally, Young Du was aware that Wee-Wee did know his name and his rep. Everything about the Green family said they were crazy, but Young Du knew Wee-Wee wouldn't be stupid enough to get work from an OG and never pay for it.

Young Du also told himself that he had a mission he was trying to complete, and he believed that the more hands moved their product, the more likely it would be to increase their customer base. While fifty grams of coke and dope weren't exactly crumbs, Young Du knew it wasn't enough to make or break them either. He knew he'd feel played if he never heard from Wee-Wee again, but what stood to be lost in that investment was less than what they'd passed out in free samples.

With all that said, though, for whatever reason catching everybody off guard, Young Du started hitting everybody up to cancel the meeting days before the leadership meeting was supposed to be held. This surprised everybody. Ski and Hoffa got a lil concerned, thinking it might have been a mistake to put everything in Young Du's hands. But Twizzy Rollack, calling from his cell phone, pretty much laughed away their concerns, telling them that Omar had convinced him that Young Du knew precisely what he was doing and that he had a trick up his sleeve.

Two and a half weeks after the shooting, Ski was home, and in his mind, he was ready to play. Unfortunately, due to being shot center mass with three forty-five caliber projectiles shattering before ricocheting off his sternum down to his lower extremities, Ski's right leg could barely support his body weight.

Despite his drive, though, Ski knew the danger of underestimating an adversary, especially considering the current climate on the streets. He was hungry as fuck, but he wasn't stupid enough to be trying to move around freely when he knew he could barely fend for himself.

Not being a homebody, Ski's first days out of the hospital were mopey and gloomy as he sat around the house with his girlfriend. But by the end of the first week, home Ski was ready to move. He was even more eager after he got the scoop on how dire things looked on the streets and was told that once he was active again, him and Young Du would be the faces of their movement, responsible for lining up and executing deals, thereby splitting the lion's share of the profit four ways with Twizzy Rollack and Omar.

This, of course, would all be done while Hoffa played under boss, becoming less involved, and Psycho unofficially took control of their response to the shootings.

Ski felt uneasy and anxious about doing something right now, though. Addressing this anxiety as soon as an opportunity presented itself, from the comfort of his house, Ski started going through his old contacts, hitting up his personal connect and making the same moves he'd been making before Hoffa spoke to him about falling back off his side hustles. This wasn't done because he was hurting for money. The bag was still coming in. He only really started making his own moves out of sheer boredom.

With all this going on, though, Ski was somewhat taken aback when Young Du unexpectedly popped up at his house.

"I'm on the way to pick up some chicken, so I can't even sit down now. I just wanted to stop by to bring you what's yours." Young Du paused as he sat a wad of cash on a nearby coffee table. "Make sure you aight and see if you can come out with me in a few days."

"Oh yeah, I'm saying." Ski struggled to stand before being cut off by his female companion.

"He can't be going nowhere like that. He needs his cane to walk, so he can't run around in the streets now. Mmm, mmm. If anything happens out there, he won't even be able to move the way he needs to and fend for himself." She hesitated for emphasis. "I mean damn, yall gotta give my baby some type of break so he can heal."

"Oh yeah, Amy, this my homie Young Du, Du, this my lil peoples, soon to be baby mother, Amy."

"I aint never been nobody lil peoples; you better tell that nigga you wired up."

Laughing with the couple, the little feeling of apprehension that had begun to grow in Young Du toward the loud, outspoken female all but evaporated as he found his way in.

"How many months 'til you due?"

"A lil less than three." She said matter-of-factly, rubbing her stomach.

"Congratulations to both y'all; I just found out I got a lil one on the way in like two months myself." He began monitoring her response. "I aint trying to take the homie out in the streets, I see the condition he in and how yall in here boo loving and shit, so I don't wanna disturb none of that. But in a couple of days, me and my people are trying to come to scoop y'all up so we can take y'all shopping."

Leaving Ski and Amy, Young Du received a call, left Newark, and headed for New York, eventually finding his way to a Bronx brownstone apartment, where a tall Hispanic man greeted him at the door.

"You don't look like your name, Dutches."

"Nah, I'm not." The man flatly said, offering no further explanation or name. He led Young Du inside to a brown-skinned female waiting in the foyer before leaving the two.

"You must be Dutches."

"And you, Young Du." She said, putting the blunt she held to her lips. "When Hoffa first said he couldn't make it here and shot your name at me, I'm like, I know this nigga, I fuck with his aunt Sam Black."

"Who?"

"Sam Black, Samantha the Neighborhood homegirl. She got a salon and some other shit in Jersey City." She explained, exhaling smoke and waving her hand in a canceling gesture. "You probably don't know her. You do look like her nephew, though, and you got a familiar ass voice. Anyway, I know I am rambling and shit, but I realized you weren't who I thought you might be when Hoffa told me that you were from Brooklyn.",

"Yeah, Marcy. I just came home a couple of months ago, though."

"A couple months ago?" The Hispanic man, now carrying a small paper bag, sarcastically asked as he reentered the room. Tell Hoffa I said I need the same numbers as before but in about half the time.

Chapter Nine

A lil over a week later, Young Du showed up at Ski's house again. After introducing Ski and Amy to Candy, the dark-skinned Hispanic female with a curvy body like the number eight, he called his partner; he called an Uber, and the four rode to New York City.

"What's good with your man, Psycho?" Young Du made small talk on the way to the city. "I keep hearing y'all talking about his family and shit like they the mob or something.'

"Nah, he just related to the Green family. Got a lil sister and two older brothers, Spyke and C-Green. Then he got like a million cousins and shit."

"You serious?"

"Facts, bro, he got at least thirty-forty first cousins." Ski laughed. "Them Green mother fuckers aint the mob or nothing but everybody in the family play. If we weren't trying to supply the state but instead we were out here off our bullshit, blowing gun smoke every day getting niggas robbed, kidnapped, or killed, the Greens would be the mother fuckers you want on your side."

"Oh yeah?"

"Yeah. The whole family lives for action. All that smoke draws the wrong kind of heat, though. We don't need any of that. That's why niggas nervous about him involving his family in any of our shit."

"I'm saying, knowing that he might involve them mother fuckers you think it's a good idea to keep him on the team?"

"Bruh, nutty as squirrel shit, but he a good ass nigga at heart. Always gon do what's right, aint too many niggas more genuine than son. As far as his family goes, I am not worried about anybody with his last name getting involved as much as Hoffa is. Cause I know none of them fuck with son."

"Yeah?"

"Facts," Ski replied and went on to tell Young Du that he knew Psycho's father before describing the man as a fly-ass old head that liked young bitches. Psycho's brothers Spyke and C-Green were like nine and ten years old when his pops robbed the cradle and shot Psycho's fifteen-year-old mother.

Ski said, Long story short, when Psycho was like five, his brothers used to torture him and lock him in the basement with their dogs. One day, something happened with his mother and his brothers. Psycho heard screams, and he snapped, stabbing his brothers.

Ski said years later, after Psycho'd been tortured by his brothers throughout his childhood, during his late teen years, while his older brothers were locked up, Psycho fucked both of their baby mothers and had a baby with one of them.

"Damn, that's family drama for you. Now, I get why you said the family don't fuck with him like that."

"He a good nigga, though. He aint do shit to them niggas that they aint have coming."

Once they got to the Experience Auto Group dealership, Ski limped across the car lot before stopping at a red Cadillac CTS.

"Damn, this a bad lil bitch right here."

"Nice, but it's a coupe, babe." Amy began rubbing the pudge in her stomach. "I thought you wanted another truck; I don't know if you need a coupe right now."

"This aint just any coupe; it's a V coupe, and I don't even know if my pockets are deep enough for a truck anyway."

"That's kind of backward, but don't let the tag make your decisions for you." Young Du whispered through a contrived smirk as he stepped between the two. "I know you brought a lil bag out here to spend, but I got something for you to blow too."

"You did play a big part in fucking up my Suburban," Ski said with a laugh.

After looking around for the better part of a half-hour, Ski settled on a black Escalade, and he and Young Du talked numbers with the dealer handling their sale. At the dealer's insistence, they had Amy sign all the necessary documents before they drove off the lot in a new Cadillac.

"Back to Jersey?"

"Nah. Take us to the Jewelers Row." Young Du directed Amy.

"Jewelers Row?"

"Yeah, the Diamond District. We still got a couple racks to blow."

"Damn, business must be doing way better than I'm hearing."

Turning to look Ski in the face, Young Du smirked and tried to sound solemn.

"Let's not talk business right now."

"Not talk business; that's a hard thing to do. Business and war is the only thing going on right now."

"Business aint a problem. We aint doing the numbers we should be doing, but it's bound to pick up. And as retarded as I think that nigga Psycho is, he handling that war shit."

"You want me to believe that?"

"Come on, bruh. You got hit, Hoffa got hit, and I took one in the shoulder, and shit slowed down, but it aint stopping. I want you back out here with me moving and shaking as soon as possible, but till then, I'ma keep making all the necessary moves that I can to hold this shit up as much as I can."

"I'm talking about that tripping shit."

"You for real?" Young Du challenged Ski's assertion. "You know what them streets looking like right now?"

"I know we put a nut in charge of a bunch of shooters."
Young Du chucked before responding.

"I think it's something like two niggas from our camp that took slugs since that shit happened in Paterson, and only one of them was serious. On the flip side, I done heard about damn near a dozen of them Neighborhood niggas getting they shit knocked off. A car full of them niggas just got tore up in Lakewood like two days ago. I couldn't keep count of how many of them niggas got shot if I wanted to. That nigga Psycho might be retarded as fuck, but he is tearing up anything repping Neighborhood on the Streets."

Stopping in the Diamond District, Young Du directed them into a jewelry store he said he'd been to before, and a jeweler quickly offered his expertise to Ski as he admired a watch display.

"Jorg Gray, founded in California, is renowned amongst novice watch buyers and timepiece connoisseurs for its aesthetic quality, trademark blends, and marriages of trends with sophistication."

"I'm saying, this shit nice, but I don't think I heard of no Jorg Gray before."

"The brand is relatively new, but the fact that they have quickly become a well-recognized name in retail watches is to their credit and shouldn't be taken for granted." The jeweler stopped to pull a watch from the display. "This specific timepiece, the Eighty-three hundred-twenty-one, isn't new; it's from the brand's cherished vaulted collection and was made specifically to commemorate their fifth anniversary. The forty-seven-millimeter chronograph is powered by a Swiss quartz movement and housed in a stainless steel case with a rose gold bezel that matches the dial, all to accentuate the enclosed sapphire crystal.

Sold on the watch, plus two G-Shocks, Ski heard Young Du in his ear.

"I fuck with them G shocks; I got a couple of them. But they aren't going to appreciate themselves like that, Jorg Gray.

"Bruh, I aint worried about none of this shit appreciating itself. Long as the bitches appreciate it, I'm good." Ski began as he turned around to savor the rear view of Amy and Candy from across the room.

A second jeweler helped the two females, showing Amy a pair of white and yellow Takat earrings with ruby centers as Candy giggled, wrapping a red-on-white Curtis and Company love timepiece on her wrist.

"Why you called shorty your partner?"

"That's what the fuck she is, that's the Brim homegirl from out in Philly. When they shipped me out of Trenton to do my last three years in P.A., my homie Omar put me on with her; we linked up, and from day one, she was kicking the door down for visits. They did everything a nigga needed and rode out with me like a champ. She's a trap star, too, fuck with the same connect Omar got us copping from. I'm thinking about bringing her on the team cause it's mad shit I know she could bring to the table. I don't know what else to tell you except that we've been rocking together since we met.

"What the fuck does that mean, though?"

"It means that's my lil bitch." He laughed. "Even if she wasn't, though, you got a whole pregnant bitch on your hands."

"Yeah, but that's different. I got a thing for chocolate."

"I'm saying your baby mother chocolate too, and she aint no slouch either."

"Yeah, but your bitch Candy different."

"What the fuck are you talking about?" Young Du said with a laugh.

"Tiffany milk chocolate but your bitch Candy black Spanish ass made of that black Godiva chocolate."

"Godiva?"

"Yeah, that's that high-quality dark chocolate."

"Oh you hitting me with all these questions to see how I'ma feel if you try to get in them draws. Nigga, I thought you was wifed up."

They laugh before Ski says he is about family because all he had was his mom's growing up, but he'd never been with one chick before, and Amy was a prune.

"I never did this relationship shit before. I aint got no other kids, though, so when Amy got pregnant, I had to level up. Not for nothing, but I never knew my father, so when Amy got pregnant, I had to make some commitment for the baby and shit."

"Oh, I can dig it, you preaching to the choir. Like most niggas, your pops wasn't there, so you wanna make sure Amy know you're there for her."

"Something like that."

"Stand up, shit." Young Du sounded supportive, looking over his shoulder at Amy and Candy touching each other. The two didn't know each other before today. But they had gone through all the introductions, formalities, and small talk during the ride to New York. At the dealership, they joked and giggled with each other, and now, here at the jeweler, they were a lil touchy-feely as Candy went from rubbing Amy's stomach to grabbing her ass.

"If you are trying to get at the homegirl or something, go ahead and shoot your load nigga. I aint gon trip; make your move. But you better hurry up and pull the trigger 'cause she is quick on the draw when she sees something she likes."

Turning around, Ski watched Amy and Candy's hand games.

"She likes bitches too?"

"All bitches like bitches. Some of them just like niggas too."

"Aight, but right now, I'm interested in the shit you were saying about her being a trap star."

"Come on, bruh. I told you where she from and what she about. You look at the homegirl and see she about here coins. You already know what time it is."

"I guess whatever shit she into is where your extra money coming from. You came out of pocket with a lot of chicken today, and I have been saying to myself, either this nigga got something else going on, or business gotta be doing a lot better than I'm being told."

"Come on, bruh, you sitting in the house all day collecting your cut, and you still wanna question what's going on?" Young Du acted annoyed, prolonging his finale. "My question is, whatever I have going on is my business. What that got to do with you, though?"

"Nigga I'm saying we must be getting our shares from different pies 'cause I can't just say fuck it, come out of pocket and blow the chicken you dropped today just because I feel like it."

"You really wanna do this now?"

"I'm doing what we all signed up for and agreed to do. You are the only one doing something different."

"Really? So you gon stand here and front like you aint been pushing bricks on the side?" Young Du challenged drawing a blank from Ski. "See what I'm saying? You can front like you don't know what I'm talking bout, but we both know what time it is. What you do on the side to put money in your pocket is your business, so what I do shouldn't concern you either."

Shifting his weight from one side to the other, Ski changed the subject, breaking his silence.

"I was surprised when I heard you canceled the meeting."

"I had to; we weren't ready for that shit. You already know none of them niggas know me like that, so that shit was doomed to fail. I would have walked in there and blown our one shot at trying to make one sales pitch to everybody simultaneously. On top of that, depending on how bad

86

I bombed the shit, it could have fucked up the lil momentum we already got built in the streets right now."

Ski told him that, under the best circumstances, if both of them made a perfect sales pitch together at a status meeting with most of the big homies in the state, it would never be as successful as Young Du thought. In Jersey, blood wasn't as united as it used to be. Ski said it was so much back-biting and homies doing bull shit to each other that niggas were too skeptical to get something accomplished.

"I see the vision and shit. I agree with the reasons Twizzy Rollack and your man Omar want us to try to focus on supplying the homies. Blood runs the state, and if we can stick with supplying the homies, it'd be quicker flips, no exposure, less overall risk, and easier access to money."

"It should be."

"If this the game plan we gon stick to, though, we got a better chance at busting it up with different big homies under different sets individually than we do at trying to go at all of them together.

"I hear you."

"I aint gon front though, bruh, even if we do what I'm describing, shit still aint gon be perfect. A lot of mother fuckers aint gon just stop what they are doing, say fuck whatever connects they have been rocking with, and start copping shit from us. It's never gon be that easy in Jersey. More than that, though, niggas are way too stupid and stubborn to see an oppor-tunity right in front of them." Ski paused, grabbing the merchandise, and they headed for the door.

"Then we gotta account for the local politics."

"That and it's a whole lot of homies that are like vultures and scavengers and shit in Jersey. As fucked up as it sounds, a lot of homies like it when we divided. For whatever reason, it may be good for their business. So they aint gon see no benefit in everybody coming together on some united shit cause they profiting off the separation."

"Good product sells itself, bruh. Compensate for niggas stubbornness by forcing the opportunity on them. Come at them with shit they can't turn away. I don't give a fuck how stupid niggas are; if we come at them with shit that just sounds so good that all they see is dollar signs while you are talking, I know most of them will be willing to fuck with each other just to get to the bag."

"You make it sound real easy. Either you are thinking about selling shit for damn near nothing, or you gon be bringing niggas in on all them dope boy moves you have been making on the side."

"I aint making it sound easy; you're just concerned about the moves I'm making." Sitting in the rear of the S.U.V., Young Du chuckled and continued. "To keep it a band with you, bruh, if it's for the betterment of the movement, my business aint off the table. But if that's what it's gon be, the shit you are doing on the side can't be off the table either. Everybody else aside, it gotta be some open book policy between us concerning your lil side hustles, any personal clients you got, or whatever you wanna call it."

"I hear you."

"If we both throw all our chips on the table, I'ma hit you with a couple of surprises and shit cause the homie Omar done pulled some shit out his sleeve, and he got a couple of things cooking up that I know you aint gon expect. Once you open up and bring all this clientele you got to the table, I'ma show you how to put all the pieces where they need to be, and it's gon seem like the money coming in doubled overnight."

They talked about rescheduling the status meeting, and Ski ensured Young Du knew he wanted to see Candy around more often. He laughed and got back to the point, emphasizing to Ski that as long as he saw him trying to integrate his side hustle and personal customers with what they were doing, he'd be able to move numbers around a lil and bring other things to the table to put some chicken in niggas pockets real fast.

"Psycho out here handling this tripping shit, and I, for the time being, I got us. Other than putting me in front of the right mother fuckers, all you really gotta do is stand with me and come up with a way to handle the lil leak we got at the Paterson trap house."

"Leak?" Ski asked as Young Du smirked.

Chapter Ten

The following weeks elapsed relatively similar to the ones after the shooting, except for a few significant differences. First, the narcotics they distributed grew from cocaine and heroin to ecstasy, molly, and marijuana. Then, at Ski's request, Candy's presence became more of a regular thing. True to Young Du's word, she immediately started earning her keep by providing them with fentanyl and a few other prescription drugs. This, along with Ski's extensive list of contacts, brought on a crazy increase in sales.

Around this time, Ski also started hitting different homies to reschedule the leadership meeting, and just over a month after the shopping expedition, Ski, with a cane in hand and Young Du at his side, limped into a large park in Newark, New Jersey, where Blood leadership meetings were sometimes held.

Every few months, or whenever pressing issues arose, the top two or three ranking homies from various sets would meet to discuss and settle relevant issues. At this meeting, Neighborhood was the only major set lacking any representation. This was obviously due to the ongoing war. The war itself and a way to end it were part of the driving premise that Ski used to call the meeting.

It was common knowledge that the back-and-forth set tripping initially started when Murder and Shine's homies tripped on the Neighborhood Homie Got Guns, and his homies, in turn, tripped back against Murder and Shine's homies. But while retaliating, the Neighborhood homies had moved on to a few Murder or Shine homies who just happened to be in the presence of other uninvolved homies from different sets.

This drew other homies and their sets into the melee. That wasn't a good thing for Neighborhood as a set. At best, it gave the appearance that the Neighborhood homies either weren't capable of executing hits on specific individuals they wanted to kill, or they simply didn't give a fuck about being discriminated against. At worst, it looked like Neighborhood as a set was at war with Blood as a whole. Either way, this was problematic.

After discussing a handful of other minor issues, the floor fell to Ski and Young Du. Ski had some rapport with most of the ranking homies there, and he had the benefit of the others knowing his name, so he made their argument and expressed the obvious to everybody there.

The war against Neighborhood wasn't helping anybody make money. The circle acknowledged that but said it would be hard to agree on ending the war without any Neighborhood homies being present. Ski stood firm, saying that the war needed to end now. Only a lil over a dozen sets had representation present at the meeting. Nobody there questioned or spoke against anything Ski said except a Spanish Piru homie named Wolf.

"Not for nothing, but it's easy as fuck for you to say you wanna end the war when you the nigga that been winning. It's hard for any mafucka with pride to say they ready to end some shit when most of the bodies that are dropping is coming from the side."

"I'm saying," Ski's big homie Wacka chimed in. "You fuck with the Neighborhood nigga Mill and the homegirl Samantha, so why you can't just try to mediate between them to end this shit?"

"Off the bat, I can tell you niggas I aint going to Mill with none of this shit. No bueno. That's my man and his lil homies out here getting slaughtered in these mother fucking streets. I go to him talking some peace shit right now; he might throw a gun in my face. That's how I'd be coming in his shoes, and most of y'all would do the same shit. Far as Samantha goes, I can reach out to her and let her know what niggas terms are and see how she feels about it, or I can just try to arrange a sit down so niggas can bust it up with her. But I can't promise shit. I don't know exactly how she is feeling over all this shit, and that's my homegirl, so I aint going to her like I'm trying to force you niggas treaty down her mother fucking throat. I aint too big on no middleman shit anyway."

"Say less."

"First off." A dark-skinned, bald Bounty Hunter homie named Zoom, who wasn't even from Jersey, spoke up. "Being that I aint from out here, I wanna start by saluting all you niggas for trying to handle shit with some diplomacy. I'm from Cali. I and a couple of my lil homies came to Jersey to see my comrade Bones, and the next thing I knew, Bones was telling me, 'Bruh, I'm going to this status meeting, and I want you to swing through with me.' I was against the shit until he mentioned the Teck homie Wacka and being that me and the homie go back, I'm like, I'ma swing through this mafucka so that I can see my comrade. Mind you, I'm walking in this park thinking I'm just gon be here to observe. But now I'm hearing some shit that I gotta respond to."

"Speak your mind."

"I don't see any Neighborhood homies here." Zoom continued after Wacka, who seemed to be coordinating the meeting, gave him the floor. "I know y'all pretty much already said that. I only repeat it to say if niggas don't even wanna show their faces to try and negotiate peace, then fuck them. You can't be wasting your time with shit like that. Keep in mind, verbally negotiating aint the only way you make peace. It sounds fucked up, but sometimes you gotta knock off a couple of the right heads before mother fuckers realize peace is in their best interest."

"It's heads getting knocked off like every other day."

"They aint the right ones," Zoom told Ski.

The big homie acknowledged that he wasn't familiar with the specifics on the ground. He told Ski and everybody else that in war, most of the niggas on the front line of the losing side want peace so the war can be over. They wanna go back to getting money or whatever the fuck they were doing before. Most of all, though, he said they want it to be over so they can stop fucking losing.

At the same time, he said as long as it's certain mother fuckers at the top making noise, all the lil worker bee's that's underneath them on the front line gotta keep up the act like they really wanna keep going to war.

"You knock off the right heads, and the worker bees will feel like they can beg for peace without getting punished and ridiculed."

"Aight. That's enough about all that shit." Wacka cut in, shifting the meeting's direction. "When y'all first hit me up about this meeting before the tripping got heavy, I was told y'all was gon have some type of proposition on the table."

"Like y'all wanted to bring niggas to the table with y'all plug or something."

"Oh, nah. That aint happening." Young Du spoke up in response to the homie named Woody, who Ski had already told him was double O.G. under Outlaw. "We got stupid low prices on all the work we got, but niggas aint getting access to no connect."

"All wars draw heat. I don't know if y'all know it or not but this tripping shit with y'all and them Neighborhood niggas aint even just between y'all and them no more. Y'all homies are getting moved on when they are in the presence of other niggas, and that's drawing other niggas into y'all bullshit. On top of that, that shit got the streets on fire right now. It's hard for niggas to move the way they want. I wouldn't have even come to show my face at this mother fucking meeting if I would have known y'all wasn't even gon have the decency to try and offer niggas a spot at the table with y'all connect."

"We are the connect," Ski replied to a Brim homie, and then he went on to list prices for various quantities of weight for the different drugs they sold before ultimately being cut off by Young Du.

"On top of them low ass prices we do got some other shit on the way that we just gon bring to the table and let homies have they way with."

"So y'all aint bringing niggas to the table with the connect, but y'all got something you just gon give mother fuckers?"

"This some type of charity shit or something?" The Brim homie joked, drawing Ski's sharp response.

"Not exactly. I don t really wanna say too much about it or what it is right now, but we do know that this tripping shit is fucking with the way niggas move, and that's getting in the way of niggas money, so we got some things lined up that'll put a lil bit of fast money in everybody pocket."

"That shit sound good."

"On that note." Wacka interrupted the Brim homie. "If aint nobody else got anything relevant to say, we can go ahead and end this meeting."

Walking away from the circle, Young Du felt some way about the fact that nothing solid had come out of the meeting. It seemed to have gone a lot worse than he'd anticipated. In the worst case scenario, a couple of sets would come together to unite in the tripping against Neighborhood instead of homies from other sets attacking Neighborhood at random when and if they saw fit.

He also thought they would walk away from the meeting with at least a few verbal agreements to do some business. But besides the Piru homie Wolf saying he'd speak to Samantha about the set tripping, nobody had committed to do anything about the war.

Even more surprising to Young Du was that, besides a few general questions about their weight, it didn't seem like anybody showed any serious interest in doing business with them. This was despite the fact that the price they wanted their homies to pay for any of their work today was almost half what their homies would pay for the same amount of work from any other connect.

Watching everybody holding personal conversations, Young Du removed his designer shades just as he heard Ski's voice behind him.

"That was better than I thought."

"How is that? We came in this mother fucker and just gave our spiel and shit for no reason. Aint nobody commit to buying nothing or doing nothing about this tripping shit. We barely got a real response to anything we said."

"Them niggas heard that shit though."

"Yeah, they heard it."

"And that's all that matters right now. We got the heads of more than fifteen of Jersey's biggest sets to come together and hear our spiel about this tripping shit and about us getting to that bag. They know what the fuck we selling, and they know how to get at us."

"Them niggas aint trying to get no money."

"What, you expected niggas to start making offers and shit right there in front of everybody else? You thought this shit was gon turn into a mother fucking action or something. I could have told you that wasn't gon happen. The left-hand doesn't want the right to know what it's doing." Ski laughed as a tall man approached the two of them. "Young Du, this me, Hoffa and

93

Ski big homie Wacka and Wacka this."

"I know who bruh is." Wacka cut in, reaching to embrace Young Du. "What's good with you nigga? I was in the county jail with your pops when he first got caught with his case back in '98, '99."

"Damn, I was a baby back then."

"I think I was like nineteen when I first met Du Wrong nut ass, and I would have never thought I'd be at a meeting trying to end a war and chopping up numbers and shit with his son. But then again, when I was on my last bid, I heard that you were making a lil noise in the penal system."

"You know the shit, I had to shake up a few spots."

"Yeah. Niggas told me you started a lil movement and shit when you was in Trenton prison on max custody with your pops."

"Yeah, I did eight in Trenton before they shipped me out to P.A."

"What's up with Du Wrong, he aight?"

"He good, going through the typical shit. I don't even know you, though, bruh, so you know I didn't know that y'all knew each other. It's crazy how shit happens."

"Nah. It's crazy that y'all think y'all can supply all the shit y'all was boasting about for the numbers you advertised."

"Real shit, bruh, we wouldn't have done all this if we aint know we could make it all happen."

"The product aint about nothing. We been had that, and we been supplying the streets with it for the last few months." Ski pointed out. "We been had the contacts to put all this shit together, but we wasn't gon bring none of it to niggas attention until the time was right and we felt as though niggas was ready to make something happen."

"It sounds good. Then, y'all volunteering to just up and give niggas some shit?"

"That shit aint really about nothing. An opportunity came at us, so we just gon drop something in niggas hands for the heat this shit causing, and it's gon be something put to the side for the homies that got bagged at our trap house too."

"This some good will shit or something. You niggas doing a whole lot."

"This what we supposed to be doing." Young Du shot back. "I'm lost on where we stand with the Neighborhood issue."

"What you mean you lost?"

"I got the impression that aint nothing gon change with the way this shit with them Neighborhood niggas getting handled and that aside from different individual homies randomly moving on them, it's just gon stay between us and them."

"Oh nah, make no mistake, we bout to deal with that shit."

"You serious?"

"Absolutely."

"So what is it about to be like Blood as a whole going against Neighborhood?" Young Du asked, putting his shades back on.

"Im saying, whether it was spoken or not in the circle, just know niggas aint smelling how this shit got the streets hot, and they aint even trying to come to the table to bust it up with niggas so everybody pretty much on the same page. But we aint about to be going back and forth with them either."

"So it's like everybody telling they homies its shoot on sight for any Neighborhood nigga you catch right now?"

"Damn, you can say less bruh. Everything don't gotta be said literally." Wacka laughed, looking at Ski. "I know you aint hear nobody give y'all commitments or nothing, but we at a fucking meeting in a park. You should have known wasn't anybody gon jump out the window and say, 'Oh yeah, sell me three of those or a half of that.' Just like you shouldn't have expected niggas to say, 'Oh yeah, we gon ride on these Neighborhood niggas over here or them Neighborhood niggas over there.' Some shit don't even need to be said. You dig me?"

"I can dig it, but it sounded like y'all was talking about still trying to sit down and talk to them mother fuckers."

"That's what it's supposed to sound like. If any unexpected mother fuckers were listening or anybody that was at the meeting left and started running their mouth, it's gon sound like exactly what you just said. It's twenty-twenty-one, bruh; I love my homies, but these duck ass niggas be telling, wearing wires, and doing all types of duck tails shit."

"Duck ass niggas looking for something to tell."

"Give it a hot minute, and niggas gon be getting at y'all about that work. In the meantime, as far as that Neighborhood shit goes, it would be foolish and attract way too much heat for us to be going around trying to wack every Neighborhood nigga. You gotta remember the people that's in power over there is stronger than the power of they people as a whole. That said,

95

all that's needed is the top mother fuckers getting hit, and that's that."

Wacka explained that after the meeting, he briefly chopped it up with the Bounty Hunter homie, Bones, from Camden. He said Zoom and the other homies were out here in Jersey on some clean-up shit. From what Wacka was told, this was their line of work. He said the Bounty Hunter homies were willing to take out one or two of the top homies under Neighborhood to orchestrate a regime change for a small price.

"What's the price?" Ski asked, getting straight to the point.

"Nothing crazy, or we wouldn't be talking about it. Let me handle the numbers, though; other mother fuckers want this problem dealt with, too, so they gon pitch in for it to get solved. I'ma oversee it and make sure everything go down smooth. But I fuck with the homie Zoom, so I trust him with executing the shit. The only thing is them niggas is cowboys, so when they come through squeezing, they gon fire at everything moving."

"That could be a negative if they spill a lot of unnecessary blood for one or two targets."

"It's a positive, too." Young Du chimed in after Ski. "If we blowing the heads off the top mother fuckers to knock the fight out of the rest of they set then it's a good thing for a crime scene to look messy."

"Long as y'all know, Zoom and his homies are indiscriminate. They aint gon know or care about who's out there. I'm gon line shit up, and y'all kick back and wait on the phone call."

"Phone call?" Young Du questioned.

"Yeah. The streets know what it is between y'all and them, so I'ma hit you niggas to give y'all a heads up before anybody gets cooked 'cause you might wanna be somewhere public with a camera or a couple of alibis."

"What's good with the other issue I chopped it up with you about?"

"You sure about the accusations?" Wacka challenged Ski.

"A hundred percent. I wouldn't speak death on lil bruh's name if I weren't positive. I've already told you about his involvement in the incident at the Newark trap house.

"Then he was feeding some type of info to the Neighborhood homies."

"That would explain how they knew to ambush y'all coming out the trap house in Paterson." Wacka agreed.

Chapter Eleven

While the four main niggas on the team, Twizzy Hoffa, Young Du, Psycho, and Ski, each did a lil of everything, they all knew and understood that they each brought different strengths to the table.

Hoffa was brought in from day one by his twin Rollack partly because Rollack and Omar planned to supply their Blood homies, and Twizzy Hoffa was what they called a Super Blood. He knew who most of the big homies under different sets were, which was typical for a gang banger. But Hoffa was a super Blood because he also knew the captains, lieutenants, and local enforcers for different sets in different cities.

Young Du was brought in simply because he was the connect to the connect. While the plug was Omar's, he still sat in a cell, so he obviously couldn't move, shake, go pick up work, or make deals on his own. Omar aimed to supply the homies in Jersey, but he didn't know Twizzy Rollack or his brother, Hoffa, enough to hand his connect over to them. Young Du was essential to the team because Omar knew him enough to trust him with the connect.

Psycho, being a trigger-happy nut case, was purely the muscle on the team. If Omar owned the team, Twizzy Rollack was the coach. In this analogy, Hoffa was the offensive coordinator directing Ski and Young Du all across the state to execute transactions. While any of them would kick for themselves if need be, they only moved freely and peacefully throughout the state because Psycho was on the team. Both who he was in name and all the crazy shit he'd done himself gave them security.

At the end of the day, though, the objective was to move as much work as they could. So, at the opposite end of the spectrum from Psycho, it was Ski, the man whose only reason for being brought on board was to move work.

Ski was their pretty hustler. The only things he'd ever been known for were getting money and being a lover boy. Not a player or womanizer, a lover boy. The pretty light-skinned hustler who tried to take everybody's bitch. As a kid, Ski watched his addict of a mother cut work and cook up for some of Newark's biggest hustlers. Inheriting her skill for cutting and cooking up when he was only thirteen, local hustlers around him paid him to do the same for them.

In no time, Ski's reputation grew. When hustlers saw that he could even perform magic with garbage work, they started admirably calling him Colonel Sanders, joking that when he cut work he or cooked up, he used thirteen signature herbs and spices; at the same time, foes of his mockingly called him Ski Love because he had a habit of not just fucking other niggas bitches but falling in love with them and trying to make them his.

By the time Ski was fourteen, he was renowned in his part of Newark for his whip game. Back when niggas was earning their stripes and getting rep for putting in work at sixteen years old Ski's name was making noise for having his own block and beefing with some of Newark's biggest hustlers because he was always trying to take they bitches.

Everybody's role on the team was defined. Though the lil war against Neighborhood was a constant nag on what they tried to do, business continued.

When their work hit the state, Candy brought it to Ski to break down, separate what they had moved from what they would sell wholesale, cut what needed to be cut, bag it all up, and put it in the hands of their hustlers.

Today was no different. When Candy pulled up on him, Ski in a tank top, gym shorts, and house slippers opened the door, and Candy wobbled her chocolate lil ass in past him carrying duffel bags. Once the shit was in his hands, Ski went to work turning on his assistant Alexa before opening packages of cocaine.

Candy made small talk, attentively watching Ski move around in his lil shorts as he got calculations from Alexa and began turning some of the coke into crack. Whenever they faced each other, Candy secretly stole glances at the lil bulge in his shorts, wondering if he was flaccid or if that was the best he had to offer. Ski was light-skinned, and he had much swag. Candy wouldn't admit it, but he was her type.

When the coke was done, weighed, and repackaged, she watched him separate ten keys of dope in three unequal piles. Again, Alexa's calculations were quickly followed, and different amounts of cut went into each pile as if he'd done it all a million times before.

A few times when he'd been facing Candy, Ski swore he'd caught her checking him out, trying to size up his dick print through the gym shorts. He didn't call her on it, or nothing cause he was still handling the work. At the same time, Candy was the shit. He wouldn't ignore the looks like he was shy or trying to curb her advances. But he still didn't know exactly how he wanted to play shit.

From the lil bullshit, Young Du told him he didn't know if they had something going on or what. More importantly, though, Ski didn't know if he even gave a fuck. He didn't know Young Du. He might have heard the nigga name before in terms of putting on for Blood and the nigga getting busy in prison, but none of that shit aint matter. Ski didn't have a problem with the homie or anything, but the way Candy looked at him made him remember that he and the homie were strangers who just winded up on the same team.

Putting packages of the work back in the duffel bags, Ski turned to Candy and spoke across the table.

"I aint the smartest nigga, but I know you could have been doing something better than sitting around this mother fucker checking me out while I was working."

"Boy bye." She giggled. "The only thing I was looking at over there was your lil ass kid feet."

"What's wrong with my feet?"

"Them shits small as hell. You know what they say about the typical nigga with lil feet."

99

"Typical?" Ski sounded offended as he reached down to stretch the fabric of his shorts over his semi-erect bulge. "Unless you have been fucking horses aint nothing typical about this."

"Nah, that's not typical." She smirked, allowing herself to blush a lil before getting an attitude the moment Ski went further and began exposing himself.

"Now you are doing too much. That's the typical nigga shit right there."

"What the fuck are you talking about?"

"Typical nigga shit. Loyal to your mans but you do all types of unloyal, dishonorable bull shit to your bitch."

"You doing the same shit I'm doing."

"Lies. I aint booed up; I aint got a whole nigga at home. If I did, I would have never even looked at you."

Chapter Twelve

In a dark parking lot outside a cheap, swanky motel, two U-Haul trucks pulled up on the side of an eighteen-wheeler, flanking the rig between them as their cargo hatches opened.

Hopping from the trailer of the moving truck driven by Ski, Young Du and two dreaded men named Slugs and Trey Eight approached Psycho, and another man named A.K., who passed a blunt back and forth as they exited the second U-Haul driven by Hoffa. Drivers included, seven men total had come to do a robbery that Young Du said would be a walk in the park because it was an inside job.

"Open, just like it's supposed to be."

Young Du noted removing a padlock from the rig's haul door before swinging the hatch open and lifting the door open. Inside the trailer, a row of boxes were stacked five across and six high to the ceiling, with succeeding rows stacked behind them.

"Told y'all it would be easy, and we aint need a bunch of ratchets or nothing."

"Well, I don't move without the ratchet."

"How much time we got?" A.K. asked, changing the subject after Psycho's comment.

"None. The dude who owns this truck is my man, and he's the one who put me on to this shit. He is in his room with an alibi, giving us time to do us without making him look suspicious. But we still gotta move quickly 'cause we don't want surprises."

"Move quick?" Psycho barked, exhaling a thick cloud of P.C.P. smoke as he lifted a stack of boxes. "Dog, you already told us all this shit. How the fuck you bitching about move quick and you the only nigga standing there talking?"

Box by box, the cargo from the eighteen-wheel rig was moved to the U-Haul trucks, and in minutes, the trailer was almost half empty when Young Du and Slugs left the group and headed for the motel rooms.

"I thought Psycho was gon go in here with you?"

"He was when I planned it. But that was when I thought he was smart enough to wait at least till we left the scene of the robbery before he started smoking that stink-ass dust."

"Point taken. He a loose cannon when he sober, so aint no telling what he'll do when he high off that shit and he got the demon in him."

"That nigga a live grenade when he high." Young Du said, stopping to knock on a door in the room. "This is it. Remember, it gotta look like a robbery, so once they are under control, we take both of their phones, money, jewelry, keys, and anything else that looks valuable."

Seconds later, a half-naked, light-skinned female who opened the door was utterly overtaken as two gunmen stormed into the almost empty room. Inside, the only furnishings were the small chair to the immediate left of the doorway, a cheap nightstand between the back wall, and a small bed.

"Get the fuck on the floor!" Young Du demanded, grabbing and forcing the female to the floor by the back of her neck as the old pot-bellied man in the room threw his hands in the air.

"Whoa! Whoa! What's going on here, young blood? We don't want no problems."

"Get the fuck on the floor, old man!"

"Alright, man, alright. This is your world, playboy." He said in compliance, lying next to his female friend as Young Du tucked his weapon in his waistline and picked up the female's large purse, inadvertently spilling its contents on the rugged floor.

"I'm scared."

"It's gonna be alright, baby." The old man whispered back to his female friend. "I think they just want our money."

"I'm scared; we gotta do something. What if they…"

"Shut the fuck up!"

"Matter fact, come here bitch." Young Du demanded as he pulled the female to her feet, directed her to the opposite side of the room, and forced her down near the nightstand. "You lay over here 'cause I don't need you mother fuckers trying nothing."

Face down on the floor, she began turning her head toward Young Du as if to argue in protest when something under the bed caught her attention.

Outside, with the last of the boxes being transferred to the U-Hauls, Psycho approached the room Young Du and Slugs had gone into and opened the door.

"What's good? What's taking you niggas so long?"

"Aint shit, we done now."

"Just tying up loose ends." Young Du noted walking around the bed to where the female lay after tossing Slug, zip ties, duct tape, and keys.

"Handle the old man, I got shorty."

Looking down and seeing something in the woman's hand, Young Du quickly realized what it was and immediately pulled her up to her feet by a fistful of hair.

"Bitch you crazy!"

"Who she call?"

"Man kill all that dumb shit; we aint got time for games." Psycho chimed in, drawing his weapon as the female wildly began swinging on Young Du.

Moving in an attempt to de-escalate the situation, Slugs stopped mid-stride as Psycho opened fire, striking the female. She let out a faint guttural scream as her body dropped. With the female strewn across the floor, Psycho quickly spun right, retraining his weapon before anybody could object.

"Please, young blood…" Was all the old man managed to say before gunfire quieted his please?

Chapter Thirteen

In a crowded room, brothers sat, opposing each other in their seating arrangements and opinions. With Rollack in the county, Twizzy Hoffa had adopted a practice of ardently bringing explicit details of drug transactions, the small ongoing gang war against Neighborhood, and other illicit escapades to his twin, and as the summer and things on the street began to heat up, these visits became more and more routine. However, Rollack voicing his opinion about his brother's risks somehow started to sound authoritative and condescending to Hoffa, rather than concerned and helpful. Today's visit, Hoffa knew, would be the worst as he came with somber news.

"I got word that Dutches locked up." He flatly said, sitting down without a greeting.

"What you mean?"

"Paydro got at me last night like, 'Yo Dutch house was hit.' He aint know why or what was going on, but she charged with a ratchet they say they found at the house."

"She got a bail?"

"She didn't when I chopped it up with him; otherwise, you already know he would have got her out."

"I don't know. Son been on some tight shit lately. Dutches said she had to go through a bunch of shit with him before he agreed to give us that last work."

"Fronting us some shit on consignment is different than bailing your baby mother out."

"You right? It's just a whole bunch of crazy shit going on right now." He admitted, shaking his head in frustration.

"My lawyer came out here this morning."

"Yeah?"

"Yeah. It aint too much new going on with the case, but he did ask me to tell you that he can't accept the package you left at his office with the secretary."

"Why did he say that?"

"I don't know. Remember, I don't even know what this package is."

"It wasn't no package. I went to his office and dropped off the rest of his counsel fee."

"The rest, what's that thirty-something racks?"

"Twenty-eight five hundred."

"Twenty-eight?" Rollack repeated with a smirk. "Damn, I aint know shit was going that good out there."

"It aint. I was paying that nigga a rack or a lil more a week. But I ran into some chicken, so I paid him off, and I'm trying to catch Samantha in the next week or so so I can give her the rest of what we owe her, too."

"Yeah?" He was challenged to do the approximate math and calculate that his brother was somewhere in the range of about forty thousand dollars. "You don't just run into money like that."

Taking a deep breath, Hoffa guarded the volume of his voice and began.

"A couple of weeks ago, I came across ten and a half boxes of cigarettes."

"Cigarettes?"

"Yeah, like ten and a half boxes. I had over a thousand cartons going for seventy-five dollars a pop."

"Hold up, bruh, you out there selling cigarettes nigga?"

"Not no more. I dropped a bunch of them on Psycho Pops Ponzi to the fence for me, and I had a couple of homegirls moving them in corner stores and shit. I wish I had more because it was a quick come up."

"So it's smooth sailing out there?"

"It aint never smooth in these streets. My biggest concern right now is keeping this nigga Psycho on a lil leash. Him and the homie Young Du keep bumping heads over some shit that happened the night we got the cigarettes."

The twins had already spoken about Young Du being Brim and Brim, Piru and Neighborhood being all West Side sets. In Psycho's mind, because they were tripping against one west side set, any homie under another west side set couldn't be trusted right now.

The first time the twins spoke after the Paterson ambush, Hoffa had told his brother how, right after the shooting on the way to the hospital, Psycho flipped on Young Du and started coming at him crazy. They both laughed it off, knowing it wasn't serious. But they also knew Psycho's suspicions about him would determine how he dealt with him going forward.

Hoffa told Rollack that immediately after the cigarette truck heist, Psycho took him and Ski to his pop's Jersey City pawn shop, where he swapped out the gun he'd used. At the same time, they read him the riot act for the unnecessary double homicide. Hoffa said that the whole time they were together, Psycho was rambling on some paranoid shit about Young Du.

He had conspiracies about Young Du trying to rock them to sleep. Conspiracies about him include that the Brim and Piru homies are not helping them in the war because they were already helping the Neighborhood homies. There are conspiracies about Young Du trying to steal the cigarettes for himself and about him not being who he said he was. Hoffa said Ponzi told them to come back to his shop anytime they had some business for him, and the twins shared another laugh when Hoffa mimicked Psycho's hysterical response, telling them they could come thru but not to ever bring that nigga Young Du with them.

Hoffa made it halfway through the story, telling his brother how Young Du had set up the heist with the truck driver, who was supposedly a customer of Candy's, before Rollack remembered seeing a story about a truck robbery turned homicide on the news and cut him off.

"I already know how the story ends. I fuck with bruh, but all he is a cannon. I don't expect him to be a thinker, and I never expect him to hesitate. Just don't let the shit between them get out of control."

"They gon be aight. It aint even a they thing. It's just Psycho being Psycho."

"Don't be out there involved in no dumb shit either, bruh."

"Here you go, preaching."

"I aint preaching nigga this real. And why is this my first time hearing about those cigarettes?"

"Not if you watch the news."

Rubbing his chin, Rollack remembered the headline from the news story: 'Two dead in apparent one point eight million dollar truck heist.'

"If you drop ten racks or more in cash at any legitimate business, they are legally mandated to file a CT report to let the feds know that somebody is spending a substantial amount of money."

"Don't tell me you about to be one of them niggas that get bagged, learn how to read, and then you wanna criticize all the moves everybody on the streets making."

"I aint criticizing shit."

"So why you talking like I aint just come from behind the wall like I don't know how to move and like all the legal shit you learning in there is new shit that just came out and only you know it." Hoffa sounded offended. "You telling me about a CT report like I don't know what the fuck a currency transaction report is or something?"

"I aint say none of that extra shit. I'm trying to tell you why the lawyer doesn't want to keep all that cash.

"That nigga in the way. When I first went to get him, he aint wanna touch your case."

"He aint think we had the chicken."

"I know. Then he started talking about needing thirty percent of eighty bands up front. He aint have no problem with cash, then. Who the fuck demand thirty percent upfront anyway."

"I'm saying he is the best in the state."

"You keep saying that. So, because he's the best in the state, you want me to pay him a couple hundred dollars a week for forever?"

"Absolutely not. But if you leave like eight with him and take the other fourteen, five hundred with a band or so extra with you when you pay Samantha, she might write the check for the fourteen five hundred for the lawyer."

"That aint happening. Psycho out here running around with a couple of lil homies slaughtering them Neighborhood mother fuckers. I aint seen Samantha in a minute. I called her a million times; I have been hitting her all over social media and everything else I could think of, but I aint getting no response."

"What you saying?"

Hoffa went on to tell his brother that he hadn't seen or spoken with Samantha since the set tripping started. He had gone to her salon a few times to drop off two or three thousand dollars, only for her homegirls to tell him she wasn't there. Rollack asked if she was ducking him, and Hoffa shot him down. Believing she was just tied up doing something every time he was looking for her, he reminded his brother that on top of trying to wage war against them, she also had a salon and auto garage.

"Every time I slide through, her lil home girls at the salon tell me the balance I owe, so I know she is getting the chicken and telling them the math to relay to me."

"It sound like you aight with her avoiding you even though you know if you paid her an extra rack or so she'd write the check for the rest of the lawyer money."

"If anything, we avoid each other. You hear about all the bullshit Psycho out here doing to her lil homies?"

"What's that got to do with you? You aint got nothing to do with the shit he out there doing." Rollack urged before reminding his twin of the most crucial detail. "The crazy shit is between you and her. If one of y'all mother fuckers is guilty by association, it's her. Her fucking son is in the county right now for killing High Five."

"You think she wanna hear that?"

"Fuck what she wanna hear. You gotta remember, as long as that nigga Charley MIA, that bitch got her whole set statewide." He hesitated for emphasis. Let her know that you and Psycho have the same status. Y'all two niggas don't get no say over what each other does. She can't feel some way towards you because of what Psycho is doing and tell you she aint got nothing to do with her son Baby Taliban and her lil homies tripping on High Five and Dre out in Camden, you and the homies in Paterson and anybody else them lil pissy ass Neighborhood niggas done moved on."

"You're right."

"Dig, bruh, that bitch about her chicken. You gotta go through there and tell her homegirls you got the rest of her money, but you need to give it to her personally. Tell them you don't expect them to tell you when she'll be there but tell them to tell her you gon come through the same time every day for the next week. Remember, all she cares about is the bottom line. So when you see her, throw her a rack or something to make it worth her while, and we'll all be able to sleep better cause fourteen racks on paper coming from a business owner look way better than fourteen thousand in cash coming from a career criminal."

"I'ma chop it up with her."

"Ask her what's good with her boy Got Guns, too."

"What up, what's popping with him?"

"I don't know, but that nigga might be working. Remember I told you Nut reached out to me when Bullet and the g Shine homie Lucky first wanted to trip down Northern?"

"Yeah, that was the shit that started all this tripping shit. They said Omar and Guns were stepping on their toes.

"Yeah, that's why they wanted to trip. But the nigga Nut was getting at me like 'I don t know why your man Omar fucking with the nigga Guns anyway' cause Bullet told him he had heard son was a rat."

"He had paperwork?"

"Nah, and I wasn't considering that shit or nothing until I chopped it up with Omar a couple of days ago, and he said his lawyer came to see him to pick his brain, asking questions about the nigga Guns like how well he knew son and whether or not he ever talked to the nigga about our case or anything else incriminating cause they supposedly trying to build some type of Rico shit against him."

"Damn, that Rico shit is scary. What's good with the homie Omar, though?"

"He good; his bitch just gave birth to their son like a week or two ago."

"Yeah, Ski just had a baby, and I think Young Du bitch just had a baby too."

"Damn, already?" Rollack began shifting topics. "Omar said his lawyer told him the whole incident concerning how he winded up in IPC seemed suspicious as fuck. When you look at that, the shit going on with the nigga Guns, and remember that we still aint even indicted yet, all this shit that's going on just look crazy as hell."

"The fact that y'all still aint indicted yet is crazy as hell by itself."

"I ran it by my lawyer, and he said with all the physical evidence, plus all of us getting locked up at the crime scene, we should have been indicted in two to three months tops. He said that based on his experience with everything going on, like that five-k-one shit the prosecutor put in a couple of months ago, it's clear that somebody is telling, and they are probably stalling to put together a bigger case or something. He doesn't know what angle they are trying to work and who is cooperating."

I get everything you're saying, but you can't just put all that together and say "son telling."

"What you think one of the homies lying?"
I aint say all that. But you can't just say you know they aint lying, either. You know homies throw shit like that around all the time just to tarnish niggas names, and for all we know, Omar's lawyer could have just been throwing random shit at him to try and find an explanation for what the fuck is going on himself."

"How the fuck you see everything that's going on with my case and everything else that's going on in the streets and shit, and you still say it aint nobody telling?"

"I never said that it aint somebody telling. I'm saying that I don't know if someone is telling the truth or not, and neither do you. You can't just see some questionable shit and say, 'Oh, it's a fact that this nigga or that nigga telling."

"Why can't I?"

"Cause you aint got no paperwork. No real proof. If you just gon say this nigga or that nigga telling cause shit look suspicious to you, them same niggas could think you telling."

"What?" Rollack demanded.

"You got suspicious shit going on, too," Hoffa said with a laugh trying to make it seem as if his previous statement was the premise of a joke. "I'm still trying to figure out how the fuck your lawyer thinks he is working out a plea deal when aint nobody has even been indicted, and the police are saying they are still looking for niggas in y'all case."

Chapter Fourteen

Turning onto Twenty-first St. in Paterson, Psycho double-parked in front of a familiar apartment building. Trying to steal himself emotionally and conceal his feelings, he lit a PCP-laced blunt as he thought about the mission's difficulty ahead of him.

"What's popping, big bruh?" M-Dot greeted entering the vehicle.

"What's good with you? You aint tell nobody you was rolling with me tonight, right?"

"Nah, but what's up with all this secret squirrel shit?"

Handing the younger man the blunt, Psycho looked at him with disgust.

"Not for nothing, but I don't want nobody knowing what I'm doing and who I'm moving with all the time. If you wanna win in this shit nigga you gotta stay ahead of the competition and the law, and you do that by keeping information on a need-to-know basis and not overlooking the lil shit."

"Don't overlook shit. So, aint nothing too small to address?"

"Hell no."

"No matter how crazy it is?"

"You got something you wanna say?"

"I don't know 'cause it might sound a lil off."

"Speak your mother fucking mind nigga."

"I'm saying big bruh; I got this nigga named Rico Brim from Cali that me and Slugs jailed with for a minute when we were making our last bid. Me and the nigga Rico locked in a cell together, so we got a good lil rapport and shit. Anyway, he finished his fed time; he is doing a state bid now."

"Aight?"

"I reached out to his bitch almost a month ago to see what's moving, send him a couple of dollars, and I told her to let him know I had seen his homie Young Du a minute ago." M-Dot paused to hand Psycho the blunt, and because he was speaking, he didn't even notice the suspicion in Psycho's eye. "His bitch hit me back yesterday like he said, 'good looking for the chicken and shit,' whatever, whatever, but he also said me seeing Young Du a minute ago is impossible. He is on the streets, but he just got out here a few days after he got my message saying I had already seen him. At this point, I'm dumbfounded. So I hit his bitch this morning, and she sent me pictures of a welcome home party that niggas supposedly had for Young Du out in Cali."

"He in the pictures?"

"Nah, he don't do pictures like that."

"So what the fuck you tell me all that for?"

"Somebody gotta be wrong. The timing doesn't line up for when they say he came home. Either they don't know what they are talking about, Young Du ain't the same Young Du they talking about, or somebody just fronting."

The conversation between the two continued similarly until Psycho began parking the vehicle while reviewing the description with his lil homie of a tall, thick, light-skinned female with long dreads. At this point, M-Dot exited the car and crossed the street, joining the crowd outside a bar.

Plucking away his cigarette, Psycho drew a revolver and sat it on his lap. His eyes darted back and forth from watching Cocaine through his rearview mirror in the backseat to looking out ahead of him at M-Dot in the distance across the street.

Pulling out a jar of PCP, he dipped another cigarette, reflecting on M-Dot's words and considering their possible implications.

"Fuck out of here." He said out loud, dismissing everything his lil homie said while looking in the rearview mirror. "What's wrong with that nigga

Cocaine? He thinks niggas don't know he is running his mouth to the law?" Psycho paused for dramatic effect, and the pit bull looked at him dumb-founded.

Lighting his second dipped cigarette, he made a mental note to talk to Slugs about the nigga Rico Brim and Young Du to see if there was any truth to what M-Dot mentioned.

"On top of that, if that shit wasn't enough, this nigga trying to play both sides in this shit against Neighborhood. Bitch ass nigga." He continued chalking up everything M-Dot had said as a game he was trying to run on him.

To what end, though, is what Psycho didn't know, and he didn't care to figure it out. All he knew was that M-Dot's actions looked more and more like betrayal.

Knowing a thing or two about betrayal, Psycho looked at Cocaine in his rearview mirror, took a deep drag on his dipped cigarette, and his mind flashed to his memory of ultimate betrayal.

When he was still running around with a snotty nose at seven, his father got locked up, and Psycho's fun childhood abruptly ended. There were no more family trips or random shopping sprees. The fun time was over. But fun wasn't the only thing that changed.

Even though he was too young to understand most of it, Psycho's father used to talk to him for hours about everything. Being the disciplinarian in the house, there were times when Psycho was in trouble, and his father would speak to him, condemning what he'd done until he fell asleep. On the other hand, instead of talking to him or even beating him for discipline when he did something wrong, his young teenage mother would leave him in a dark room for hours with no TV, phone, or toy for punishment.

After a while, when dark closets and rooms weren't scary enough any-more, Psycho's mother started throwing him in the basement for doing anything that pissed her off. His brothers Spyke and C-Green bred pit bulls back then, and one of them had learned taxidermy in boot camp, so there were always a bunch of scary half-stuffed animals all over the place and a handful of angry pit bulls running around in the basement.

None of this stopped Psycho from being thrown down there. Before long, whenever his mother or brothers saw fit, whether it was because he asked too many questions or they simply grew tired of looking at him, they'd lock him in the basement with the dogs and mannequin animals.

At first, it scared him to be in the dark, damp basement with pit bulls and creepy dolls. After a while, Psycho got used to the dummies and started getting along with the dogs better than he did with his brothers. This continued for so long that it became a common practice. The days became months, and before anybody knew it, over a year had passed full of days when Psycho was sent to the basement as soon as he came from school and wasn't seen until late that night when he ate and went to bed.

Even as he sat in his car waiting on M-Dot, Psycho could still close his eyes and smell the dogs in the basement. He puffed away, and the embalming fluid continued to haze his mind. Drifting to deeper depths of his PCP high, he could hear the screams that got his attention years ago as he began to relive the day he was betrayed.

Sliding the steak knife in the doorjamb, nine-year-old Psycho wiggled it around until he heard the lock click. Opening the basement door, he heard another scream, followed by another. He ran to the living room and didn't see anybody. Then, he turned on his heels to check the bedrooms.

Psycho's heart began to sink as he ran past his brother's open bedroom doors, and as much as he wanted to break down and cry because of the possibilities, he pushed himself forward, noticing what sounded like a rhythm to the screams.

Opening his mother's door, Psycho was dumbfounded by what he saw. His mother was on top of his brother Spyke, and C-Green was behind her in her ass. This was the ultimate betrayal. Psycho didn't know exactly how it all happened, but he remembered running up and swinging indiscriminately swinging wildly at his brothers.

By the time his mother was able to get from between his brothers and try and stop him, there was blood all over the place. Psycho could still remember looking down and realizing he held the now bloody knife he'd used to pick the basement lock.

Just as he finished his cigarette, a burst of gunfire erupted, snapping him out of his trance. Psychos thumb immediately cocked the hammer on the revolver he held, and he began to pull out of the parking spot just as M-Dot ran up to the vehicle opening the door. In one fluid motion, Psycho's hand rose, brandishing the revolver, and abruptly pressed it against M-Dot's head, pulling the trigger twice before he could sit down.

"Bitch ass nigga." He said, pushing the man's body from the vehicle, closing the door, throwing the car into reverse, and hitting the gas.

Chapter Fifteen

Two months after Young Du and Candy had taken Ski and Amy shopping, Twizzy Rollack and his codefendants, Omar and Dough, still sat in cells, hadn't heard anything from Black, their other codefendant, and hadn't been indicted or received any substantive information about their case in months. Although there hadn't been another court date for the two to talk face-to-face, Omar and Rollack regularly spoke via cell phone. By this means, they stayed current on what was going on with each other and followed the events on the streets. But as much as they tried, they couldn't micro-manage the interactions on the roads as much as they'd envisioned.

From what Omar told him, Rollack believed that Omar and Young Du spoke almost as often as he spoke with Ski, Hoffa, and Psycho. Yet, despite all this communication, shit on the streets wasn't running nearly as smoothly as they thought it could. In the beginning, Omar had sold Rollack on a vision of them having a couple of traps where their hustlers would sell shit straight to fiends. This vision also said that the bulk of their fast money would come from other hustlers, who they hoped would be their homies, purchasing weight from them at wholesale prices.

They wanted to be the connect for their homies, and after the meeting, they supplied more of them. The problem was that most homies who brought work from them were copping with them individually. Money was money, but as good as the traffic was, they aimed to supply the hoods and sets moving birds at a time, not ounces, quarters, and halves.

By echoing Omar's voice, Young Du had been telling Ski since day one that with their connect, it was beneficial for them to buy as much weight as possible with each flip, because the bigger the quantity they purchased, the less the connect charged them.

Since the status meeting, big homies from three of the state's smallest sets, One-Eight-Third, Outlaw, and Families, had reached out to Ski and started copping from them. But being that these were the smaller sets and their footprints weren't that big, the weight they regularly brought was only really like a handful of individual niggas copping shit at one time.

In any event, though, their product spoke for itself, so what they missed out on in serving entire hoods and sets, they made up for in individual sales. After what Young Du had thought was a failure at the status meeting, many individual homies repping different sets from different cities started copping weight from them. When the flow increased, this created demand for Ski and Young Du to open new trap houses in Jersey City, Irvington, New Brunswick, and Asbury.

They also still had the same traps in Newark, Paterson, Lakewood, and Camden that they'd had since the beginning, where their homies sold their products hand to hand. Because of this uptick in business, Ski moved his lil homies Nickels and Blood Money up in rank and put them in charge of managing the two traps that saw the most traffic in Newark and Camden. All in all, the money flow was good. But as time passed, the heat from the ongoing war became more of a problem.

One homie randomly tripping on another homie under any set was something that often happened. However, all-out wars, also known as set tripping between entire sets or all sets against one, usually didn't happen without the statewide leaders giving the green light for authorization. Though that authorization wasn't verbally given at the status meeting, Wacka did tell Young Du and Ski that he was gon handle it and get the authorization.

About a month after the status meeting, the original team Omar had put together to manage their traps and run the day-to-day operations was relatively removed from the war when it wasn't brought to them directly. This wasn't the case for Psycho, who seemed to be taking personal responsibility for wagging the war against the Neighborhood homies.

With what seemed like a handful of Neighborhood homies shot every week and two or three killed every other week, young homies under the Neighborhood set began switching their set to a different one or dropping their flag altogether in fear. Blood, as a whole, hadn't officially committed to tripping on Neighborhood. But that didn't affect the war regarding who won in the streets because Psycho and the handful of homies running with him seemed to be quickly racking up a serious body count.

With the Neighborhood homegirl, Big Red, recently being killed outside a bar and M-Dot found executed up the street, it was clear who was responsible for the killings. This meant that things would escalate before they improved.

More and more, the war against Neighborhood was looking one-sided as Psycho and his goons dominated the scoreboard, but there were casualties on both sides. A trap house in Camden that sold their work had been hit in the last month alone. Two blocks they had workers on in Newark had been shot up. After M-Dot's bar shooting, one of Hoffa's lil homies was shot dead execution-style as he strolled through a mall with a female. And just yesterday, two Murder homies delivering dope that was already paid forgot, ambushed, and shot dead as they sat at a red light in Jersey City.

What was being called a war was being dominated by one side. While Neighborhood lost the casualty count by five to one, homies opposing Neighborhood wouldn't show their faces anywhere near Jersey City, Atlantic City, or Lakewood. Neighborhood as a set ran those cities and while they were losing the war throughout the state their control over those cities didn't change.

That said, sliding through a city controlled by a set you were at war with was akin to visiting a housing project knowing you had a conflict with somebody who lived there. If a fight broke out and you had to retreat you'd find yourself trying to run from the entire projects. In this instance, if a gun was drawn, you could be fired on by a substantial amount of the people in the streets as you tried to flee the city.

Despite all that was happening, the thrill of making the next dollar allowed Ski and Young Du to operate efficiently somehow. When the idea to supply the leaders of all the sets didn't seem to take off as quickly or easily as they'd envisioned, they displayed business-like shrewdness in revamping their sales strategy. Everybody at the status meeting knew they had the best work in the state. Yet, for many different reasons, only a handful of these same homies pursued them and started copping from them after the meeting.

Following the cigarette heist, Young Du decided to give boxes of their cigarettes to statewide leaders of various Blood sets as compensation for the heat their war was causing. Ski then suggested expanding their sales base by selling the weight of a slightly diluted version of their dope and coke to some of their homies' competition. This, Ski believed, would stir things up and increase the need for more homies to cop from them just to keep up with their counterparts.

With Omar's blessing, Young Du agreed to lower the prices on the diluted products, knowing they would recoup any lost profits in the long run as their customer base grew. In the course of about two weeks, Ski and Young Du sat down with various statewide leaders of Latin gangs, different Crip sets, and a handful of neutral movers and shakers in hopes of them becoming new customers. This immediately proved to be a good strategy, as some meetings concluded with deals being made.

After a few of these transactions led to more of their homies coming to their trap houses or reaching out to them to cop some weight, Ski got an unexpected phone call from somebody under one of the state's biggest sets.

On a bright July morning, Ski turned his SUV onto a quiet street in Newark and began addressing his passengers.

"From what I was told, the Piru homies heard about us from the nigga Wee-Wee."

"Psycho, cousin?" Young Du asked.

At this point, he dismissed the work he put in the man's hand as a loss. Ski said Wee-Wee reached out to him, saying he'd talked to his big homies about them, vouching for them, and had set up a meeting. Ski said the last thing Wee-Wee noted was that they needed to make it to this meeting to get some Piru money.

"It's about time we gon see some kind of profit from the lil shit I put in that nigga hands."

"Yeah, but this aint just some kind of profit. We are going to meet No-

122

vella."

"Who the fuck is that?" Candy asked from the backseat.

"The Mob Piru home girl. She gets to the bag. I got a restaurant; we are going to meet her at the lil diner slash brothel shit she owns right outside the hood. Y'all might not have heard of her, but Young Du should have crossed paths with her big nigga Lord Ru when he was jailing. He one of the niggas who brought that Piru shit out here."

"Brought it out here?" Candy challenged, noticing Ski eyeballing her in the mirror.

"Well, that shit was out here, but you know what I'm saying. Lord Ru, one of the niggas who made it official."

"So he got the state?"

"Yeah, but it's really like the bitch Novella got it 'cause she has been making all the moves since he has been locked up," Ski said while parking. "I don't know if she is looking for weed and pills or coke and dope, but they are trying to do business, and if we can lock this down with her before we know it, we could be supplying half of the Mob homies."

"Ain't no if we are coming to some type of agreement about whether she wanted us to meet her here." Candy chimed in.

"The home girl got a crazy reputation for being careful and secretive, though. She doesn't do much talking, and she aint into mother fuckers being on phones and shit in her presence or nothing either."

"I heard."

"Fuck whatever the nigga Wee-Wee said to her. I know all the shit we are pushing is top of the line, but I think the only real reason the homegirl is checking for us is because of the shit that just happened with the nigga Boss."

"Boss?" Young Du sounded confused.

"Nigga named Boss. Streets saying he was a rat, somebody just blew his shit off on Facebook live."

"Yeah? I missed that one."

"You heard about the shit bruh." Ski reminded him as Candy showed him the video on her phone. "That was him that got whacked with that telling ass Neighborhood nigga Alpo."

"They both got killed, and three bitches got shot in the process."

"Oh aight, I did hear about this shit." Young Du gave the device back, recalling their conversation in Ski's hospital room.

"I just wanna know why it had to be so damn early?" Candy shifted around in her seat, feeling Ski's eyes on her cleavage as she eyed the face of his wristwatch while he pulled the keys from the ignition.

"I don't know, but this is the time I was told. They got some coffee or Red Bull or something in there, though. We gon be aight."

"Iced coffee is good."

Exiting the vehicle, the trio crossed the street and looked admirably at the name 'V Diner' on the burgundy awning that hung above the door they were about to enter.

"Welcome to Vagina Diner, satisfying your appetite is our desire. How may I help you?" A dark-skinned petite female greeted them, and Candy watched Ski Zone in on her lil bubble ass.

Within minutes, Ski was flirting with the dark-skinned chick, and in between flirting back, she found time to get Candy a cup of iced coffee and was explaining the rules anybody going upstairs needed to follow as she led the three to the back of the establishment. Half paying attention to the woman and what she was saying, Candy watched how Ski almost gawked at her with no shade and realized he had a thing for darker skin.

In the back of the establishment, the woman who greeted them told them to go up the stairs, and Ski's cell phone began to ring.

"What's good?" He greeted the caller after the screening. "What, right now? I can't. Wacka, I can't, I can't hear you." He said, looking at the phone's screen, dumbfounded. "Young Du, that was Wacka."

"Yeah?"

"Yeah. You know we have been waiting for that call from him. He said something that sounded like what we had been waiting to hear, but the call got dropped."

"It wasn't dropped; it got jammed." A corn-rolled, dark-skinned figure said from the top of the staircase. "It's a signal jammer in the building. Somebody downstairs should have told y'all we don't like phones and shit in this part of the building."

"It's people on phones and shit downstairs." Ski blurted out.

"You got cameras and everything in that mother fucker."

"Yeah, it's a business nigga. We can't stop customers from using phones and shit downstairs, and it's cameras down that mother fucker to monitor the business. Just like every other restaurant. But don't none of that shit, cameras, cell phones, or no other type of communication or recording gadget get past this point?" The figure said, waving a foot-long paddle like a black object.

Young Du, the first of the three visitors to reach the top of the staircase, realized the voice belonged to a bulky female.

"Leave your phones and shit on the table." She pointed the wand at the small coffee table at her side as she spoke. "And stretch your arms out."

"What?"

"Put your phone on the table and lift your arms so I can wand you down."

"What the fuck is that?" Young Du asked, putting his phone on the table and beginning to remove his watch as Ski reached the top of the flight behind him.

You can keep your watch on as long as it isn't connected to your phone or anything. This is an electromagnetic frequency wand. It detects electronic waves." The female said, waving the device around his body.

BEEP!

It screamed as it got near his waist.

"What's that?"

"Shit, that's my other phone." Young Du admitted removing a small burnout from his waistline. "Damn, I turned that shit off anyway before we came into this building."

"Turning it off aint good enough; them shits still transmit signals. As long as a battery is in a cell phone, it's sending signals to a tower."

"You sound like you know what the fuck you are talking about." Ski joked, and just as he sat his phone on the table, Candy, who stood to his left, somehow spilled her coffee on his arm.   "God damn. You got that shit on my watch and everything." He complained, removing his watch and setting it next to his phone.

After the three were wanded down without a hitch, they were led into a room where a tall, brown skin female stood waiting.

"Young Du and Ski, right?" The bulky female said, standing next to her tall, brown-skinned friend as they faced the group of three.

"Yeah, I'm Ski. He Young Du, and that's Candy."

"What's pimping?" The bulky female greeted them all. "I'm sure y'all

125

probably already know this, Novella, but she doesn't do a lot of talking. I'm Beefy, and I'm gon be chopping it up with y'all on behalf of Piru."

. . . .

In a small office, an older, brown-skinned female spoke adamantly to two male faces on her tablet's screen.

"I know it's fucked up, but as hot as it is right now, you can't even afford to be thinking about what's going on in the streets of Jersey."

"Fuck the streets, I'm thinking about the family. I got a gang of lil homies I can't just leave for dead."

"What you think about that?" She challenged the older of the two.

"I agree with you now. But I'd be fronting if I acted like I wasn't feeling the same way Charley felt before me and you talked face to face at the party. Niggas up there manipulating my mother fucking homies to get them involved in some dumb shit; I wouldn't even be me if I aint at least think about shooting up that way to air some shit out real quick. Especially when I haven't heard my name or seen my picture in the news."

"Them pussies saying they are looking for two dark skin bald head niggas." Charley hesitated. "Not for nothing but them niggas up there tripping on Neighborhood homies at will. All three of us already know if something happened to you, Sam, or if the wrong Brim nigga got they shit knocked off, aint nothing nobody could do to stop this nigga from coming up there."

"Samantha." A dark female stood in the office doorway, interrupting the video conversation. "Somebody here to see you."

"Who is it?"

"Hoffa."

"Who"

"Twizzy Hoffa." The brown skin male declared from behind the female.

"Well, god damn. Take him back to the front; I'll be out there in a minute."

"Who was that bitch?"

"And what that Teck nigga doing in your shop?"

"One question at a time, please?" Samantha smirked, addressing the younger face on the screen. "That's my nephew's friend Tasha. She related to the Greens, so I be trying to keep her close to me to keep her lil ass out of trouble."

"And why that nigga Hoffa at your shop?"

"The only reason I could think of him coming through here is to bring me some of my chicken. I did let him hold a lil bag before all this crazy shit started." She stated flatly.   "More importantly though, you know it's always a bunch of lil' Neighborhood homies out front and all up and down this block trapping. This nigga coming to drop off my money, he aint stupid."

Samantha told Charley she understood how he felt about losing Big Red and all the other homies. She reminded him that they were her homies too and emphasized that unless he was trying to go to jail and not ever be able to retaliate himself, he needed to stop letting what was going on in Jersey make him forget why he'd left in the first place. Taliban agreed with her, reminding his brother that Got Guns was already sitting on a new Rico case.

Shifting her attention to Taliban, Samantha told him she'd heard that there was a break in their son's case, so she'd be visiting their son in the county jail tonight and meeting with his lawyer tomorrow morning. Ending the conversation, she tucked a small handgun in the front of her jeans where it would be visible and exited her office.

At the end of a short hallway, barber chairs sat almost at the center of a large room as waiting chairs sat beneath the picture-framed windows that lined the far wall. Rinse sinks and salon-related materials lined a mirror-covered right wall alongside a fifty-inch smart TV. Hung in the middle of the left wall.

"What's that?" Samantha asked, noticing that the five people in the room were watching the screen.

"It's a news clip." Tasha clarified, pointing to a remote to restart the video.

"One month ago, a man who had been the state's star witness in an upcoming Rico trail was found dead in Camden, New Jersey. Then, two days ago in Jersey City, a man who was scheduled to take the stand in a Newark murder trial against Terrance Johnson, a.k.a. Baby Taliban, was found dead inside his home after being shot in the head. Normally, these two cases happening at opposite ends of the state would appear to be unrelated. Still, we and other news crews have gathered here at the state capital today for answers after reports surfaced that evidence left at both crime scenes, as well as at apparently up to three or four other locations, appears to link them all together. This is leading some investigative authorities to whisper about the possible existence of a serial killer."

"You got a lot of nerve coming through here." Samantha interrupted the program, drawing Hoffa's attention.

"Nerve? I came through here, checking for you every day at the same time for the last week. I left you messages and told your homegirls I had the rest of your chicken, but I wanted to sit down and bust it up with you."

"It still takes nerve. You just gon walk in here to talk after all the shit y'all niggas out here doing to my homies."

"You can't put this tripping shit on me, Sam; you know I aint into that goofy shit."

"I don't know shit bruh."

"So you gon put all the spilt blood on my hands?" Hoffa eyed the gun on Samantha's waist and measured the demeanor of the room.

"Your hands aint clean."

"Clean?" He shot back, legitimately sounding offended. "I can dig you feeling some way about your homies, but you can't flip it on me like I'm accountable for everything every one of my homies does. My hands aint got half the authority as yours. If anything, I'm less responsible for the dumb shit my homies are doing in the streets than you are for yours." He hesitated, trying to show sincerity. "I can dig you feeling some way about your homies. I'd be coming the same way if I was in your shoes. But you know I'm out here for the chicken. I aint never been into none of the dumb shit."

"So what's rolling?" Samantha challenged sitting in the first barber chair, which provided her with a clear view of the men outside the window behind Hoffa. "You came here to watch the news, or you got something for me?"

"You already know I got the rest of your chicken."

"Yeah? That's a lot of money."

"I'm out here making a lot of moves."

"So I hear." She stated that it sounded like a question more than a statement.

"I wish I could bring you in on something."

"I don't see that happening right now."

"I know right now isn't the best time for us to do no business, but I'm trying to put a couple of dollars in your pocket.

"Well, time is money nigga. If you got something to say, speak your mafuckin mind."

"You are basically asking for a quarter of the bud and pills we cop every flip, and you are only trying to pay a couple of dollars more than we do."

"What's wrong with that?"

"The math doesn't add up." Candy interrupted. "I mean, of course, it does on y'all end. But not for us. We aint taking trips to transport the best shit over this mafucka from state to state to unload a quarter of the weight for only one or two points in profit."

"So you wanna up the price for the risk you're taking to get the work to Jersey?"

"You know how this shit works; it aint charity. We hustling, we aint trying to get hustled." Ski shot back as Novella whispered into Beefy's ear.

"I can't argue with you charging us based on the risk you are taking, but at the same time, you can't front like y'all don't benefit a whole lot just on the strength that y'all doing business with us."

"Explain that benefit." Ski challenged Beefy as Candy and Young Du quietly exchanged words at his side.

"We can't promise that nobody gon start doing business with you just cause we rocking with y'all. But we all know the deal. Us fucking with y'all is like us vouching for y'all."

"You putting a value on the possibility that mother fuckers might wanna cop from us just because we doing business with y'all?"

"Absolutely. We only reached out to y'all cause we heard y'all got the best shit on the streets. We aint gon waste time debating that. But at the same time, for some reason, y'all only supply a couple of nondescript homies chasing coins."

"We are getting money."

"Y'all getting pennies. Based on the shit you got, you could probably be supplying half the state if y'all could get your hands on enough of it. Y'all making a lil noise, got the streets buzzing a lil, but aint nobody that's official copping from y'all. That's why you aint doing half the numbers you should be doing."

"What's that got to do with this?" Young Du tried to control the narrative.

"We can go back and forth with you acting like you don't understand what the fuck I'm saying, but you mother fuckers know if we rock with y'all on any level, it makes you legitimate to other mother fuckers."

"You can't put a price on that, though."

"One of you mother fuckers did enough homework to know we got another shop in Camden identical to this one. If the math works out right from us pushing your shit, in a month or so, we'll be ready to double up so we can supply the other location too."

"We might have heard a lil about y'all, but..."

"So you know it's upstairs and downstairs in each of our establishments." Beefy cut off Ski before going into detail about the numbers they did at the Vigina diner.

She told them that this was one of two locations they had and that each had two different establishments. As Beefy gave them the layout upstairs, telling them it was six apartments and eighteen rooms, Ski remembered hearing that the Vigina Diner could see the most money blocks seen in half the time.

The cocky female boasted that along with food orders, small individual purchases of weed, pills, and other party drugs were made downstairs while pussy and large quantities of party drugs were sold up here in the apartments.

"This shit runs twenty-four-seven, and we always booked. If we move your shit through here, the streets gon buzz more, and your demand gon shoot through the roof. In no time, we probably gon be buying all the weight from y'all that y'all getting from the connect right now, and in the process, y'all gon fuck around and double or triple the shit y'all picking up now."

"Probably." Candy rejoined the conversation with backup from Young Du.

"The real problem is we came here thinking y'all was trying to cop some coke or dope 'cause that's where the real money at for us. I mean, I can dig it if it aint what y'all trying to do, but after hearing a lil bit of what you into, I think we might have a proposition for you."

"I don't know about no propositions, but all that whispering shit y'all two had going on while we was talking was rude as fuck."

"Pardon the rudeness, but he's trying to tell you..."

"You can't tell me what he's trying to tell me, lil momma." Beefy cut off Candy. "You are a lil overdressed, but these negotiations could end with you getting a job in this upstairs establishment. We got a welfare line of mother fuckers I know that would pay just to get a lil taste of that candy."

Candy laughed before Novella's heavy Hattian accent interrupted her.

"We listen to proposition."

"Every month or month and a half, we take a trip out west, and besides the coke and dope we are getting, we end up dropping like fifteen racks and come back with a lil more than four times the bud, molly, and pills y'all looking for."

"How far west?"

"Texas border." Candy volunteered. "If y'all serious about the numbers you was quoting, we can work it out where you'd be getting what you want, but the ticket would be a lil more expensive than the shit you threw at us. The only thing is you can't step on our toes by wholesaling the shit you copping, and you gotta get in on some of this risk."

"What risk?"

"As of now, I take all of the trips out west. You bitches are less conspicuous. With other female drivers, we could double the weight we bring in, and we all already know y'all got access to an abundance of bitches that wanna work."

"Why the fuck would we agree to that?"

"Cause you're trying to get this money."

"Oh, we gon get this money regardless." Beefy sounded insulted. "Don't get it fucked up."

"And we gon do the same shit. Even if we gotta hit the streets passing out free samples for us to have this shit take off the way was talking about."

"We do deal." Novella's accent was heard for the second time. "Make concession, no wholesale and bitches to drive for you."

"Now the only issue is this tripping shit."

"Oh, that aint an issue. Our homies aint getting involved in that shit."

"I'm saying we had to ask because..."

"I know why you had to ask." Beefy cut-off Ski. "Niggas was saying when all this tripping shit started down Northern state prison, it was a Piru homie getting money with the Neighborhood nigga Got Guns."

"Yeah, that's what happened."

"No, it aint."

"Fuck you mean, no it aint?" Young Du almost yelled. "I know the nigga that was there."

"Well, we don't know the nigga."

Seeing how fast the temperature in the room changed, Ski jumped in to save the deal. "Fuck it, it don t matter. Y'all don't know the nigga, and y'all aint tripping, but we do got a deal."

. . . .

Handing Hoffa a check, Samantha exited her salon behind him and addressed the two men outside.

"Do y'all gotta smoke that shit right here?"

"It's all gone now." One of them said with a laugh.

Directing her attention back on Twizzy Hoffa, Samantha looked at him sideways.

"I still don't know how you got your hands on the chicken to pay me back and pay off the lawyer so quickly."

"I told you I'm out here with the movers and shakers. If you aint heard, I'm out this bitch winning. Got a nice lil' money team."

"Money team?"

"Yeah. Me, my nigga Ski, Young Du."

"Whoa. Whoa. Who the fuck is this Young Du you talking about?"

"The Brim nigga Young Du."

"Tall, cocky, bald-headed?"

Looking at a picture on her phone, Samantha pulled up, and Hoffa responded.

"Nah, nah. I don't think that's the homie. I'm saying he looks like the nigga. The homie I'm talking about is tall and cocky, but he aint all that big." Looking a lil harder, he paused before continuing. "He got a baldy and shit, too; the niggas look just alike. But the homie I'm talking about aint as big as son in that picture."

"Well, I don't know what Young Du you are talking about, but the real Brim homie Young Du is my nephew, and you can't talk about him," Samantha said with a chuckle as rapid gunfire erupted.

Hitting the ground, Hoffa found shelter crouching along the driver's side of a parked van and quickly realized that the shots were coming from across the street. Cursing himself for leaving his gun in his car, which was three vehicles down, he looked around and found Samantha lying in the middle of the sidewalk, reaching for her waist. Grabbing her arm, Hoffa managed to start pulling her body just as the storefront windows of her salon began to shatter, sending heavy shards of glass to the ground.

Taking her gun, Hoffa looked to return fire and realized a small sedan sat in the middle of the street on the other side of the van he hid behind. As the gunfire increased and bullets pierced the side of the vehicle, Hoffa moved to return fire, but just as he looked around the rear of the van and let off his first shot, his heart sank at the sight of the mac totting gunman firing at him as he walked toward him.

POP! POP! POP! POP!

Single shots rang out, sounding closer than the burst of the Mac, and as Hoffa turned to put his eyes on the shooter, he watched the home girl he'd followed into Samantha's office get shot down. With her now laid out next to the two lil Neighborhood homies in front of the salon's entrance, another mac-toting gunman stepped to the curb in front of the van to finish off the three, and Hoffa seized the moment.

Pulling his trigger three times, Hoffa managed to hit the gunman, sending him into a backward stumble before Mac fire tore into Hoffa from the back.

. . . .

Even though Novella and Beefy refused to buy any hard drugs like coke or dope, after they'd agreed on the deal, Novella whispered into Beefy's ear. The bulky woman told Ski, Young Du, and Candy that because they were doing business, they would pass the word on to their homies about the coke and dope they had.

Following the meeting with the Piru homies, Ski dropped Young Du off at his car, and he and Candy went to Paterson to grab some work from Candy's storage room. They were supposed to pop up in a couple of Blood hoods to pass out some fentanyl, opioids, and other prescription drugs that Candy had brought to the table.

This was Ski's first time at her storage room. Being that Candy would be making the first trip out west with the Piru home girls a couple of days from now, Ski wanted to get Candy's spiel on all the work she had so he'd know exactly what the fuck he was dealing with before she hit the road. Pharmaceuticals wasn't Ski's twist, but that was precisely what his lil bruh Blood Money was used to moving, so when Candy was gone, the plan was to put Blood Money in charge of moving the medicine. Anticipating walking into a storage room full of pharmaceuticals and seeing it were two different things, though.

Up till this point, anytime they spoke about the new shit Candy was bringing to the table, Ski always jokingly referred to it as medicine. He knew how important she was to them getting their work from the connect and imagined she might have a bunch of pill bottles stacked up in her storage room, probably totaling a couple of thousand pills. But inside the room was one lone table and a foldable chair surrounded by large garbage bags full of pills stacked shoulder-high.

"What the fuck?"

"Yeah, tell me about it." She said, resting her ass on the edge of the table.

"You is the mother fucking medicine lady." Ski laughed, grabbing one of the heavy bags and sitting in the chair.

"You gon joke all day?"

"Nah. But this a whole lot of mother fucking pills."

"How long is it gon take you to turn it into a whole lot of mother fucking money?"

"Be easy," Ski said, licking his lips and looking her up and down. "This what the fuck I do."

"I hear you, but like you said, this, a lot of mother fucking pills."

"It's nothing, cool out."

"All that shit sounds good." As always, Ski had been eyeballing Candy the whole time they were around each other, but with them alone in this hot, tight storage room, she could practically feel his eyes crawling all over her. Even worse, now it seemed as though he wasn't trying to hide it. Then, on cue, Ski's phone went off, and the room fell silent.

"What up?" He said, holding the screen in front of his face.

"Unless we eating takeout tonight, I'm gon need to hit a grocery store cause it aint enough shit in here for a full meal."

"Fuck you talking about, we just went shopping. It's so much food in that kitchen you can't fit no more shit in there."

"She saying she don't wanna eat what the fuck y'all got in the house." Candy cut in, grabbing Ski's phone so she could FaceTime with Amy. "What's up, girl?"

"Aint shit; what's up, Candy." Amy sounded happy.

"You know the shit, another day. Trying to get that bag. I had to grab the phone though 'cause I heard this ungrateful nigga giving you excuses about why you don't need to go shopping after you did push out his baby and you are trying to slave in a hot kitchen to cook something for him."

"So why don't you get her and take her shopping?" Ski challenged.

"What he say?"

I told Candy why she doesn't come to get you and take you out, then?

"Oh shit, that sound like a date." Amy sounded anxious.

"I don't know if y'all want that. I get my hands on Amy, but she might not come home the same day."

"Or the same way!" Amy yelled, giggling.

"She ready."

Chapter Sixteen

Pulling up outside of an auto body detail shop, Beefy exited her vehicle and ducked underneath the only partially open garage door. Squinting her eyes to look around the dark shop, she called out to the man she'd come looking for.

"Mill!"

"What up, what's popping?" The tall, slender man said, appearing right in front of her.

"You tell me nigga. You got a bitch getting out of character coming here in the middle of the night all incognito on some secret squirrel shit."

"What's pooping Beefy?" A deeper voice called from the other side of the room.

"Who the fuck is that?" She demanded, drawing her weapon as she struggled to make out the face.

Then, just as the overhead lights flickered on, illuminating the room, she retucked her weapon and eagerly approached the man for a greeting.

"Damn, Taliban what's good with you nigga? A bitch been hearing all type of crazy shit in these streets about you and Charley."

"Yeah, and I just started hearing crazy shit about you and Novella fucking with the niggas that shot up Samantha shop."

"Really?" She laughed casually resting her hand on the but of her weapon.

You know I ain't come for no action, or it would have started by now. You also know it's way too many eyes and ears in these mother fucking streets to think nobody would catch the niggas that started the lil war against Neighborhood coming in and out the Vagina Diner."

"I know the streets talk but we aint got shit to hide and if you being told that the niggas we fuck with had something to do with the shooting at Samantha shop, somebody playing you for a sucker. I was literally in the room with them mother fuckers talking business when that shit at Sam salon was taking place so it couldn't of been them. On top of that, Twizzy Hoffa fuck with the niggas you talking about. Last time I checked, he got shot at the same shooting, and I'm hearing he is in worse condition than Samantha is."

Knowing that was a valid point that he'd already considered and realized didn't make sense with his theory Taliban bit his tongue and let her continue.

"A minute ago the lil niggas called a status meeting with two or three mother fuckers from every hood except Neighborhood. Long story short, the nigga Ski started flexing talking about all this work they trying to move for damn near nothing. One of them flipped the script and went on a lil rant, trying to convince everybody to come together and go against Neighborhood."

"Really?"

"Nobody said nothing there, but behind the scenes Wacka got a couple other homies to get involved with that shit and that's how it grew to what it is now. But you already know if it aint about the coins Piru aint really with it, so we did our homework and found out them niggas did have some quality shit. I let them know we was checking for them, so the bitch Candy, Ski and Young Du came through."

"Young Du?" Mill challenged.

"Yeah, the Brim nigga. He supposed to be somebody under that shit."

Punching commands into his cell phone, Mill rejoined the conversation, showing Beefy the screen of his phone.

"That's him?"

"Nah. He look like the nigga, but I don't think that's him though. He aint that big."

Quickly weighing the pros and cons of exposing their hands, Taliban and Mill briefly made eye contact, considering what they'd just heard before ending the conversation.

"We might need to bust it up with you about something later on, but we never had this conversation. Aight?"

You don't even have to say that bruh. Loose lips sink ships."

Chapter Seventeen

Leaving multiple people dead and others hospitalized, the shooting at Samantha's salon had the streets in a frenzy. The two homeboys who stood outside smoking, as well as two of the four homegirls from inside, were dead, and the other two were still hospitalized. Samantha, now in the hospital's recovery ward, had a list of injuries she'd been recovering from for months. However, she was doing way better than Twizzy Hoffa, who was still comatose and in grave condition after being operated on and removed from the trauma unit.

Ski was on fire about Hoffa's condition. He had wanted a couple big name Neighborhood mother fuckers to get whacked, but he never could of anticipated Hoffa getting shot in the process. With shit playing out the way it had though, his hands was tied. Yeah, Hoffa was his homie, and he was willing to knock heads off for him, but their big homie Wacka had been in on it too. Being that none of the Bounty Hunter niggas responsible for the fuck up had been killed or arrested it seemed like Wacka was just willing to let the shit play out and let the pieces fall wherever they may.

Given the circumstances what the fuck was Ski supposed to do, tell Rollack? In the best-case scenario, Rollack would get a bunch of Murder homies involved, and it would be Ski, Rollack, and some Murder homies against Bounty Hunter and most of the Teck homies because Ski knew the majority of his set, including Psycho, would go along with whatever Wacka told them. What was more likely to happen, though, was Twizzy Rollack flipping on Ski too for being involved in any way with getting his twin shot. Either way Ski was in a fucked position.

In the days that followed, numerous major traps, known hangouts, and apartments used as headquarters for different Blood sets in northern New Jersey were raided. This gave the appearance to some that a statewide crack-down was in effect. At the same time, with Run, Nut, and other random statewide leaders of different Blood sets being snatched up and questioned by gang unit or homicide, the individuals who should have been feeling the heat believed that the cops didn't know what was going on.

To them, it seemed that it wasn't a coordinated operation, but instead that the police from different cities were merely collaborating with depart-ments from neighboring cities to grasp at the unknown blindly. That said, Ski and Young Du began to move with a higher degree of caution as they tried to stay below the radar.

Entering their Newark trap house to make a drop off Psycho, Trey Eight and Slugs greeted the short dark skin doorman, Ski's lil homie Nickels who managed the trap from behind a bar top and the two customers he was dealing with. Psycho and Trey sat on the couch to the right of the doorway, and while Nickels concluded his transactions, Psycho dipped a cigarette from the jar he had pulled out of his pocket and began smoking. Minutes later, after wads of money were exchanged for work and the customers had left, Psycho gave Slugs who stood in the middle of the floor the duffel bag he had thrown over his shoulder, walked over to the chest high bar that separated the open floor panel kitchen from the living room and broke the silence.

"I see that money coming today."

"It's like this all day, every day."

"We gon need more smack before the night over," Nickels said from the other side of the bar resting a small handgun on the island top and chimed in following the doorman's lead. "I been trying to get at Ski all day. I've hit him on every platform, and I've been blowing his phone up, but I keep getting his voicemail.

"I was with him earlier." Psycho exhaled a cloud of smoke, deciding to play with the man's head and see where the convo could go instead of just giving him the work and leaving.

"Well he aint been through here in a couple days and he know how fast this shit move. If we don't re-up in a lil while we gon have to close up shop and start turning niggas away."

"I'm saying, it's a lot of shit going on right now. Son can't just drop shit and move whenever the fuck you call."

"Oh, nah. Nah. I know, I know bruh probably got a lot on his plate and I can dig niggas moving with some caution or whatever."

"Caution or fear?" Psycho laughed, seizing the opportunity to bait Ski's lil homie. Then, after his question went unanswered and an awkward silence filled the room, he blew another cloud of smoke and continued. "With all the bodies dropping I aint surprised niggas keeping they heads low, so they shit don t get knocked off."

"Whatever it is it's about to start fucking with this money."

"Oh, naw, that aint happening. Even if you gotta get at me to track them niggas down and get some more work to bring through here, make no mistake we out here for this chicken. We can't be turning away money just cause Ski and that nigga Young Du missing in action." He confirmed resting a MAC ten on the bar top as he made eye contact with the light-skinned man. "Y'all the only two in here?"

"Yeah, but we good." He tried to sound confident, but Psycho swore that the man's eyes had betrayed him, darting from Psycho's Mac to his short friend who still guarded the door.

Stretching across the island Psycho quickly grabbed the man's gun and cocked it in front of his chest in one fluid motion.

"Fuck you so nervous for nigga?" He demanded, waving the weapon with hand gestures as if it wasn't deadly. But before he could get a response, a loud knock was heard at the door behind him.

Gripping the handle on the Teck that dangled from his neck, the short, dark-skinned man turned to look through the peephole just as pellets from a shotgun blast tore through the door.

Diving headfirst over the bar, Psycho quickly gathered his wits and found himself ducking beneath the bar, crouching next to the light-skinned man. Handgun shots, along with what sounded like a teck, were heard before another roaring shotgun blast went off and was followed by a burst of fire from some chopper.

As bullets sporadically ripped through the wall that supported the bar, Psycho realized this wasn't shelter and reached over the bar top to try and steal shots. Out of pure reflex, he quickly ducked back down when the shotgun roared again. The quick measure of the room had unsurprisingly shown the doorman strewn out across the floor, Slugs a few feet away awkwardly laying on the duffel bag with the doorman's tech pointing at the doorway and Trey-Eight diagonally across the room crouching behind the arm of the couch with his gun trained on the door.

Reaching over the bar again to return fire Psycho grabbed his mac from the bar top and when he crouched back down he gave Nickels back his handgun and cocked his weapon. Coming up for the third time, Psycho sprayed a quick burst of mac fire to suppress the gunmen before his weapon abruptly stopped, causing him to duck as he began struggling to unjam the charging pin. With that, the room awkwardly seemed to fall silent before kicks at what remained of the door were heard.

"Bruh, them niggas make it in here we dead and if they don't kill us I'm a kill your bitch ass for not shooting at them," Psycho told Nickels.

"Fuck that." He yelled, answering Psycho's war cries, stood up to fire, and was knocked backward by a barrage of bullets.

Two gunmen, the first tall with dreads and the second with no distinguishable features, entered the apartment shooting. Pausing over the doorman's body, the dreaded gunman squeezed the trigger of his Kalashnikov and made the man's head explode. After kicking the weapon from Slugs' hand, the second gunman pointed his gun down at Slugs' head to do the same just as Trey-Eight rose from behind the couch, firing on him. Hit with two shots, the man collapsed as his dreaded companion fired back at Trey.

Knocked backward by the first three projectiles, Trey hit the ground when the second trio struck him and was still somehow holding his weapon, struggling to aim at his target until another barrage of seven-sixty-two bullets tore into him.

Un-chambering the round that jammed his weapon, Psycho pulled the charging pin and reached over the bar, firing on the dreaded gunman who was now dragging his companion out of the apartment in retreat. Rejoining the sawed-off toting gunman who'd shot down the door, the three took off down the hallway for the staircase. Without thinking, Psycho jumped over the bar and tried to chase them down.

Catching them before they got anywhere, Psycho opened fire on the three as they ran past the building's elevator. Psycho's Mac fire struck the dreaded man, making him stumble forward, but he continued trotting down the hallway, half-carrying his companion.

Only feet away from the stairway, the third man was hit by a trio of Psycho's bullets that made him collapse against the wall. Out of bullets, Psycho reached to pull his second clip from his pocket as the door to the elevator beside him began to open. Slamming the clip in his weapon, his eyes darted inside the elevator. Then, in his peripheral, he saw the man leaning on the wall, turning around, and waving his sawed off.

Diving into the elevator as the shotgun roared, Psycho's ears rang loud as he took momentary cover. Pulling the firing pin on his MAC, he felt the rumble of the shotgun blasts tearing apart the wall outside the elevator. The blast's impact violently shook the elevator. After the next blast, Psycho peaked around the doorway, gun first, squeezing just as the dreaded man and the one he half-carried entered the stairwell at the end of the hall. But before he could aim to get off the money shot, the shotgun roared again, and Psycho could almost swear he heard ball bearings ricocheting off the elevator's door frame.

A few more blasts went off in rapid succession before the firing abruptly stopped. Taking a quick look, Psycho saw that the sawed-off man was on the floor, leaning against the wall, apparently reloading his weapon. Seizing the moment, Psycho stepped out the elevator, squeezing the trigger, and didn't stop until the man with the sawed-off slumped down and dropped his weapon.

Running to the stairway, Psycho leaned over the railing looking down and found no signs of the other two.

Chapter Eighteen

A little before midnight, Candy was up making final arrangements to head out west to re-up in the morning. She thought hitting the road early helped her blend in with the work traffic. So, the night before a trip, she always double-checked everything before going to sleep so she could get up with the sun and hit the road right away.

That night, after doing the math on the money the Piru homegirls had brought her from Novella and calculating the difference from the amount she needed to retrieve from their safe for the connect, her phone began ringing with calls and alerts for social media updates. Everybody was talking about the shooting at their trap house.

Candy immediately tried to hit Ski, but he didn't pick up. Young Du was the first person she spoke to, and he told her he'd Face Timed with Psycho, but nobody had been able to get in touch with Ski all day. They both knew how close Ski was to his lil homies and it was early as fuck so him not answering his phone was concerning. A quick social media check told Candy that it was Ski and his baby mother's anniversary. This was why he'd been inaccessible all day.

Still, it was early, though. And because Candy was concerned that Ski might do something rash if he found out about the shooting on his own, both she and Young Du agreed that she should find Ski and try to get into his head.

Because of his attraction to her, Candy could almost always get in touch with Ski, so today shouldn't have been different. Except it was. It was Ski and his baby mother's anniversary. After getting a babysitter and spending the evening together they was on a few tonight and was in the middle of a couple hour fuck marathon. While Candy was making preparations to head out west, Ski was laid up in bed with his baby mother riding him.

Candy hit his phone, checked for him on social media, and hit his baby mother before deciding to just pull up at his house with something to take his mind off the bad news of his lil homie getting shot.

Since the money for the connect was kept in a safe, only Candy and Young Du had the combination. At a storage room that Ski had the only key to, Candy technically had to see him before she hit the road anyway. Under the guise of this, she decided to lure him out of the house with a ruse before dropping the bad news on him.

Ski's face was soaked in sweat when he opened the door in nothing but gym shorts. It was clear what was going on in his house. But Candy, unabashedly, kept looking down at the bulge in his shorts. After she had told him her plans to take a couple of the Piru homegirls out west to re-up, Ski tried to postpone her mission due to his current involvement.

Candy smiled, batted her eyes, licked her lips, looked down steeling glances of his bulge, and flirted almost every other way she could just enough to keep him hard and feed the idea that something could happen between them tonight. Standing in his doorway, she knew Ski was twisted around her finger when she slapped his sweaty chest and told him to put on a shirt and come with her, and he complied.

When they got to Candy's car Ski was surprised to see the dark skinned Piru homegirl from the Vagina Diner in the back seat. Since the day they'd locked eyes and exchanged little comments back when the trio first went to meet Novella Ski, and the homegirl had been in each other's DM's talking shit to each other.

Her complexion, features, and body weren't as dark, attractive, or curvaceous as Candy's to Ski, but she was physically his type. Besides being black and sexy than a mother fucker Ski liked the fact that she was sexually ag-

148

gressive as hell and had sent him a few videos making sexual threats about what she would do to him.

"Damn. What up, big bruh? You been hiding from me?" Her sultry voice almost drooled into his ear as she reached over to fondle him before he could even close the passenger door behind him.

"Can't hide now." Candy taunted pulling from the parking spot as Ski reclined his seat to accommodate the homegirl who was already leaning over to reach for his dick.

Chapter Nineteen

While Candy and two of Novella's Piru homegirls were on their way out west to re-up, Ski had his lil homie Blood Money moving Candy's pills and helping Psycho re-supply everybody that trapped for them. At the same time, him and Young Du drove up and down the state delivering product to their non Blood customers and tried to secure new deals. After making rounds through a few Latin king hoods in Newark and Patterson Ski and Young Du were now headed to Atlantic City to make drop off's in various Crip hoods.

It had only been about three weeks since the meeting with Novella, barely a month and a half since they began hearing from Alpo and Boss's old customers, and Ski had already started introducing Young Du to his clientele. Yet, the amount of product they usually moved had already more than tripled.

Novella had the venues to move a lot of work, and her flow was consistent. Alpo and Boss were big in central and southern New Jersey, so their deaths put a sizable dent in the amount of product on the market. While some of Alpo and Boss's clientele withered away after they died, many of their customers flocked straight to Ski and Young Du. All this gave them the network to grow precipitously on an entirely different level.

Though the amount of money Novella brought them for party drugs and the influx of new business they got after Alpo and Boss's deaths helped them skip a few stages, Ski and Young Du were making some strategic moves on their own, too.

Being that most of Ski's personal customers were high ranking members of rival gangs, once they got them copping from them, Ski came up with the idea to pull a bait and switch on them. Majority of these customers were foes of their homies so when deals were struck with them the first few deliveries that they got was of a product more potent than the shit they sold their own homies.

But after a few transactions, once they'd built a sense of brand loyalty with the customers and dealings became almost normal, the quality of the product gradually decreased until it was a little less potent than whatever work they sold their local homies in that area. That said, however, all of their wholesale products were still a couple of steps above any competition in the state. But even though that wasn't comparable to the quality of work, their hustlers stood on corners slinging hand to hand.

The summer was theirs, and more and more, it began to seem like everybody else was running in place instead of playing catch up. Twizzy Rollack and Omar, from jail cells, had successfully worked through Ski and Young Du to move pieces across the figurative chess board that put a significant amount of the state's wholesale drug trade in their hands.

Yeah, there was still a little war going on against Neighborhood, and they weren't only supplying their Blood homies with their product like they had envisioned. But money was coming in like crazy, and every time they turned around, customers were increasing the amount of money they spent with them, or someone new was reaching out to try to do some business and ride their wave.

While they worked toward their goal of only supplying their homies, it seemed like Ski couldn't care less about who it was that bought their work in the meantime. Young Du, though, always made sure to remind Ski of what the ultimate goal was.

The only real downside to supplying their foes was the potential that at any minute these dealings could get contentious, and shit could go left. So, Ski and Young Du had to make these transactions personally, and at this point in the summer, there was so much set tripping going on that the two of them would rather stay low and have someone else make these moves from the luxury of an unknown location.

As they swerved in and out of lanes down the state's turnpike, Young Du sounded sincere speaking about the shooting at their trap house and Nickels getting shot. After Ski had filled him in on Nickels' status, Young Du went on to update Ski about what he'd been hearing about the events around the war they'd been wagging against Neighborhood. Although they were still losing the war, the Neighborhood homies had recently taken a few significant shots at them.

Since the shooting at Samantha's salon, Neighborhood homies had shot up their trap house in Irvington, and over a half dozen blocks they sold work on throughout the state. The one trap house Ski had boldly set up in Jersey City had also been shot up two days back to back, leaving three fatalities. On the third day, with a police paddy wagon sitting right on the corner, the shooters brazenly returned, pulling triggers to inflict more damage. In total, since the shooting at Samantha's shop less than a month ago, more than seven homies on their side had been killed by Neighborhood homies.

Of course, the shooting that hit closest to home for them was the one at their Newark trap house. Though Psycho's lil homie Slugs and Ski's lil homie Nickels were shot there as well, of the four people who died in the shooting, only Trey-Eight and the doorman were on their side. Psycho'd been so excited by the shooting that he sent Ski cell pics of the slumped man in the hallway he'd riddled with bullets and was upset he couldn't get a chance to get pics of the other assailant who died in their getaway car.

While timelines and Twitter feeds of anybody with close proximity to the streets were full of insinuations that the neighborhood homie Mill was responsible for the Newark shooting, the oblivious gossipers with no connection to the matters were all over social media, speculating about it possibly being a robbery gone wrong.

Anybody really in tune with the streets, though, knew it was likely some retaliation for the shooting at Samantha's salon. Birds were even chirping false stories on social media about it being Ski's lil homie Blood Money who got shot in the Newark trap house instead of his lil homie Nickels.

Most people who were somebody in Jersey were familiar with Samantha and her reputation. Even those who didn't understand that her reputation as a ranking member of a Blood set from California meant she could have dozens of homies from other states flown in. This told most people that the shooting at her salon couldn't go unanswered.

This being the conversation, Ski segued to what he felt was a related topic, telling Young Du that he'd spoken with Hoffa's mother.

It was two slugs in Hoffa's head, and while the doctors refused to operate while he was comatose, the moment he did come out of his coma, they had a surgery planned to remove the projectiles from his brain. Before he went into a coma, Hoffa kept repeating to his mother that he needed to talk to Ski. The problem was, Hoffa's mother said there were armed guards outside his room and all over the hospital, for that matter, because he was technically under arrest.

Still though, she told Ski that she'd falsely listed him on her son's visit list as his brother. She promised the moment Hoffa woke up from his coma, she would call Ski and let him know so he could visit before the surgery.

After that somber conversation was had, Ski told Young Du that Twizzy Rollack had said he'd been in contact with Nut.

Ski said Rollack was trying to talk the Murder O.G. into having a sit-down so they could discuss the possibility of them being the Murder homies' only supplier statewide.

With impeccable timing, Ski's cell went off just as they jumped back on the turnpike, leaving Atlantic City headed north. Ironically, it was Nut, and after being given directions to a meeting location, Ski hung up the phone.

Ski told Young Du that, despite the money the Murder homies could bring to the table, he'd been hesitant to reach out to Nut directly because he wasn't sure if they should align themselves with him. He told Young Du it was a lot of niggas with mixed opinions about him. When Young Du asked what he meant by that, Ski reminded him of what Wacka had said at the meeting about certain shit that shouldn't be said around certain mother fuckers.

When Young Du's face said he remembered the conversation with Wacka, Ski told him a lot of mother fuckers thought Nut was the type of person who shouldn't hear certain information.

"So what, is he a rat?"

I never saw anything that said that, and I haven't heard anybody credible say that they saw anything, so I don't think so. Otherwise, we wouldn't be having this conversation." Ski paused, looking at Young Du. "I'm just giving you everything I know and I'm looking at the shit like if the Murder niggas thought Nut told on anybody, they would of been got him whacked. Plus Rollack is in the best position to know what them Murder niggas think, and he would of never been reaching out to the nigga trying to put us together if he thought it was any credibility to that shit. But then again, nobody can say for sure.

"Can't be for sure about nobody but yourself."

"You're right."

"We'd be missing out on a whole lot of chicken if we just didn't fuck with the Murder niggas right?"

"A lot of chicken? Bruh it's like a million Neighborhood, Brim and Piru mother fuckers in Jersey. Aint none of them getting more money in these streets than Murder, Teck or G-Shine though."

"Really?"

"Hell yeah. It's a difference in having numbers and being heavy in the streets. We getting money with Novella and them but as much money as the Piru homies get, most of they shit aint in the streets. They own business and all that clean cut blue collar shit. Meanwhile, any Murder nigga you meat is knee deep in the slums. That nigga Nut could make the call and the Murder homies in south Jersey alone could probably top what all the Piru homies dropping on us. The streets is all the Murder niggas do."

"I heard."

"You see how fast the shit we dealing with quadrupled after Alpo and Boss died and we started supplying Samantha and a couple other mother fuckers? We can probably fuck around and double what we doing right now if we got the Murder mother fuckers copping from us."

Minutes later, Ski exited the turnpike in Lakewood, circled the Kennedy projects apartment complex, better known as KP's, and turned left, entering the complex's big parking lot that was surrounded by project buildings on the other three sides.

Seeing that a lone five-series Benz sat in the center of the lot, seemingly by itself and facing them, Ski instinctively knew that it was Nut. Pulling up and coming to a stop within feet of their passenger-side front bumpers touching, Ski and Young Du exited the Escalade. Noticing the words "MOB PIRU" spray-painted on the ground on his side, Young Du turned

155

his head just as two men exited the vehicle.

"What's popping?" Nut greeted him, extending his hand to the two men he'd last seen at the meeting a few months ago. "This my lil homie Raw."

"What's popping? What made y'all decide we should have this lil meeting in the Piru hood?" Young Du asked with a handshake.

"Why not, we fuck with the Piru homies, and I know you niggas getting some kind of chicken with Novella, so I figured it'd be a good atmosphere for a lil powwow." Just as the signature handshakes concluded, another sedan entered the parking lot from the lone vehicle entrance behind Ski and Young Du.

"And these my lil bruh Bullet lil homies." Nut added lighting a blunt as the new vehicle came to a screeching halt beside Young Du, thereby lining up almost hood-to-hood with Nut's Benz.

"They good, aint nobody trail them here." The driver said as the two exited the vehicle.

"Ski and Young Du, obviously my lil homie Bullet aint here right now cause he still behind the wall, but these his two lil homies Wu and Ant."

"What's popping?" They greeted.

"What you meant when you said, 'they good aint nobody trail them here?'" Ski inquired, and with a chuckle, Nut answered.

"You niggas got a lot of shit going on with y'all and as much as I been wanting to chop it up with y'all to see how we could get some chicken together my nigga Raw been hesitant from the jump. He feels like y'all have been attracting too much of the wrong type of attention. It's like everybody that fuck with y'all get drew into set tripping against them Neighborhood niggas. But I aint here for none of that. Long story short you niggas should know although I don't got my hands involved in too much of what go on in north Jersey I got rank for my set on the streets statewide so my homies like Raw aint comfortable with me exposing myself or them to unnecessary risks. They aint even want us to have this lil powwow."

"Really?"

"Yeah. But then I got this persistent mother fucker Twizzy Rollack getting at me like 'yo, you gotta fuck with my niggas.' Wu and Ant being the closest to the streets keep telling me about this drip you niggas got and all they hearing is good shit about the product you niggas pushing. Again, Raw in my ear cautioning me like, 'bruh, them niggas hot and they come with a lot of extra bullshit.' Until I finally say fuck it, we gon bust it up with these niggas somewhere neutral and secure and since Raw feel like the bullshit travels with y'all I told Wu and Ant to wait by the turnpike exit and trail y'all here to see if something followed you mother fuckers here."

"You serious?"

"Calm down, killer." Raw stepped forward, resting his hand on his tucked weapon to counter Ski's advance.

"Yeah, you niggas good though. You should be happy somebody was watching your back to make sure nobody followed you here."

"Nobody except the nigga on the bike." Ant chimed in with a chuckle after Wu.

"What you talking about?"

"This nigga bugging," Wu answered Nut before Ant could respond.

"I aint bugging, it's like five minutes from here to the turnpike. A dreaded nigga on a Ducati followed y'all off the turnpike to a block or two away from the projects."

"Well the nigga aint here right no." Looking around in a sarcastic gesture, Nut seemed to scold his lil homie. "Besides Twizzy Rollack you was the main nigga pushing for us to bust it up with these niggas so we could talk about these moves. Now you talking about niggas getting followed and Jamaican mother fuckers on motorcycles, don't tell me you got cold feet?"

"Never that. I want us to get this chicken, but security is priority, and I got a bad vibe from the nigga on the bike."

"Bad vibe? Nigga you strapped, you supposed to be a gangster. Shit, yo hood is only a couple blocks from here, along with five other homies you in the middle of the Piru projects that you agreed would be good for the meeting and some nigga on a bike got you nervous?" Nut paused to take a drag on his blunt before turning to Wu. "You ready to do this?"

"Absolutely."

Wu took the lead, apparently speaking for him and Ant. He told them that him and Ant had a few spots in Lakewood and out in Asbury. Because of this, he said they'd both need to start off with about a key and a half of dope and almost three of coke. Young Du responded, telling him if handling work wasn't a problem on the strength of who Rollack was, they were willing to match what they copped on consignment and just getting the remainder of the chicken from them when they re-up.

Of course, the Murder homies loved the sound of that. Even Nut said him and Raw would get some work so it could be matched, and they would flood their homies throughout South Jersey so Ski and Young Du could eventually start supplying a large amount of Murder homies. Coming to an agreement, Nut turned to Ski and gave the man a dap.

"If y'all can supply the shit y'all saying it's gon bubble. In no time I can have y'all shit in Murder hands all over the state." Just as Nut took his last pull on the blunt and plucked it away, a Chrysler Town and Country minivan sped into the parking lot and swerved to a complete stop so that the passenger sliding door was facing the meeting.

Without hesitation, Raw pushed Nut to the ground and raised his weapon, squeezing on the three men who hopped out with assault rifles. Ducking behind the hood of the Escalade, Ski and Young Du momentarily found cover.

Wu and Ant did the same, ducking behind the hood of their sedan until a stray seven-sixty-two slug ricocheted off of something and loaded itself in Ant's side, collapsing him on the passenger side of his car.

Drawing a forty cal, ski edged closer to the passenger side of the Escalade's hood, which was where the assailant's gunfire seemed to be trained. Peeking around the corner of the hood, he barely aimed and began steeling off shots. Small caliber glock in hand, Young Du on the opposite end of the truck's front hood, turned the driver side corner and crept toward the SUV's rear.

Just as Wu prepared to pull Ant back into cover, one of the assailants came around the rear passenger side of the sedan, training his fire on the passenger side of the front hood in an attempt to hit Wu. But when Ant raised his nine, squeezing the gunman, he retrained his AK-47 and dumped four slugs in him.

In a split second, Nut seized the opportunity, running around the hood of his Benz and reaching into the driver side. When he spun back around, holding a Tec-9, Wu immediately rose from his crouch behind the hood, and him and Nut squeezed their triggers until the gunman fell. Just as they stopped, squeezing the faint roar of an engine could be heard from behind them, but before they could turn to put eyes on the source, forty-five-caliber MAC-10 slugs tore into Nut from behind.

Dropping to a squat, Wu found cover in front of Nut's Benz, and after peeking around the driver side beyond Nut's strewn body, he laid eyes on the motorcycle-riding shooter. The same dreaded man that Ant had thought was following Ski and Young Du. For a brief moment, Wu thought about rising to return fire when the gunman on the bike stopped shooting, but in an instant, the man released one clip, jammed a second one into his weapon, and reopened fire.

Raw had the same thought as Wu, but instead of hesitating, he miscalculated and rose from cover, opening fire on the dreaded gunman. Being a moment too slow, he caught the man after he had reloaded his weapon, so now, after Raw's first few shots missed their mark, the assailant trained his fire on Raw until he collapsed between Wu and Ski. Struck in the arm by one of Raw's nine millimeter slugs, the gunman popped the clutch and throttle, pumping gas into his bike's engine.

The two remaining assailants from the van retrieved their fallen comrade and repositioned themselves behind Wu's sedan to offer cover fire to their comrade on the bike. With Wu and Ski ducking for cover from the seven-sixty-two slugs that shredded their way through cars, the dreaded gunman sped past the Benz, Nut and Ant's body, and then eventually around Wu's sedan toward the van. Seeing his only opportunity, Young Du stepped out from cover behind the rear driver side of the Escalade, aimed his weapon for a clear shot at the dreaded gunman, and was struck by three shots, knocking him backwards.

Chapter Twenty

"What up, what's gang banging nigga?"

"Same bullshit." Ski began sitting across from Twizzy Rollack.

With Hoffa hospitalized and out of commission, Ski was the one visiting Rollack to keep him up to date on things. Given that this was his first visit, he didn't have a good gauge for measuring Rollack's demeanor.

Even without having a gauge to go off of he expected to see a whole lot of anger, grief and pain displayed by his friend, specially being that his twin brothers shooting was still fresh when the meeting between Young Du, Ski and the Murder homies was ambushed leaving the top Murder homies on the streets dead.

"Don't come in here with that quiet shit dog. I got some good news from my lawyer, and I don't need you coming in here trying to kill my vibe."

"Pardon my soul," Ski said, taken aback by Rollack's up demeanor. "My mind was just somewhere else. What's good with your lawyer, though?"

"He came through this morning all jolly and shit and surprised me with news that we just won a pretrial motion. You know we been bagged for this shit with no bail since October last year?"

"Yeah. It's like ten months."

"These fuckers been getting all type of extensions and shit, so they don't have to indict us and at the same time they been playing about giving us a bail. The prosecutor requested an extension yesterday. My lawyer argued against it, and for some reason, the judge ruled in my favor."

"What that mean?"

"If I don't get indicted in the next ninety days, they gotta cut us loose or give us bail."

"Just like that?"

"Hell yeah nigga. My mother fucking lawyer already talking about getting a bail hearing in the next couple weeks so we can put some more pressure on the courts and speed up the process."

"Wow." was all Ski could say. Now, understanding why Rollack, knowing the losses they'd incurred in the streets in just the last few weeks, still seemed to be in good spirits.

"My mom's told me Hoffa kept saying he needed to talk to you. Have you been up there to see him yet?

"Nah, I'm trying to wait till he wakes up. Your moms said they aint gon do surgery until he come out the coma and as soon as he do she gon let me know."

"Yeah, she told me it's like a million cops in that mother fucking hospital so watch yourself when you go see son. Tell that nigga he gotta hurry up and recover, I'm on my way out that bitch, aint no time to be on injury reserve right now." He paused to flash his devious smirk. "I'm hearing you niggas getting a whole lot of chicken out there."

"Oh yeah, we doing that. It's just a whole lot of heads getting knocked off out here."

"Heads get knocked off every day," Rollack said dismissively.

"You right. But OG's and big homies don't just be getting they shit knocked off every day. Bang in peace to Nut and the other Murder homies that fell the other day."

"Yeah, BIP to the homies that fell. But niggas been saying Nut wasn't right for years so for all we know that whole shit could of just been orchestrated to blow that nigga head off."

Listening to Twizzy Rollack speak, Ski began to realize that Rollack couldn't be aware of the severity of his brother's injuries. Ski also thought he heard a hint of glee in the way Rollack spoke and believed that this might be somehow due to the deaths of Nut and Raw.

Gang banging for almost two decades now, Ski had long ago dismissed naive ideas about all homies being his homies and all blood being his blood type. The grim realities of the streets had long ago taught him that human nature was too cutthroat for every dog to be his dog.

That said, he had also understood the power structure of Murder in Jersey. Like a few sets in the state, Murder had two leaders at its helm. While Rollack's big homie C-Green, who controlled north Jersey, was locked up out of state, Nut, who typically ran south Jersey, really should have had executive power throughout the state if he'd only exercised the authority.

Now, with Nut and Raw entirely out of the picture, though, there was no OG or Captain for Murder on the streets. Having no first or second in command on the streets naturally put authority in the hands of Twizzy Rollack and Bullet, the two Captains who were at least locked up in the state.

Having the same rank, one might have thought that Rollack and Bullet would run the state the same way C-Green and Nut had before. But Rollack played on a completely different level than Bullet did. Rollack felt insulted that he and Bullet shared the same rank even though it was only in title. The leader he was and the power and influence he had far eclipsed anything Bullet was capable of. On top of all that, with his big homie Nut dead, Bullet's status as a Captain was in question now, and Ski knew Rollack would either raise the issue about its legitimacy or strip him of it.

For whatever reason, before the visit, Ski hadn't considered the implications of the shooting in Lakewood. Still, in this moment at this visit with Rollack, it became abundantly clear that Murder in the state of New Jersey was under the tutelage of Twizzy Rollack.

"What's good with the nigga Young Du?"

"He aight, he took a few to the chest but he good."

"Yeah?"

"Yeah. He had on a vest, shit hit him square in the plate, but they was chopper slugs so one pierced him a lil. He took it like a gee and brushed it off though."

"Yeah, his man Omar hit me last night and told me he took a couple to the chest."

"The homie Omar aight?"

"Yeah, the homie max out on his other big in a couple months, so he should be back up here in the county with me."

"Shit, the way you talking y'all might not even be locked up."

The remainder of the visit continued in a similar fashion. The conversation between the two went from Psycho, the shootings he'd been involved in, distribution of the money they was making and how much of said money was appropriated for and sent to the growing number of homies who had got locked up while fucking with them.

After covering the details of the recent shootings at their trap house, Rollack and Ski agreed then and there that it made sense to completely separate Psycho and the work he ran around putting in from their distribution efforts. But knowing that Psycho was only trying to ride for them and the homies they'd lost, Rollack and Ski also agreed that him and the homies riding around with him just putting in work on the Neighborhood homies would still see the same amount of money.

When the conversation shifted to the specifics of the money being made on the streets, Ski told Rollack that a lot of Villain, Seven-Nine-Three, Bounty Hunter, and Teck homies were now buying weight from their trap houses.

"That aint enough. Remember, we are trying to supply whole sets." Rollack reminded him.

Then, Ski told Rollack that since the meeting, they'd sold a few keys of dope and almost a dozen of coke to the Outlaw and One-Eighty-Third homies only to have Rollack dismiss those accomplishments as well, reminding him that they were among the smallest sets in the state. But when Ski told Rollack about the details of their meeting with Novella, his childhood friend flashed his signature smirk of approval.

They both knew Piru was one of the heaviest sets in the state. Even though Murder and other sets were probably stronger in the streets, the Piru homies had clean money and were way more influential. Ski told his friend that since the meeting with Novella, a lot of her homies started coming through their trap houses buying weight of almost everything.

This meant that they were getting some hard drug money from the Piru homies, too. But to Rollack just the meeting and deal alone with Novella somehow represented longevity and told him that shit on the streets was on the right track.

Rollack told Ski that from the moment he heard about Nut and Raw's death, he'd been working the phone and had spoken to a couple Murder homies. As a result of these conversations, he said a bunch of the Murder homies in north Jersey committed to copping from them. He also said he'd spoken with Wu and a couple of Nut and Raw's lil homies all over south Jersey and was confident that after Nut, Raw, and Ant were laid to rest, the majority of their homies would be copping from them in some capacity.

Though it had just dawned on him during the visit, Ski knew that all the Murder homies were now only coming into Rollack's fold for one reason. The moment Nut and Raw's deaths were announced, every Murder homie on the streets in Jersey knew that Twizzy Rollack was in control. That said everybody wanted to kiss ass and get in the good graces of the new nigga on the throne.

Being a lil disturbed by how easily Rollack spoke about his recently deceased homies, Ski took note of the slight but didn't ponder its possible implications. At the end of the visit, Ski assured the man he'd known since childhood that he'd handle things with his lawyer and pick up all the other responsibilities that Hoffa had.

Chapter Twenty-One

Hours after the visit with Rollack, Young Du and Candy led Ski into a Spanish restaurant in Harlem, New York. After Candy exchanged words with the clerk behind the front counter, the trio followed the clerk through a door that led to the back of the establishment.

"What's all this?" Ski whispered to Young Du.

"You put all your cards on the table and been connecting the dots between the shit we got going on and your personal customers, so Candy and the nigga Omar felt like it was time for you to meet the connect."

Entering a dimly lit room where two Dominican men played pool, the female clerk who'd led the group whispered something to the older pool player who sipped on a corona. The clerk then turned to leave the room, but before she could clear the doorway, the older man uttered something to his pool opponent in their native tongue, prompting the man to follow the clerk's lead.

"What's up, Carlito?"

"No-ting much," Carlito replied to Young Du, chalking the end of his pool stick once he was alone with the three guests. "I see you and miss eye Candy bring company to my establishment."

"This my homie I been telling you about."

"The reason our sales have been picking up like crazy recently," Candy added.

Lining up a shot, the room fell silent until Carlito's pool stick struck the q ball, sending it across the table and knocking two balls into one hole.

"So he is dee one responsible?"

"Yeah." Young Du and Candy said in unison.

"I still do not know why he is now before me in my establishment." Looking at the three faces for an exaggerated second, Carlito saw surprise, nervousness, and a hint of what he thought was fear before he dropped his pool stick, cracked a smile, and embraced Ski with a hug. "'Tis okay, hombre. I joke, you know. You make mucho denaro. I happy with you. I want to meet you."

"So what's good, Carlito?"

Pulling a duffel bag from beneath the pool table, Carlito turned to Candy and answered her question.

"Little while ago, I come across opportunity for me. So I fly all dee way here, call you here because I have new opportunity for you to make mucho-mucho denaro." Downing the last of his Corona, Carlito sat the bottle on the table, cracked open a new one, and continued. From now on, for every purchase, I will give you fifty kilos. Thirty cocoa, twenty heroin, and you give me six hundred..."

"Whoa. Whoa, Carlito." Young Du interrupted the connect. "All due respect, Poppy, I don't think we can handle that much every flip."

"You tripping." Ski outburst before Carlito could respond. "We can do that."

"Ah, ha. I forget you are dee one responsible."

"Ski, I don't know how we gon juggle all them birds."

"You must ahhh, how do you say it... Spread you wing, expand horizon."

"I'm saying, I'm thinking about where we gon get you that six hundred thousand from right now."

"I expect you to say this." Carlito laughs and sips the corona before unzipping the duffel bag. "New opportunity for me. I give you one million fraudulent U.S. dollars; you take it home to Jersey to sell, you know? In five, six, maybe seven or eight week you know, you come to regular meeting place and give me two hundred thousand for the money and six hundred thousand for kilos."

Chapter Twenty-Two

Though he was ambitious and had the hunger to take the connect up on his offer, Ski had no clue how he was going to get the man his money. He knew they'd get the money for the drugs, but just unloading the extra keys would be enough to keep them busy for a minute. Then, the new hustle of managing and trying to move a million dollars' worth of fake bills was a completely different hustle with its own unique problems.

That said, Ski knew the confusion and stress that came with the extra responsibilities he'd put on all their shoulders. But unlike Young Du, he was savvy enough to know that this was all good stress. Also, unlike Young Du, Ski knew that it was better to get everything from the connect first and then wreck your brain figuring out how to move it.

Ski knew that everything didn't have to be sold, and it didn't matter where the money came from as long as the connect was paid. He knew it wasn't going to be an easy feat, but the way he saw it, all they had to do was give the connect the first eight hundred thousand they touched, and he still had almost five percent of that put away, just from his cigarette money.

As soon as they leave the meeting with Carlito, Ski jumps on his phone. After a few conversations during the ride back to Jersey, he'd found hands to put a hundred and seventy fraudulent bills into, in exchange for over ninety thousand dollars. In the next few days, Ski met with his big homie, Wacka, and more than a dozen other big homies, managing to put together another $290,000 for Carlito solely off the sales of the fraudulent money. Ski couldn't believe how fast that shit was moving itself. Unfortunately, though, everything wasn't going as smoothly as the distribution was.

The day after Young Du and Candy brought Ski to meet the connect, Candy called Ski early in the morning to vent. Young Du didn't want them to introduce Ski to Carlito and had only gone along with it because Candy threatened to go over his head and talk to the man whose connection it was. While Ski and Omar didn't know each other, Candy reminded him that Omar wanted them to supply all the homies in Jersey. That said, it only made sense that he would agree to their introduction of Ski, who was responsible for most of their distribution, to Carlito.

Candy said even though the meeting had gone off without a hitch, the next time she was alone with Young Du, he was furious. She told Ski that Young Du fucked with him, but he didn't trust him enough to wanna introduce him to the connect.

Telling Ski how Young Du had got in her face confronting her, telling her to stay in her fucking place almost threatening her Candy sounded emotional and a lil scared. Ski thought she sounded so much unlike her usual self that more than once during their conversation, he asked her if she was crying and if she was alright.

Once she sounded a lil better, Ski tried to thank her for trusting him enough to tell him how Young Du was coming, but she cut him off.

"Nah, you don't need to thank me. Besides being loose with Tiffany stick you a real ass nigga. It's only right for a real bitch to stand up for a real nigga."

By the end of their talk, Candy had calmed down enough to half-laugh at Ski's unfunny jokes and make him promise not to confront Young Du or say anything about what she'd told him.

On the flip side of their operation, barely a week after the Newark trap house shooting, Psycho, with Cocaine in the backseat following a hearse and numerous limousines that made up a funeral procession, drove into the gates of a Jersey City graveyard.

Stopping a second later, he finished off a PCP laced cigarette, hopped out his car, leaving Cocaine, and walked a few yards to the plot where Trey-Eight would be buried. Standing with his lil homies, Slugs and A.K., Psycho looked around the group at the faces of Trey-Eight's family, and his gaze rested on his mother for a moment as she held onto Trey's brother, her only remaining child.

Psycho found himself thinking about all the services he'd been to in just the last few months. Footing the bill for the services, seeing to it that homies financially contributed to the fallen homies' kids, and ridding to ensure that the other sides' casualties more than doubled theirs usually gave Psycho a lil solace. But he hadn't seen Blood on Blood all out set tripping last this long and maintain a regular body count like this before. More and more, it was seeming like every other week, another homie or two on their side was dying, and Psycho was petitioning Ski and Young Du to give up funds for them.

Psycho, of all people, understood that set tripping was part of gang banging. He was part of the Green family, so naturally, some of the violence that came with gang banging was normal to him. But this was different somehow. Though he wouldn't admit it, on some level, Psycho understood that long-term set tripping did a disservice to the unity they were supposed to have.

Yet, as much as he knew that wagging all-out war against one set for this long didn't make sense, he would never put his gun down first. Thinking about all this made him wanna kill even more, and he wanted to kill something now.

As Trey's brother wrapped up his ceremonial speech and brought that part of the service to a close, people began tossing flowers onto the descending casket, and something caught Psycho's attention. Out of the corner of his eye, he spotted a man on a motorcycle near the entrance of the graveyard. From afar, the man seemed to be watching the service, but everything about him appeared to be out of place.

Then, just as Ski and Young Du's words about the main shooter from the Lakewood hit being on a bike rang in Psycho's head, the man turned his bike around and sped away. Without thinking, Psycho left his homies to mourn with Trey's family and found himself back behind the steering wheel of his Audi A8, but before he could shift the vehicle's gears, the passenger door opened, and Trey's brother jumped in.

In a suit and hard-bottom shoes, Trey-Eight's brother pulled a small three-eighty from his waistline and spoke straightforwardly.

"I seen the nigga on the bike and you already know I'm with the shit so don't waste time trying to talk me out of riding."

Being somewhat familiar with the man, but more importantly, understanding and respecting the urge to ride, Psycho didn't respond. He backed his vehicle out of the graveyard and took off after the man on the bike.

Right in front of them, Psycho spotted the bike turning left a few blocks ahead. Just as he approached the block himself, Psycho was relieved when the van in front of him made the left turn first, allowing his Audi to separate from the motorcycle and thus helping him remain inconspicuous. Speeding up the block, the van turned left, and Psycho reached the corner just in time to see that the motorcycle had turned right and was now turning left just two blocks over.

Grabbing the Mac from the floor and sitting it on his lap as he approached the intersection that lay within the block, Psycho could feel his adrenaline pumping, and Cocaine could, too, as the pit bull stood in the backseat, growling. Just as Psycho turned his steering wheel to enter the block, he realized it was a dead end and hit the brakes. Before he could move to retreat, his passenger door swung open, and the long barrel of an AK-47 came through his driver's side window and poked the left side of his face. Momentarily glancing into his rearview mirror, Psycho knew that the fix had been in when he saw that the van that once separated his Audi from the motorcycle now sat behind him, boxing him in.

· · · · · · · · · · ·

In less than half the time the connect was saying he expected them to be paying him back, they had more than half of what they owed him, just from the fake money. Ski or Young Du couldn't believe how fast that shit moved. Every time they put some of it in somebody's hands, it seemed like hours later or the next day, somebody around that person was calling them for just as much if not more than that person had gotten. This, in turn, helped the distribution pick up for the extra keys they were getting now.

Since the status meeting, Ski and Young Du had been tearing up the pavement, meeting and trying to make deals with just about everybody. They were supplying something to most of the Tech and a substantial amount of Piru homies. Then, after the visit with Twizzy Rollack, Ski'd eventually chopped it up with Wu and a couple of other Murder homies. Following these conversations, they started copping from them on the terms Nut, Raw, and Ant agreed to before the ambush in Lakewood.

At this point, they had leaders from three of the states' top six sets copping from them, and they were doing some regular business with almost all of the smaller sets. Aside from what their workers sold on the few blocks they controlled, they still distributed shit to Ski's clients, members of rival gangs and anybody else who wanted to buy something.

Of course, Neighborhood, being the set that they were tripping on, wasn't doing any business with them. But Ski saw no reason why they still hadn't done any business with the next biggest set, G-Shine.

G-Shine, as a set, having been involved in the tripping against Neighborhood since the war began, still had a number of their homies running around, putting in work with Psycho. At this point of the summer, everybody knew that Ski and Young Du had the best work on the streets. Yet, as obvious as it seemed that they'd be doing business together, Ski or Young Du hadn't sold anything to any G-Shine homies.

Although it was one of the largest sets in the state, the G-Shine homies didn't have many of their own blocks or hoods where they were known for making a lot of money. Their homies were scattered on different blocks, in different hoods, throughout different cities. Still thinking about putting their product in as many hands as possible, Ski arranged a sit-down.

Inside a small chicken shack in Trenton, N.J., Ski and Young Du sat at a table across from Hak-Shine, the top G-Shine homie in the state, and his lil homie, Lucky. The four had only been talking for minutes. They had already come to an understanding that, because Shine as a set had so many homies under it in Jersey, different groups of G-Shine homies in different cities largely did their own thing on a day-to-day basis.

That said, Hak couldn't do anything about getting G-Shine as a set or even a substantial portion of his homies under the set to commit to copping from Ski and Young Du. Hak and Lucky, however, were interested in getting their hands on some of the fake money that Ski and Young Du had. But before they could agree on a deal, Lucky had a question for Young Du.

"Don't I know you from somewhere?"

Smirking, Young Du seemed surprised that the question was directed at him.

"If you gotta ask something like that, you don't know me, bruh."

"What type of answer is that?"

"What type of question was that?" Hak-Shine chuckled glancing at his lil homie. "If a nigga look familiar, you lead with the questions cause he could be your enemy or he could be the fuzz. You don't know why the fuck he look familiar, so you don't talk to him for a minute and wait until after we don chopped it up about all kind of illegal shit and then say 'yo, don't I know you from somewhere?"

"I'm saying, the homie might of seen me in passing or something. But I'm some different type of fly nigga, so I think everybody who ever met me remember me. Plus, I just came home off a twelve-year bid, so I know you don't remember me from nowhere."

"What's good with getting to this money, though?" Ski chimed in bringing it back to the business and within a few minutes they'd agreed to sell the G-Shine homies almost twenty thousand fraudulent bills in fifties, fifteen thousand in twenties and about five in tens for twenty-five thousand dollars with the caveat that Hak-Shine and Lucky would give some of Ski and Young Du's work to their lil homies.

"That don't sound bad," Hak said, smirking. "Lucky could give whatever work you got to a couple of homies, and if they wanna rock with y'all, we'll plug them in."

Just as everybody seemed to agree, Lucky, still suspiciously looking at Young Du, spoke up again.

"Where you was locked up at?"

"In Jersey, I was only in max custody in Trenton, then they shipped me to P.A. to do my last couple years."

You weren't never down in Northern State Prison?

"I wish I was nigga. From what I heard that shit was like the streets compared to Trenton."

"Didn't the shit with them Neighborhood niggas start down Northern?"

"Absolutely." Lucky proudly responded to Ski. "I was there when it started, me and the Murder homie Bullet made the calls for three G-Shine homies and two Murder homies to pop off on the Neighborhood nigga Got Guns."

． ． ． ． ． ． ． ． ． ． ．

In a dark, smoke-filled room, Psycho and Trey-Eight's brother sat side by side, tied down in chairs in the middle of what appeared to be an auto body garage as the dreaded man they had followed walked around the room, circling them.

"I need names, and you can walk, lil bruh."

"Really?" Psycho laughed sarcastically, first looking down at the sheets of plastic covering the floor, where Cocaine's dead body lay, then looking around at the three other unmasked gunmen standing around the room.

"Yeah, really. I aint gon front, for a second I wasn't sure if I wanted to kill you or not. Your last name is Green so I'm sure you done did all type of shit you need to die for but I aint sure if your bullshit calls for you to die from my gun. Now these niggas with me got a completely different opinion. They want your mother fucking head, no question. But I'm thinking they might be overreacting just a lil bit, and we might be able to help each other."

"You think so?"

"Hell yeah." He assured him, pulling up a chair to sit right in front of Psycho. With the two practically face to face, the dreaded man looked down at Psycho's gun, cell phone, jar of PCP, and pack of cigarettes sitting between the two. "Let me get a dipped cig." He said, grabbing the jar and cigarettes before Psycho could reply. "I don't think you know why you here, lil bruh."

"Let me guess, you one of them Neighborhood niggas and I'm here cause we been slaying you bitch ass niggas all over the state."

"Hear that shit?" The dreaded man laughed, dipping a second cigarette in the jar as he looked over his shoulder at his henchmen. "Told y'all this nigga was different."

"So why we here?"

"Well, I don't know your man. He wasn't part of the plan; wrong place, wrong time." He shook his head, looking at Trey-Eight's brother. "I guess he is somebody you picked up at the funeral. Probably part of the fam or friend of the deceased. Either way, he's a victim of circumstances now."

"Fuck you nigga!"

"Yeah, that barking shit tough as hell. You see what the dog got for doing that shit right?" The dreaded man paused with a smirk as he lit both cigarettes and put one in Psycho's mouth.   Whoever you are, I'm happy you're here now. Even though you don't know me, I know exactly who the fuck you is, and I know about all the tripping shit you been running around doing. But I aint here for none of that."

"Who the fuck is you?"

"Taliban. I aint Neighborhood, I'm Brim. Even though you don't know me I know you done heard the name enough to know I could of made a call and had a gang of niggas pick you the fuck up. If it were as simple as me just wanting you dead as soon as one of my niggas seen you they would of just knocked your shit off. But none of that dumb shit you niggas been out here doing aint involve me or nothing I gave a fuck about until recently." He lied. "Now though, somehow, someway, y'all done fucked with some-body and caused them to trip on your man Hoffa when he was with my peoples Samantha and that led to her getting shot up and shit."

"A couple different mother fuckers got shot at ol girl salon. You can't just say that shit had something to do with my niggas."

"That salon aint never been shot up, and nobody was targeting her for nothing. We both know that shit connected to something you stupid moth-er fuckers done did. So I'm like if I can't get my hands on the trigger man one of you niggas gotta pay. But on the other hand I know if I knock you and your homie shit off right now I probably aint never gon find out who shot up the salon."

"You think I know who did that shit?" Psycho asked as Taliban reached down for his phone, unlocked the screen with Psycho's thumb, and began scrolling through it. "How the fuck would I know who did it?"

"You smarter than that lil bruh, I know you don't want my niggas to go through this phone and start picking off your peoples."

"Really?"

"Tell me something." Taliban began with a line of questioning that he knew would wipe the smirk from Psycho's face. "What's up with that old lady you bring breakfast to every morning? That's your grandmother or something. Yeah, I took a page out your family playbook, and I followed you to her house the last couple days, so I know how to hurt you if you force my hand, but I aint here for that."

"Bruh, you know I don't know who did that dumb shit at that salon. Hoffa my mother fucking homie if I thought I knew who the fuck..."

All I know is that I came here with questions, and you're not giving me any answers.

"Answers?" Psycho raised his voice, smiling through a cloud of smoke. "How the fuck you kidnap us and hold us at gun point talking about give you answers, and we can help each other and all this goofy shit?"

The men in the shadows noticeably began to grow anxious and guns could be heard cocking before Taliban began his response.

"I'm trying to be cool lil bruh but you making this shit real hard. I came in here thinking if this nigga act like he wanna play ball and give me something to go off, I'ma cut him loose, I can help him end this tripping shit against Neighborhood and I can even line shit up so him and his mans could get some of that real Brim money and stop penny pitching. But you coming crazy and these niggas behind me is like sharks smelling blood. All this back and forth shit only making it worse for you."

"More threats?"

"Damn, I keep forgetting you one of the Greens," Taliban said rising from his seat drawing twin glocks. "That mean you supposed to be like a tough guy or something right?" Resting his weapon's barrels on Trey-Eight's brother's kneecaps, the Taliban pulled both triggers.

"Whoa! Whoa! What the fuck you doing, why you shoot him!"

"Incentive! I know this. Your dead lil homie brother. Either you gon do the right thing for your fallen homie family or you gon make that sad ass lady burry her last kid."

"What!?" Psycho yelled over his moans.

"I'm giving you some mother fucking incentive. You might need a lil extra reason to do the right thing. You can be tough and act stupid but he gon bleed out unless you help me, help you save his fucking life."

Taliban was right. The two spoke quickly, and minutes later, Psycho hit Ski on speakerphone, found out where he was, and told him that he was with a Brim homie who was ready to single-handedly bring them most of the state's Brim money if the two of them could meet up. Ski wasn't in the area and tried to get Psycho to settle for meeting with his lil homie Blood Money, but that wouldn't work.

Psycho said that for everything the Brim homie was bringing to the table, he would only meet with Ski now. In exchange for all he offered them, he wanted them to discuss ending the war against Neighborhood by Brim, helping in any way possible to find out who the shooters were that had shot Hoffa and Samantha. Ski said he'd try to make the meeting but insisted that if he couldn't, Blood Money would be there in his place.

While this was being done, Taliban's goons were getting Trey-Eight's brother ready for the hospital. Before they left Taliban gave them Psycho's cell phone with instructions on exactly who to kill if they didn't hear from him in an hour.

Chapter Twenty-Three

Not understanding all that Psycho said but excited about the opportunity to do business with one of the biggest sets in the state, Ski hit Blood Money when he got off the phone with Psycho. While driving he spoke to his lil homie on speaker phone so Young Du could hear the exchange but when the conversation was over both Ski and Young Du had doubts about his ability to seal the deal so they postponed what they were about to do and hit the gas to make sure that Ski would be the one at the meeting.

They were in Jersey City, so Ski chose to meet in Audubon Park, which was right in the heart of his sets hood in Jersey City. The sun had just set when Ski left Young Du in his truck and walked along the paved walkway entering the park. Heavily treed though, Audubon was already really dark, so less than a minute into his walk he reminded himself that this weird ass, last minute meeting, at night, was set up by Psycho's crazy ass so he didn't know exactly what he was in store for.

Thinking like this, Ski began to wonder if it was a good idea for Psycho and whoever he was here to meet with to be able to see him approaching long before he could see them. Knowing the answer to that question was no, he instinctively began to walk in the dirt just along the side of the walkway through the heavily treed park.

Questioning his idea to meet in this location, Ski pulled out his cell phone and began to call Psycho just as he realized that the park ahead of him opened up wide to a benched off section designed for barbecues and similar functions. Directly ahead of him now, he spotted what looked like Psycho seated on a bench. But there was something else too, or at least what looked like someone else. There was another figure at the end of the bench where Psycho sat.

Getting closer, Ski saw what looked like dreads hanging from the figure's head. Then he realized that the figure standing over Psycho held what looked like a weapon, and as he reached for his own, Ski noticed a motorcycle off to the side. Without hesitation, he quickly reflected on the bike from the Lakewood shooting and fired his weapon, sending spent projectiles into the side of his target. Taliban stumbled sideways, dropping his gun before falling.

"Fuck you doing nigga!" Psycho demanded in shock, kneeling at Taliban's side and grabbing his glock forty.

"Fuck you mean what I'm doing! What you doing!"

"I told you what the fuck I'm doing!" Psycho rose from Taliban's body, pointing a shaky gun in Ski's direction.

"That's the nigga who moved on us in Lakewood! He was with the shooters that whacked the Murder homies!"

"I know who the fuck he is!" Psycho confirmed not sounding like himself as he looked back and forth from Ski to Taliban's body.

Then, just as Taliban appeared to be trying to say something, a figure quickly approached from behind Ski. Psycho, half caught off guard, pointed and fired his gun with no regard for the target. Psycho's bullets only narrowly missed Ski, who had dived to the right behind a thick patch of bushes.

Looking to the figure who'd been shot after approaching him from behind, Ski immediately recognized him as Young Du.

"Nigga you shot the homie Young Du!"

"Why the fuck you bring that nigga with you!"

"Fuck you mean why I bring him! Nigga you shot him!" Ski yelled back at Pyscho just as Young Du began to stand.

"I'm aight."

180

"That, that nigga aint Young Du."

"What?" Psycho turned to ask Taliban who had drawn his second weapon and was waving it in Young Du's direction.

"That nigga aint!!!" was all he managed to say before three quick shots tore into him.

Spinning around, Psycho trained his weapon on Young Du and pulled the trigger before being struck by fire that knocked him backwards. Hunched over and holding a wound, Psycho looked to the bushes where Ski hid, trying to follow his voice.

"Psycho, what the fuck! What's popping with you nigga!"

"Awww, fuck you nigga!" he groaned in pain.

"Fuck me? Nigga you tell me to meet you by myself and you show up with the nigga that squeezed on us in Lakewood. How the fuck is you coming!"

"Fuck you! We under the same hood you bitch ass nigga and you ridding with this nigga you just met!" These were Psycho's last words because as he moved to re-aim his weapon, desperately trying to follow Ski's voice and make out his outline in the bushes, Ski pulled his trigger until his weapon had emptied.

Chapter Twenty-Four

The day after Psycho's death, nobody heard from Ski. Young Du had called and reached out to him all over social media to try to get in touch, but Ski barely picked up his phone, updated his accounts, or posted anything. When they did speak, they briefly discussed business; other than that, it was almost like Ski was doing everything he could to avoid Young Du. Today was no different. Young Du had told him he wanted them to sit down so they could go over some numbers and he could bounce a couple of ideas off his head, but Ski hit him back, saying he was going to be busy all day checking out new trap houses.

Their Newark trap house had been closed since the shooting there. Before it closed, that trap was their main breadwinner. Ski had needed to find another local spot to open up in its place, but it seemed like there were always a hundred things going on, so he'd been putting off the search for a new one since the shooting.

With Candy riding shotgun and his lil homie Nickels in the backseat, Ski drove all around Newark. After checking a couple of spots and not finding what they needed, they agreed that they should check a few spots in Jersey City. A lot of the traffic that came through the now-closed Newark trap house had come from Jersey City, so finding a new spot over there makes things convenient.

That said, leaving the first spot that was a bad fit because it was located right outside a neighborhood-controlled area, they found exactly what they were looking for in the second Jersey City apartment. It was a small, rundown tenement in a crime area, so all in one meeting, money was exchanged, a lease was signed, and keys were handed off.

Leaving the new trap, Ski got so caught up talking to Candy and Nickels that he wasn't paying attention as he approached the corner. Slowing down for the red light, he uncharacteristically pulled up extremely close to the rear bumper of the van in front of him.

Before he was old enough to sell drugs on the streets of Newark, Ski'd played bumper tag and escaped numerous cop chases in stolen cars, so he always left more than enough room to maneuver between himself and other vehicles. Just as he dismissed the importance of his error, a sedan a few cars behind him in traffic swerved right out of the lane, pulled up, and rammed into his passenger side.

The impact rocked his SUV, jolting everybody in the car. Jerking his head back after banging it against the steering wheel, Ski looked around, gathering his wits. Equilibrium jarred, and Ski was lost for a second as to what was going on when he saw Candy raising her small three-eighty to fire out her window. Nickels yelled in Ski's ear, and before he could respond to anything, Candy was half in his lap, still firing her weapon.

Spinning the wheel right, Ski reversed his Escalade, pushing both the car behind him and the attacking car on his passenger side. With bullets ripping through his SUV, he quickly turned left, threw the truck in drive, and accelerated forward, jumping the curb as one of the gunmen climbed from the assailant vehicle and ran behind the Escalade, firing.

"Who the fuck is that!?" Candy screamed, jumping in her seat and firing from her window back at the assailants as Ski swerved around the corner pole that held the traffic light, completed his left turn, and drove off the curb back into the street.

Now, around the corner from where the ambush had taken place, the vehicle accelerated forward, leaving the would-be assailants behind.

"Gotta be them Neighborhood niggas." Ski finally opened his mouth before looking at Nickels in his rearview mirror. "What the fuck!" He yelled, almost crashing as he looked at his slumped lil homie bleeding out on the backseat.

Chapter Twenty-Five

Being the only person on their side hit in the ambush, Nickels died after catching eight slugs. Ski knew he was dead as soon as he looked at him in the mirror.

The day after Nickels's death and five days after the Audubon Park shooting, Young Du had only seen Ski once. Though up till this point, the limited communication they'd had by means of messaging and face timing was enough to keep business moving at a steady pace, it was weird for two men who'd been making moves together and had been around each other just about every day. Still, Young Du understood that Ski had been distancing himself to grieve over Nickels and Psycho and emotionally move beyond whatever had happened in the park.

Being from out of state and not knowing the two men before he came home and his homie Omar and their homies Twizzy Rollack and Hoffa put them all together, Young Du didn't know exactly how deep Ski and Psycho's bond was. But knowing they'd the same big homie and hearing the way they reminisced about past wars they'd engaged in together against this gang or that set, he knew that to some extent they'd come up together, and if nothing else, that alone bred loyalty and a sense of devotion. It appeared to Young Du that these were the things that Ski was struggling with.

Losing one close homie to the game by any means was enough to rile up some of these emotions. But Ski was dealing with the loss of two. Then, adding insult to injury, in most instances when a homie's lost, the ones who live to grieve at least have a clear enough idea of who was responsible, needed to be targeted, and who they could direct their rage and retaliatory shots at.

Ski could grieve over Psycho and Nickels, and he could avenge Nickels, but being that Ski himself was the triggerman in Psycho's death meant this wasn't like most instances. He couldn't avenge Psycho's death. That being the case, Young Du also knew that the anti-climactic feeling of it all had to be weighing heavy on Ski. Who could he target for the death of his homie when he was the gunman?

With all this on his mind on the morning of Psycho's funeral, Young Du spoke out of the window of his SUV, placing an order for food before maneuvering his vehicle forward to the next window at the restaurant's drive-thru, where he paid for and received his bag of breakfast. Before he could even put his cup of coffee in the cup holder, the vehicle behind him was blowing its horn.

Glancing at the sedan through his rearview mirror, Young Du let up on the brakes, and his SUV slowly accelerated, leaving the drive-thru and approaching the intersection when a small sedan pulled up in front of him, cutting him off.

Just as he realized what was happening, a man, gun in hand, hanging out the window, opened fire. Ducking for cover, Young Du instinctively threw his vehicle into reverse and stomped on the gas. Hitting the sedan behind him, his SUV pushed the car back a few yards before they both came to a stop. Shifting gears again, Young Du's SUV jerked forward, picking up speed before smacking into the rear of the vehicle that had cut him off, sending the sedan into a tailspin.

Turning onto the intersection and accelerating in the wrong direction, Young Du glanced at what he'd left behind him in his rear view mirror and sped away from the apparent blitz.

Swerving in and out of lanes, Young Du reached for his phone and made a few calls. He considered going home but decided against it, knowing that Psycho's funeral and wake were far too important to miss. He also knew that he needed to speak with Ski face-to-face.

Less than an hour later, Young Du was making his way into the church where the services were being held. He'd heard that this was the largest church in Newark and had seen pictures all over social media of the crowd of people who had come to pay their respects. But seeing crowds of people outside waiting, on top of all the people seated in the pews of the church, Young Du oddly felt a newfound respect for Psycho.

He'd heard all the rumors about how big and revered Psycho's family was, but he'd never expected a turnout half as big as this. The thought even crossed Young Du's mind that he might be in the wrong place until an usher handed him an obituary and ushered him to a seat up front next to Ski and a bunch of other Teck homies.

Reflecting on the delicacy of the conversation he needed to have with Ski Young Du, he barely paid attention to the service as person after person went up to the pulpit and spoke about Psycho until the pastor delivered his sermon and the choir sang their hymn. Before long, the services had concluded, and walking behind the pallbearers who carried Psycho's casket, Young Du spoke quickly into Ski's ear.

"You know Rollack and them got a bail hearing tomorrow?"

"Nah, I aint know that."

"Omar hit me, saying he spoke to Rollack last night. He said he had been trying to reach out to you, but he couldn't get in touch with you."

"I'ma hit him after the burial." Ski nonchalantly said, coming to a stop at the curb as everybody watched the pallbearers put the casket in the hearse.

He wasn't trying to ignore what Young Du was talking about, but his attention was somewhere else. The night Psycho was killed, without even thinking, Ski fled straight to Psycho's pops pawn shop to get rid of the dirty guns. Ski had left Young Du outside and while Psycho's pops Ponzi wasn't around D-Green was there to unknowingly help his cousins murderer swap the weapon he'd just used to knock his shit off for a new one.

Ski was surprised he hadn't heard nothing from the Green family about this and chalked it up to D-Green keeping his mouth closed, the family not giving a fuck about Psycho or somebody not putting two and two together. That said though, he was weary as fuck about running into D-Green at the funeral and having to answer questions about that night.

"I know Omar and your man Rollack are happy as hell they might finally be getting a bail." Young Du said, interrupting Ski's thoughts. "At the same time, Omar was telling he concerned about the homie Rollack. He said he think he stressing over that shit that's about to happen with Hoffa but he trying to hide it."

"What's going on with Hoffa?"

"You aint know bruh woke up from the coma yesterday? They saying they getting him ready for surgery so they can pull the slugs out his head today."

Without saying a word, Ski turned around to face his baby's mother, Amy. As the two spoke, Young Du, still standing at the curb, made note of the abundance of people, apparently relatives, all wearing 'In Loving Memory' t-shirts that bore images of the same older lady.

"Where your G-ride at?" Ski asked, interrupting his thoughts. Minutes later, the two were in his truck, flying to the hospital.

"I don't know how I forgot about this shit with Hoffa," Ski said breaking the ice.

"I'm saying Rollack and them know it's a lot of shit going on right now. Niggas at war and we trying to supply the whole fucking state. Everybody is entitled to have a slip of mind and forget something once in a while."

"Fuck happened to your G-ride?" Ski demanded, looking up from texting long enough to notice the bullet-ridden hood.

"You tell me why the fuck all them people wearing RIP t-shirts in memory of other mother fuckers at the homie funeral?"

Young Du was surprised to find out that since Psycho's death, his grandmother, one of his uncles, and his lil homie Trey-Eight's brother had all been killed. Before Young Du could say anything Ski assured him that Psycho's family, the Greens, was handling that shit. Psycho had siblings, aunts, uncles and cousins that was Bloods and Crips. Anybody who knew them knew that their family, the Greens, was as thick and as deep as a gang itself.

Ski told Young Du that he'd spoken with a bunch of Psycho's relatives, who all had death in their eyes, and that was just the ones who appeared to be old enough to be his parents. There was also a bevy of relatives in their thirties, twenties, and teen years who looked like they were dressed to put in work right there at the funeral.

After a brief moment of fake sympathy for Psycho's fallen relatives, Young Du explained the morning's shooting at the drive-thru, and they both agreed that the Neighborhood homies were responsible and that the payback for the last shootings had to be swift and devastating.

When that was done, Young Du told Ski about the news he'd heard that morning. Apparently, the Neighborhood homie Mill had somehow got arrested for the shooting at their Newark trap house and charged with the Murders of M-Dot, Trey-Eight, Taliban, and Psycho.

Ski couldn't believe it. He'd heard that the nigga Mill was a cannon and since they'd been set tripping Ski just pretty much assumed that the nigga probably had a hand in some of the biggest attacks against them. But this didn't add up to Ski because him and Young Du personally knew exactly who was responsible for at least two of those murders. His mind went to Psycho's cousin, D-Green, and the night he had gone there to swap out the dirty guns. He'd heard the nigga D-Green was a piece of shit and Psycho told him he always brought his used guns there so D-Green had the opportunity to do something foul but what the fuck and why.

Ski also thought it was something a lil weird about the way Young Du spoke about Mill's arrest. The man was Neighborhood, so he was naturally their foe at the time, but Ski thought something in Young Du's tone sounded a lil too animated or excited speaking about the man's unfortunate run-in with the law. To Ski, everything about that was principally wrong.

Chapter Twenty-Six

A nervous man full of guilt and compunction sat behind his steering wheel in the parking lot of the largest hospital in N.J., thinking of recent events. Having a moment of solitude, he found his thoughts drifting as he began to reflect on his childhood and the events that had crushed the family he had known. He thought of his arrest nine months ago and him being, what felt like, interviewed more than interrogated, broken, and eventually turned by the FBI.

Knowing that what he was doing was not only completely wrong and cowardly but also abhorrent in every way, the man regularly had moments when internal conflicts within himself came to a head. He found himself struggling to find and hold onto the few things that he told himself somehow justified the bullshit he was doing.

He tried to tell himself that his current state was everybody else's fault. He said to himself that it wasn't him that was at fault for all the cowardly things he'd done, but that his actions and who he had become was the result of everything that had happened to him. In his mind's eye, everything that had occurred throughout his life was like events on a timeline that could have only led to this moment. Anxious and full of guilt, he tried to get his mind off of the approaching conversation he needed to have and the mission he needed to execute by reliving his last official debriefing.

From the lobby of the FBI state headquarters in Newark N.J., the man made his way to the elevator and pushed the button for the sub-basement. He had visited the building over two dozen times at this point, yet he had never been to its sub-basement before being summoned there today. When the elevator doors opened, he was surprised to see that this level held nothing but a bunch of double-wide cast iron trailers.

Approaching him with two men, his handler, Helen Holmes, extended her hand and introduced her two coworkers.

"Thomas White special agent with the DEA and Robert Smith from the ATF this is government asset Omar Brown undercover in the field operating under the identity of gang leader O.G. Young Du a.k.a Abdul Myers jr., son of triple O.G. Du-Wrong, real name Abdul Myers sr. who are both members of the Brim set of the Bloods street gang."

"Pleasure to meet you." The DEA agent greeted shaking Omar's hand. "I been with the agency in Jersey since ninety-seven, so I remember the Du-Wrong case enough to know that the state wouldn't have put him away without your testimony."

"I think a jail cell was too good for him."

"I've seen the case file. I thought he was like a father to you." ATF agent Smith asked. "What were you like, eight or nine, when you took the stand against him?"

"Off by a few years." Helen Holmes said, leading the three men into the nearest trailer.

Inside, Young Du saw what appeared to be a small, technologically advanced shooting range. Watching him look around, seemingly amazed, Agent White stepped forward so Young Du could hear him over the gunfire as he spoke.

"Seventy foot double wide ballistic enclosed shooting modular. Equipped with three firing lanes, bullet traps, rifle and pistol-rated shooting stalls, and target retrieval systems. It has simulation systems, live firing games, and target and training scenarios. It can also double as a panic room or storm shelter."

"Lastly." Helen chimed in, yelling over the gunshots to introduce the man responsible for them seconds before he stopped shooting. "This is special agent Chris Wiggins, and Wiggins, this is..."

"I know who he is."

"Well, now that everybody's met, I want you all to know that I was against this briefing. But Wiggins convinced me that it was necessary, so without further delay, the floor is his."

"You all know that the secret service isn't as familiar with or prepared to deal with street crime as your agencies are. Yet, without really knowing what we were getting ourselves into, we joined this investigation solely based on the word of our fearless leader, Helen Holmes. I'm not sure exactly what's going on. Still, I've recently started receiving a lot of heat from people who have some serious concerns about the limited progress being made in this case, as well as the scope of our investigation and the number of bodies that are dropping. Then, on top of all that, its whispers being heard about a serial killer in the state that the local news is calling The Rat Hunter."

"Serial killer?"

"There's no serial killer," White assured Young Du.

"Can't be sure about that, we got what four or five very suspicious murders that all took place in the span of months in different cities throughout the state and they all appear to be linked."

"Linked?"

"A dead rat thrown on a dead body and rat poison or whatever it was sprinkled on a dead body is a bad idea of a cruel joke. There's nothing linking the murders other than the local media saying that it's a serial killer who they chose to nickname The Rat Hunter."

"It is kind of suspicious, though."

"Yeah, but we're professionals." Helen reminded. "Professionals don't concern themselves with suspicions. Details of the cases aside, because you're not talking about evidence, a profiler might reasonably surmise that different perpetrators committed the murders."

"It's likely copycats. After the first murder, somebody or multiple people saw the amount of publicity the first case got just because something associated with a rat was left at the crime scene."

"I don't know, guys."

"What I don't know is why the hell I'm standing here with three professional peers talking about bogeymen in front of our asset. Especially when it was you who requested a debriefing with the other coordinating agencies, she put Wiggins in the spotlight.

"I've told you, the powers that be are concerned."

"Come on, Wiggins, from the beginning, your agency wanted as least involvement as possible. You didn't want to be hands-on, and you didn't even want to be involved in the oversight. This is your first briefing. So nobody believes that you asked for this briefing to say that simple shit."

"Yeah, you could have said that in an email, or we could have Face Timed or something." Agents Smith and White teamed up to tag Wiggins.

"This is our first time meeting Mr. Brown, but Smith and I have been to every briefing, so it's hard to believe that you asked for this briefing so that you could say something so basic."

"You didn't come for a briefing, and you didn't come just to say people in your office were concerned about the investigation."

"Simply put, we know it's always people in our offices who are concerned about all our investigations."

"I think you wanted us all in this room so you could deliver a message."

"The floors yours." Helen ended White and Smith's onslaught, and the room's eyes rested on Wiggins.

"I'm very interested in the progress of the case. Unfortunately, however, people in my agency who outrank me have already made up their minds, and there may not be anything I can obtain here today that will change their minds.

"What exactly have they made up their minds about?"

"They want to pull the plug on us. They're already discussing reaching out to directors in your agencies this week to express their concerns and suggest that this matter be resolved, allowing our manpower and resources to be retooled and put to better use.

"Are you serious?"

"Absolutely."

"Wait a second. All the Secret Service has contributed to this investigation is some fraudulent currency.

"So the agency that's invested the least and is doing the least wants to end the investigation?"

"You got to buy us some time. We're not even close to being ready to wrap this up, are we?" Smith asked, and everybody looked at Helen.
wants

"Wiggins, are these powers that be lower than your director?"

"Yeah."

"And your director at the service is the older Polish guy, Podsy or something like that, right?"

"Director Thomas Podlesny. But where are you going with this?"

"Maybe I'm mistaken, but White, didn't you two work together on the old mafia Pistone case back in the day?"

"Sure did. Joe Pistone a.k.a. Donnie Brasco."

"And the goal of the Pistone case was to take down the leadership of the mob families?"

"Exactly."

"So, White, you and Wiggins together will speak with director Podlesny. Bring him the file I'll supply you with and tell him everything you're about to see and hear."

Dimming the lights and pointing a remote at the far wall, which instantly converted it into a projection screen, Helen panned the room, looking at everyone's face as she spoke.

She began recounting that at the onset of their nine-month investigation while sitting in Northern state prison, the bureau provided Omar Brown with narcotics to build and bolster his reputation. Both his codefendant Twizzy Rollack and his then roommate Got Guns, unaware of the investigation, helped him buy narcotics, and the Feds facilitated the means to get the drugs to him inside.

Rollack involved his sister in the transactions by having her secure narcotics, and Got Guns, a high-ranking member of the Neighborhood Bloods, did the same with his baby mother, thereby giving the government leverage over them. To further the investigation, the Feds gave Omar cell phones to sell to the leaders of different gangs. At that point, Guns was getting close to his release date, but the bureau couldn't afford to have him on the streets just yet if the case was going to go to the next level. That said, when Guns was assaulted in Northern state prison, the Feds used that opportunity to pull him out of the jail from state custody, ship him out of state, and slap a federal detainer on him.

"All this is why the case is just eating away money and resources."

"You didn't hear anything yet," White assured Wiggins.

"The wiretaps and everything else I mentioned so far have long ago been passed on to local and state departments. Our investigation, however, known as Operation Street Sweeper, has almost sixty active wiretaps. We got apartments and cars mic'ed up and cameras in a few pairs of Omar's designer shades. We have active surveillance on approximately twenty individuals, and we're paying for some form of passive surveillance on about another thirty.

"There's the money."

Turning to fix her gaze on agent Wiggins, Helen exhaled and slowly continued.

"You got to bear with me. I'd only intended to give a brief summary today, as some of the success this case has already seen is unbelievable. Some of the trust I initially placed in our assets' ability to deliver and do what was needed may have seemed presumptuous and even misplaced. Still, I'm pleased to inform you that Operation Street Sweeper has successfully infiltrated the Blood gang. She paused, pushing buttons as images of faces appeared on the wall in a pyramid shape. "As of today, we're targeting a little under three hundred individuals in some capacity."

"That's a lot of defendants."

"Many prosecutions."

"Many conditions." She corrected Smith, who tried to correct Wiggins.

As Helen continued her spiel, she informed them that, due to the number of defendants in the case, U.S. district attorneys had requested that she categorize the targets separately.

"The targets are categorized based on their rank and status despite what set they're a part of. Then, for clarity, I've also taken it upon myself to separate the categories into two different tiers, depending on the degree of evidence we've on them, the counts we can convict them of, and the amount of time we reasonably believe we can obtain from them.

As she went on and on, Wiggins, who wasn't used to being involved in actual investigations to this degree, zoned in and out, just trying not to miss anything significant. Ten minutes into her spiel, when she described the category of criminals who'd face twenty years and up for charges like murder, racketeering, and conspiracy to everything under the sun, Wiggins listened more closely.

Helen stated that the thirty or so individuals in tier two of this category led about eight of the state's largest Blood sets, and the remaining individuals in tier one of this category controlled three of the state's top five most ruthless, strong, and powerful Blood sets.

"Do we have these guys yet?" Wiggins asked.

"We have them, but all of them aren't completely nailed down yet."

"This is why me and you are going to convince your director to give us a little time."

"If we can convince him that we're going to get the leaders of the most violent sets, I'm sure he'll give us another month or so as long as there's no more surprises."

Chapter Twenty-Seven

Still sitting in the driver's seat, the man known as Young Du watched Ski walk across the parking lot and approach his SUV. Being that the Feds had both Samantha and Hoffa's hospital rooms bugged Young Du knew from details of a conversation Samantha had, had with someone that before the shooting at her shop, Hoffa had told her something about Young Du that made her tell him that the man he'd knew as Young Du wasn't who he said he was.

Young Du assumed that Hoffa would share whatever he knew with Ski during this visit. Because of this and the limited time the investigation had left, Young Du had been instructed to come completely clean with Ski and try to flip him.

"What's popping, bruh? The homie all aight?" He asked as Ski got in the car.

"He breathing. They kicked me out cause they were prepping him for surgery. Got my boy in there doped up talking crazy and shit."

"Really?"

"Yeah, really. He said some crazy shit about you too."

"Yeah, he told you who I am?"

"What?" Ski frowned, remembering Hoffa hysterically repeating, 'He aint the real Young Du.' He aint the real Young Du' as he left the room.

"You know what I'm saying, Ski. I don't know exactly how much Hoffa knew, so I don't know how much he could have told you, but I'm aint the real Young Du; that aint even my name. That's just my cover. The real Young Du is still locked up in P.A."

"Your cover!"

Knowing that Ski had left his gun under the seat before going into the hospital, Omar drew his weapon and sat it in the center console before continuing.

"This gon be hard to hear, but for the last nine months, I been working for the Feds."

"The Feds?" Ski repeated, grabbing Omar's gun and putting it in his face.

"That's not what you wanna do."

"What!" He barked cocking the gun.

Ski, it's a van full of agents right behind us. If you pull that trigger, your life is over." Omar calmly said, and Ski quickly stole a look over his shoulder to confirm the warning as Omar continued. "My name aint Young Du, its Omar. It's only three different ways this shit can play out bruh. We both know I done damn near been your shadow for the last couple months. I witnessed you in enough drug transactions to put you away for like fifteen to twenty. I know the details of conversations you had with homies about getting mother fuckers moved on. I watched you get Wacka to label M-Dot and give Psycho the green light to blow his head off. I have been with you in a couple of shootouts, and I watched you kill Psycho. I watched you put in all types of work, and on top of that, you've been wired for sound for months.

"What the fuck!?"

"You been bugged, nigga its wires everywhere. I took you to New York to get a G-ride and you got a couple watches and shit. But all that shit wired for sound, anything I missed they caught. You already know they got way more than enough shit to put you in a cage forever. But it don't gotta go like that."

"Nigga is you crazy!" Ski barked as the gun grew heavy, and his fingers began to sweat. "You a fucking rat, I should kill you right now!"

"I wanna help you, bruh, but it's only one good way out of this."

"Fuck what you talking about nigga!"

"I know you wanna go home." Young Du raised his hands in submission, trying to calm the man. "You pull that trigger, you never going home again. You aint gon be here to raise that son you just had. If you drop the gun and get out the car right now, them Feds behind us gon snatch you up, and you never going home again. The only way this shit end good for you, without you ever going to jail is if you drop the gun and sit here and hear me out."

"You got me fucked up!"

"You got a newborn at home, think about that shit Ski. That baby needs you here for him. It aint about you no more; you wanna be here for him and be the father you aint have. Everything you do is supposed to be for him now. Remember telling me all that?"

Chapter Twenty-Eight

Awakened from his deep sleep in the wee hours of the night, eight-year-old Omar lay in bed for a second, motionless. He was frustrated and confused. From the top bunk, he couldn't tell if it was the oppressive project heat in their apartment, which labored his breathing, or his lil brother constantly fidgeting around on the bottom bunk that kept waking him from his sleep every time he dozed off.

Regardless of what initially brought him out of his sleep, during these late-night, early-morning hours, hearing the heavy breathing, moans, and groans coming from his mother's room always kept him awake. Even though he wasn't the savviest third grader, Omar knew that the sounds he was hearing were his mother and stepfather doing the nasty. 'Ewww,' the thought almost made him say it out loud while rolling over in the bed before climbing down.

Just as his feet hit the floor, he heard the early morning cries of his infant baby sister two rooms away. Tip-toeing to the window, his little fingers grabbed hold of it and lifted it as high as the safety braces would allow.

"Ooo!" His brother's annoying voice wined behind him. "You gon get in trouble. Why you opening that?"

"Cause I'm hot."

"Well, I'm gon get cold."

"No, you are not."

"I'm telling Mommy."

"I don't care if you tell. If you wanna be a snitch, you gon be the one who get in trouble for tattle telling."

"Nuh unh." He whined.

"Well go tell then." Omar climbed back to his top bunk, calling his brother's bluff as he heard footsteps moving around throughout the house. "You know Mommy hates it when you tattle, tell."

"It aint that cold, anyway."

Minutes later, after his little brother had squirmed around, Omar heard Abdul's breathing turn into the light, five-year-old snoring, just as he heard his mother and stepfather's distant voices speaking. Then came the loud bangs.

BOOM! BOOM! BOOM!

Sudden bangs were heard at the apartment door, and then his mother's footsteps could be heard marching to answer it. "Who is it? I said..." Omar heard her last words before what felt and sounded like an explosion rocked through their apartment, destroying his world as their front door was rammed in and a barrage of gunfire went off. The next few minutes felt like their bedroom was in a war zone.

When the gunfire finally stopped Omar peeled his body from his piss soaked bed and jumped down to the floor. A second later, he stood at their cracked bedroom door, peeking out into the hallway at his mother's body. As a million questions filled Omar's head, he heard his brother Abdul's cries and felt his presence creeping up behind him.

"What the fuck." A grown Omar said, wiping his eyes as he sat up from his reclined driver's seat. Reflecting on the dream he was having, a dream from something long ago that he didn't call a nightmare only because it was the last time he'd heard his mother's voice, Omar quickly looked in his rear-view mirror, adjusting himself, and saw his face looking back at him. But it was also the face that he'd been telling people was Young Du.

"Damn, open the door bruh." Candy barked at Young Du, tapping his passenger-side window until he let her in.

"How the fuck I tap the window to wake you up, then you wake up and look straight in the mirror wiping your face on some diva shit. Like you don't even acknowledge that I just woke you the fuck up."

"I'm tired as hell. I hadn't slept in a couple of days, so I shut my eyes and dozed off for a minute. It's mad bull shit going on."

"That's exactly why it aint time to be sleeping and shit. You might close your eyes and miss something."

Chapter Twenty-Nine

At the end of Ski's short visit with Twizzy Hoffa when he mentioned that Young Du was outside waiting on him Hoffa had kept repeating 'he aint the real Young Du, he aint the real Young Du' almost hysterically but being that he was heavily sedated, had slurred through most of the visit and had said a few other things that didn't add up Ski'd dismissed it as the medication talking. But after hearing Young Du say it for himself, there was no mistake about it. That nigga was a rat.

Following the exchange between Ski and Young Du in the hospital's parking lot, Ski felt more than betrayed. It wasn't like he'd known Young Du or Omar or whoever the fuck that nigga was for years. But on the strength of Twizzy Rollack and Twizzy Hoffa, men he did know forever, he'd began to fuck with and even embrace that weird ass nigga.

Struggling to wrap his head around everything that was going on and what it all meant, Ski had been low for the next few days. After Young Du told him who he was and how deep shit went Ski aint have nothing to say and he just listened to Young Du going on and on until he dropped him off at his car.

Driving around for hours with no destination, Ski only stopped to get a bottle to drink and something to smoke as he thought about everything he was told. 'This nigga a rat' a voice kept repeating in his head. Then, remembering what Young Du said about his watch, Ski pulled it off his wrist. 'This nigga a fucking rat' he heard the voice and after a while he remembered that Young Du said they had wires everywhere, and he pulled over to park on a random street, got out and walked.

The way he saw it, things could only play out one of two ways. He was going to prison forever for killing Young Du and whatever else the Feds had on him, or he would get killed in the process of trying to kill Young Du. It wasn't any other way. The hoe shit Young Du was talking about wasn't even an option. In Ski's mind, that nigga had to die for thinking he could talk Ski into being a rat just as much as he needed to die for being a rat his self. He was dead; it was just a matter of Ski finding the perfect way and time to do it. Snitch ass nigga.

After walking around aimlessly, Ski looked up to see a familiar light halfway up the block he stood on. Throwing his head back to finish off the remainder of his liquor he dropped the empty bottle and crossed the street to get to the Vagina Diner.

Following a wild night with two Piru homegirls who worked at the Diner Ski slept from about four till six in the afternoon before he was woke up by the same dark skinned homegirl who sucked his dick in Candy's car before they went out west to re-up. Ski was a sucker for big asses and dark complexions, these were the reasons he had a thing for Candy. While the Piru homegirl wasn't as sexy, dark and didn't have an ass as big as Candy's she was still nice as hell and from the way she tried to swallow his whole dick during that one brief escapade he knew she was a freak.

That said, when he stumbled in the door last night, he was hoping to see her so they could have a lil session.

"You need to get up and wash your ass." She said, handing him a rag, towel, and toiletries.

"Straight hotel treatment, huh?"

"You could of woke up in my mouth if your dick wasn't smelling like all type of twat." She replied, leaving the room.

Damn. Ski thought to himself as he jumped in the shower. He couldn't wait to wash up and get his hands on the home girl. It was a whole lot of good pussy in the Vagina Diner, and he would of had a lot of fun trying it all out while they continued to do business with the Piru homies if this bitch ass nigga Young Du wasn't a fucking rat. That fucked everything up. Now Ski knew it would all end with him locked up for killing Young Du or with him being remembered as a martyr who died doing some real nigga shit trying to kill a rat.

Fucked up as it was, Ski had done time before so he could picture Amy bringing their son to see him in some prison. He had taken care of other homies' kids and their baby mothers while they were locked up or because they had died, so he knew how the game went. He also knew he was affiliated withstand up niggas so he knew Amy and their son would be taken care of. Hard as he tried, though, he couldn't picture Amy and his son's life with him being dead as a martyr.

Ducking under the shower to let the water hit his head Ski remembered Psycho and M-Dot and wondered how Wacka and other homies under his set would react knowing he killed his homie and got a lil homie under his set murdered for some nigga who was a rat all along. Then, he thought of Psycho's family.

Psycho was the second youngest of three siblings. His brothers, Spyke and C-Green were both locked up and didn't fuck with Psycho too much when they were home anyway. Still, his extended family, the Green family was deep as fuck in Jersey City, Newark and Paterson and was renowned throughout northern New Jersey for one thing. Action.

Psycho didn't come from a typical family by anybody's standards. In different ways, Ski probably knew over a dozen of Psycho's cousins, aunts, and uncles, and as far as he could remember, they were all knee deep in the streets. With a lot of them being known for robberies, home invasions, kidnappings, and murders, the Green family was like a tribe of goons.

"Fuck." Ski blurted out, jumping from the shower. He realized that even if he got bagged for killing Young Du a bunch of suspicious shit would come into question about the circumstances of Psycho's death. He'd been lucky that nobody had cared enough to connect the dots thus far but he knew if he got bagged for killing this rat ass nigga it wouldn't be long before somebody did the math. If the truth came out, his killing of Young Du wouldn't do any justice to his name, reputation, legacy, or safety.

As he was getting dressed without really drying off, all these thoughts flooded his head. He could practically hear his homies saying 'fuck the fact that you killed him or got bagged trying to kill him. That nigga worked for them people and you let him use you to get two of your homies killed and you introduced him to a million mother fuckers so he could set them up.' What the fuck was Ski thinking about?

Anybody that fucked with him who didn't wind up in prison wasn't going to look out for his son or baby mother or remember him as a martyr. His name would put a bad taste in their mouths. He would be remembered as the reason this whole shit happened so if Amy and his son wore 'Free Ski' or 'In Memory of' t-shirts they might get chased out the hood for wearing it and if anybody ever painted a mural for him in the hood niggas he once called his homies would use it to piss on.

Almost running out of the Vagina Diner Ski found his truck, hopped in and took off. Then, re-lighting a blunt from last night, he found a liquor store and put more alcohol in his system.

Chapter Thirty

Unlocking the door, Ski, still holding his liquor bottle, had barely stumbled in and closed the door of the apartment when he heard what sounded like moans. Ski knew Amy watched a whole lot of porn, sometimes till she fell asleep. Because of this he'd come home countless nights to find her sleeping with porn on the screen.

As he walked down the hall, approaching the living room, the moans he heard grew louder, and Ski almost thought the actress sounded fake and a little overdramatic until he could see where the moans came from.

The first thing Ski laid eyes on when he turned the corner in the candle lit living room was a big chocolate ass bent over. Amy was bisexual; Ski knew she'd been with females before they got together, and she still flirted and played. But she'd acted like a prune since they were together, so he never thought he'd walk in on her like this. With Amy on her back sprawled out on the coffee table, the chocolate goddess between her legs sucked hard on Amy's clit and ignored her plea's to stop when she seen Ski in the doorway.

Ski took a few steps into the room, stepping over a double-sided dildo and rabbit vibrator until he stood right behind the dark-complexioned female. From this vantage point, he could see everything. Though in a candle lit room Ski was close enough to see what looked like the ring and base of a ring pop protruding from her ass hole, but she was still oblivious to his presence. The moistness between her black cheeks glistened in the darkness. Turning his head to the side, Ski watched juices ooze from her box and trickle down her inner thigh.

Amy's moans turned into what sounded like plea's for the woman eating her pussy to stop. Her hands even grabbed the woman's head, seemingly trying to push her away. But none of this worked.

Ski watched a black hand grab the dildo already protruding from Amy's pussy and began to fuck her harder with it as the other hand under her ass lifted her cheeks and pelvic area off the table. All this happened as Amy's pussy continued to be sucked on. He watched Amy's grip tighten around the woman's head in a way that he was familiar with, and Amy's moans that had turned into pleas now became cries.

"Don't stop, don't stop, don't stop!"

Minutes later, when her cries had calmed to heavy breathing, Ski stepped back and took a swig from his bottle.

"Where you going, baby?" Amy asked out of breath prompting the face attached to the black creamy ass to turn around. Ski almost stumbled looking into Candy's face, her dark features glistening wet in pussy juice as she sat bare ass on the floor trying her best to look innocent nibbling on the nail of her index finger while looking up at him.

Feeling his lustful eyes crawl all over her body, Candy abandoned the coy role and crawled over to Ski, quickly undoing his pants. Before he could even try to help, she already had him in her mouth. Feeling the head of his dick brush past her tonsils Ski watched her eyes tear up as she refused the urge to gag. Spitting his manhood out, one of Candy's hands crawled up Ski's inner thigh and cupped his nuts, massaging them as she spat into her other hand and began jerking him off with it. Looking down, Ski watched Amy crawl over and try to kiss the woman, but Candy wasn't missing a beat.

Amy gave up on the kiss and crawled behind Candy sliding the rabbit into Candy's pussy causing her to moan while sucking on Ski. Ski grew harder being jerked off with spit and saliva and almost dropped his liquor bottle when Amy crawled back around, and her mouth wrapped around his balls sucking them one at a time while Candy's tongue danced up the bottom of his dick before he felt her lips sucking along the side of it.

Candy's lips ultimately wrapped around the head of Ski's dick and sucked him all the way into her mouth. Moaning from the rabbit vibrating inside her pussy and working her clit she drooled and slurped loud trying to eat his whole dick. With Amy sucking his balls and Candy moaning and slurping as she sucked his manhood Ski couldn't hold out and came in her mouth. Candy never stopped her sucking or slowed down though seeming to savor his taste still sucking on him once he shot his load until he went limp and began to stiffen up again.

Amy got up from the floor, took the bottle from her baby's father, and poured another swig of liquor in his mouth before sitting the bottle on the floor and kissing him passionately. Finally standing from her knees Candy grabbed a pillow from their couch and with it positioned under her lower stomach she threw her torso across the coffee table so that her full ass was tooted up in the air on display. Ski watched her reach back and slowly pull the rabbit from her sticky box before licking it clean of her girl cream.

Holding his dick, Amy guided her baby father across the room. Considering all the drinking he'd done Ski was surprised how sober he felt on his feet, it was almost as if Candy had somehow sucked the intoxication straight from his dick. As Ski grabbed her whole ass and spread her cheeks Candy moaned feeling him pierce her pussy lips.

"Ohhh yeah!"

Curling his fingers to grab the top of her ass Ski quickly found his rhythm and was driven by her moans to pound deeper and deeper into her tight pussy as she tried to throw her ass back at him. Grabbing her ass tighter, he watched waves ripple across her big soft black ass every time he thrust into her. Throwing one of her legs over Candy's waistline, Amy straddled her backwards so she could kiss her man and help him spread Candy's heavy cheeks. Pulling away from the kiss Amy grabbed the ring protruding from Candy's ass dislodging it a little as she spat down in her ass crack and began fucking Candy's ass with her anal plug.

"Oh Shit! Oh Shit!" Candy screamed and Ski felt the explosion inside her as her pussy began to twitch around his dick which only made him fuck her harder until they came together.

The three found their way to Ski and Amy's bedroom, and their tryst continued until they were all spent.

Chapter Thirty-One

About eight the following day, Ski was woken by his ringing cell phone. Answering it, he spoke with Beefy and was told that the Piru homies wanted to talk to him this morning. Right when he thought about telling her they would need to reschedule, she urged him on, telling him she thought he was trying to secure the bag. Beefy went on to tell Ski that the meeting was in their best interest because the amount of money on the line was at least equal to what they were already spending with them.

Ski didn't think he was in the right headspace to hit the streets, but he knew the phone call with Beefy sounded like this meeting would present opportunities far too beneficial to pass up. Still, he was hesitant after getting off the phone, but when he heard Candy's phone going off immediately afterward, he made up his mind to go. Despite what was going on and how he would eventually decide to handle that nigga he'd been introduced to as Young Du, Ski knew a chance to get a bag and lock in a new custy was always good news.

As Ski got dressed, his phone went off again. This time, it was Rollack, which in itself was strange because Ski knew he usually only pulled his phone out at night. Ski had seen that Rollack and his mother had been blowing up his phone since the night he left the hospital. But being caught up and trying to process what he'd learned about Young Du, Omar, or whatever his name was, Ski had intended to call back but never got around to it. Now, speaking with Rollack for a few seconds, he received the depressing news that Hoffa had died.

Something went horribly wrong during his surgery; a vessel ruptured, and he began hemorrhaging. The doctors tried to suture or even cauterize the vessel, but the events happened so fast, and Hoffa bled so profusely, that they never got to seer the wound and stop the hemorrhaging before he bled out. Rollack was hurt, and for once, Ski could genuinely hear pain in his voice.

Surprisingly though, when Ski suggested that he fall back from business today and go see Rollack's mother before coming to visit him, Rollack insisted that he stick to the script. He said as long as the shooters paid the price, him or his mother didn't need a shoulder to cry on.

Instead of weakening him, losing his twin seemed to strengthen his resolve. Rollack told Ski that having lost his twin, it was more important than ever before that they capitalize on every opportunity they can. Otherwise, it would be like Hoffa had died for nothing.

A lil over two hours later Ski pulled up outside the Vagina Diner. Ski hadn't worked out exactly how he wanted to handle Young Du, but he'd agreed to come to the meeting so he could show face and keep up appearances while he figured things out.

"This nigga here already huh?" Ski said, nodding his head in Young Du's direction as he and Candy walked through the doors.

Minutes later, after the greetings were out of the way, the three were led upstairs, searched, and taken into a room where Beefy and a light-skinned man with cornrows waited.

"Young Du, Ski, and Candy, this the Piru homie Prince-Ru. Novella aint here 'cause what we here to discuss aint necessarily gon change the agreement we already got with y'all."

"Aight."

"Whether or not we need to have a discussion depends on y'all's answer to one question. Under the existing agreement, we can't wholesale any of your work. Question is would y'all feel some way if we did wholesale some of the shit in another state?"

"Nah," Candy quickly blurted out before Ski or Young Du could say anything.

"Hold up, what state you talking about?"

"New York."

"Damn, that's too close for comfort. New York is the backyard. You supplying niggas that close could fuck with our numbers and get in the way of shit we trying to do."

"I'm saying, at the end of the day we aint trying to supply the fucking state or sell nothing to nobody that's trying to complete with y'all in selling y'all fucking work. But we do got some homies over there that like y'all shit, so we trying to cop from y'all and put it in they hands while pocketing a couple dollars in the process."

"What's in it for us?"

"It aint even that complicated. They wanna move shit in a whole different state and they can't undercut us with our shit so it aint effecting nothing we trying to do over this mother fucker."

Watching Ski and Candy go back and forth in disagreement, Beefy didn't want to interrupt the two, who almost looked like a couple, but she needed to make sure she sealed the deal.

"You niggas say you trying to be the mother fucking connect for the homies, so you supposed to be playing the bulk game chasing the next flip. But I'm trying to help you unload a whole lot of shit and it's sounding like you worried about a couple pennies. You already know what me and my sis been spending, and if we can come to a deal today, we gon drop a lil more than double that starting next flip."

"We can't do that without more drivers." Candy quickly shot back, doing the approximate head math.

"It's done. We got three more homegirls for y'all. So we got a deal?"

"It's a deal." Young Du said, and with that part of the deal concluded, Beefy gave the floor to Prince-Ru.

Prince-Ru began telling them though he was Piru him and his homies basically did they own thing independent of Novella. While she and Beefy don't have an interest in harder street drugs like coke and dope, they were Prince's bread and butter. After the numbers were crunched, he agreed to buy a key of coke and dope with the promise to at least double his purchase in less than a week if the product was half as good as he'd heard.

With arrangements made for them to meet later to finalize the sale, Young Du, Candy, and Ski descended the back steps and walked through the eatery to exit the establishment. Halfway to the front door though, Omar, under cover as Young Du, walked past a man seated at a table and stopped dead in his tracks.

"Junior?"

Turning his head, the man stood to look the fake Young Du in his face. "My name Abdul bruh."

Amazed and barely believing his eyes, Omar, a little lost in the moment, remembered he was playing the role of Abdul, a.k.a. Young Du, and looked at Candy and Ski waiting at his side. "Y'all go ahead and get shit ready for that move with ol boy. I'ma get with y'all in a minute; I need to stay here and bust it up with son about something."

That was like music to Ski's ears, he was seething and couldn't wait to get away from this rat ass nigga. He noticed the crazy resemblance between Young Du and the cocky nigga he was talking to, even on a quick glance it was hard to miss. But Ski aint give a fuck who it was. He just wanted to get away from this rat.

Even though he didn't know how he was going to get rid of this nigga, yet Ski felt like his blood boiled more and more every second he was in this nigga presence. Grabbing Candy's arm, he pulled her away, and the two of them were out of the door before Young Du turned back to the man he called Junior.

I don't think you know me, bruh.

"I don't know you." Young Du challenged himself by allowing himself to be Omar as he looked at the man who looked just like him, with a preppy slant, and dominated him by at least forty pounds of muscle. "Nigga I'm your fucking brother."

"My brother?" Abdul laughed, squinting his eyes to scan Omar's face.

. . . .

"You know who that was?" Candy asked Ski as he pulled from the parking spot.

"Nah, I aint never seen him. Fucking with Young Du though, that nigga could be anybody."

"What do you mean?" She challenged picking up on the shade.

"I mean what I said, fucking with Young Du that nigga could be a homie, a pastor, a custy or any mother fucking body else. For all we know that nigga could be the police."

"Whoa, whoa. Flag on the play bruh. You don't think the homie just kicking it with the police like that?"

"Nah, I'm just talking." Ski laughed uncomfortably, trying to clean up his statement as his eyes darted back and forth from Candy to the road. "That nigga look like he could be his mother fucking family."

. . . .

"You telling me you been right here in Jersey all this fucking time bruh?"

"Nah, I wasn't always here in Jersey. I was back and forth between here and New York. My pops' mother lives over here in Hoboken, and the rest of my pops' family lives up in Brooklyn.

"Bruh, I aint even know if I still had a mother fucking brother or not. I sat in a hot ass cell thinking about coming home and getting an investigator or something to try and find you and I aint have no idea where you could be at."

"You sat in a cell?" Omar acted surprised.

"Nigga I just came home. I got bagged for manslaughter a week after I turned fifteen. They waved me up, tried me as an adult, and gave me thirty. I appealed it and fought them in court until I got some relief.

"And here you stand?"

"Here I stand."

. . . .

"Them niggas look just alike. If I aint know better, I'd think they was brothers or something." Candy said with a dry laugh.

"I can see that."

"Whatever it is, you two niggas aint really have too much to say to each other at the lil meeting just now. Once it was over, as soon as he said he was kicking it with son and he'd get with us later, you couldn't get away from him fast enough."

"Aight, what you saying?"

"I'm saying, sensing a lil shade between you and the homie. I hope that shit aint got nothing to do with what happened between me, you and Amy." Candy began resting her hand on Ski's thigh as emergency lights flashed and sirens screamed behind them.

Ski's eyes darted to Candy, who clutched her designer handbag. Thinking quick, he made the calculation, shook his head, and began to pull over.

"This some bull shit."

"We aight," Candy said, trying to calm him. "Long as everything straight on your car and shit we good nigga."

Seconds later, a tall black cop stood at Ski's window, and as Ski tried to hand him his papers through the window, the cop opened Ski's door.

"Exit the vehicle."

"What?" Ski challenged, reaching with his right hand to grab the gun on his side.

Quickly drawing his service weapon, the officer pointed it square in Ski's face.

"Keep your hands where I can see them and exit the vehicle."

Dropping his gun between the seat and center console, Ski complied.

"It's aight." Ski heard Candy's voice as he got out of the Escalade. "I hope you mother fuckers know I'm recording this shit with my phone."

Leading Ski to the back of the truck, the cop gave him a quick pat down before holstering his gun and turning Ski around to face him.

"What the fuck is your problem? You wanna die in prison?"

"I don't know what you're talking about."

"Now you gon play stupid?" The cop reached for his neck and pulled out a chain that was tucked into his shirt so that the badge medallion with the letters "FBI" across it could rest on his chest.

"You FBI?" Ski asked, thinking the man barely looked twenty.

"Listen, this is not a back and forth. If you wanna go to prison forever, like for the rest of your fucking life where you'll be somebody's bitch instead of having a bitch sitting with you in your car then keep on acting like you're thinking about obstructing justice and interfering with a government investigation by exposing the identity of a government informant."

Chapter Thirty-Two

Walking through a growing crowd of second- and third-graders, Omar was anxious to get away from his school. They only lived about a block or so away from the school, and Omar and his little brother, Abdul, usually waited until Abdul Sr. came and picked them up, but not today. Today, Omar was out of there; he was walking home. There was supposed to be a fight between Omar and another kid, and Omar wasn't trying to engage in it.

As he pushed through the crowd that seemed to be walking in the opposite direction, he felt like they were all against him. This was the only reason Omar was trying to avoid fighting.

Major was the cool kid in class, and Omar had unintentionally offended him by accidentally stumbling into him and spilling his lunch tray on him after somebody'd bumped into Omar in the lunch line. In elementary school, it was hard to look cool with tuna salad all over your clothes, so Major told everybody he was going to beat Omar up. Major was bigger than him, and Omar was well aware of that, but that wasn't the problem Omar was worried about.

While Major was the cool kid, everybody knew Omar wasn't from New Jersey. They always laughed when he talked and said the way he talked and dressed was country. That being the case, in Omar's seven-year-old mind, he believed if he fought Major, win or lose, all the kids there would jump him. He felt hands on him as he walked through his peers, and a few of them called him "punk" after he'd passed them. Looking down to pry someone's hands off his shirt, Omar looked back up to see the crowd open up in front of him and Major, tuna stains all over his shirt, walked towards him.

"You trying to run from a fight, punk!" Major questioned, pushing him back.

"I'm going home."

"No, you aint. You messed up my shirt; you gotta pay for that."

"Stop playing, move, man," Omar said sucking his teeth and trying to walk around Major again before being pushed again.

"Fight!" Somebody yelled.

"Fight! Fight! Fight!" Other voices began to chant, and just as Omar began to take a step and try and walk around Major again, somebody grabbed him from behind and spun him around.

"You scared to fight that boy?" Omar's stepfather Abdul demanded. Looking up into his eyes, Omar was both happy to see him and ashamed to be caught trying to walk away.

"He scared, he a punk!" Someone yelled out, followed by laughter, as Abdul pulled Omar away from the crowd.

"Snitches get stiches." Another kid warned.

"He aint no snitch, and he aint no punk. I promise you lil niggas if he don't fight that boy today his lil brother gon fight him." Abdul told the kids before addressing Omar.

"What's wrong with you? You scared to fight?"

"No."

"What? Put some base in your mother fucking voice boy and stop mumbling like a bitch."

"I said no, I'm not scared to fight. I thought they was gon jump me."

"Well, aint nobody jumping you now. Either you gon fight that boy, or your brother gon fight him. This nigga already bigger than you and your lil brother just turned five so you know he like half this lil nigga size. If you don't fight him I'ma make you watch him whip your lil brother ass."

Before Abdul had finished talking, Omar dropped his book bag and was halfway out of his jacket, diving back into the crowd. As soon as he reached Major, he jumped on him, swinging before he could even throw up his hands.

Seeing his little brother, Abdul Jr., a.k.a. the real Young Du, after all these years, Omar, who had been telling people that he was Young Du, was flooded with memories, thoughts, and emotions. Omar vividly remembered the fight with him and the kid, Major, but more importantly, he could still recall what Abdul had said to him in the car after the battle as they waited for Young Du to be dismissed.

"I know I aint your pops and shit Omar and I aint trying to be him. But I know what it's like to be a seven year old nigga so I know it be mad shit going on that you don't know how to talk about. You should know that you always have my ear, though. You always gon be my lil man, and I hope you know you can talk to me about anything. As a matter of fact, I would like you to discuss anything with me. Abdul paused for emphasis as they both watched Young Du run towards the car once the kindergartners got dismissed.

I wish you hadn't had to fight that kid today; you're probably mad at me for making you fight. But it was necessary. When you get older, you'll understand. You the number two man in the house, Omar, so if something ever happened to me, I gotta know you can fight for the family."

Swerving his vehicle in and out of lanes, Omar, who was headed to a meeting with Ski, Candy, and the G-Shine homies, was inundated with old thoughts because he knew he had a briefing with his FBI handler, Helen Holmes, immediately after this meeting. There were a few things he needed to get off his chest. Omar was happy about reconnecting with his brother, but he was mad that they'd just ran into each other by chance. He scoffed at the thought of all the times he'd heard Helen mention the FBI's intel. If the FBI had missed the fact that Young Du had come home, what else might they be missing?

This was his life they was playing with, and Omar was going to make sure Helen understood how fucked up it was that somebody in the FBI wasn't doing their job. First, though, he had to see what the G-Shine homies were talking about.

Pulling into the same chicken shack where they'd met before, Omar saw Ski's truck, and after parking, he looked up in his rearview mirror, mentally calling himself Young Du to get into his role, and exited his truck.

"What's up, what's popping?" Young Du greeted the four people as he sat at the end of the bench across from Lucky.

"What's popping? Your peoples just got here a couple of minutes ago, and I already told them we trying to double up on what we got the last time, but I need it for a lil cheaper. Problem is, your homegirl aint saying shit and Ski talking about y'all can't budge on the numbers."

"It's like he only brought the homegirl so we could have something pretty to look at while he telling us no." Lucky chimed in after Hak-Shine as he stood from the bench before heading to the front counter of the eatery to get his order.

"I'm saying, y'all been spending money, so we gotta find a way to make these numbers work. I'll even eat the loss if I gotta." Young Du said, looking at Ski and Candy before he stood to follow Lucky to the counter. Pulling out his phone, Young Du pulled up his photos and handed the device to Lucky.

"Fuck is this?"

"Me and my brother. His name Omar, he Piru." The honest Omar said in character as he took his phone back and followed Lucky back to the table. "I said something to him about what you said to me when we first met up and he said if you was the same Lucky that was in Northern state prison fucking a couple of them c.o. bitches and flooding the jail with that loud then yeah, he was down there with you."

"I'm the only G-Shine nigga named Lucky." The man said with a smirk, and Young Du knew he'd properly stroked his ego.

The remaining of the meeting went so well that they came to an agreement where the G-Shine homies not only handed over five wads of cash each totaling nine thousand dollars in exchange for ninety five thousand fraudulent bills that Candy pulled out of her bag, but Lucky even jumped on his phone and arranged sales for five birds of coke and three of dope.

Outside the restaurant, Ski, Young Du, and Candy stood around discussing the operational details of who would be picking up and delivering what to whom over the next few days. Hak and Lucky had already left, and once Ski, Young Du, and Candy got on the same page, they were ready to part ways as well, but just as they approached the parking lot, two minivans, both with sirens screaming, lights flashing, and sliding doors already open, pulled up fast, cutting them off.

226

Before Ski or Young Du's weapon could be drawn, over a half dozen men in police uniforms stood in front of them all gripping assault rifles.

One man stood out, moving a lil slower and waving around long revolvers as he spoke.

"Whoa, whoa, chief. Please keep your hands where I can see them. These nigga with me is real trigger happy, I don't think y'all wanna make none of them nervous. I'm finally meeting you mother fuckers and y'all trying to pull out guns and shit?"

"It's like eight of you mother fuckers with choppers and shit pointing at us."

"That's different." He dismissed.

"You niggas cops or something?"

"Cops?" He frowned his face. "Is you niggas cops, asking all these fucking questions."

"Come on bruh, you niggas hopping out of cop cars wearing uniforms and shit."

Oh, you're smart; you must be Ski. Witty, a lil quick on your feet always got some shit to say, my mother fucking cousin loved you nigga. And I guess you supposed to be the Brim nigga from Cali that just came home right? What's your name again?"

"Young Du."

"Young Du?" He laughed dismissively. "Whatever you say, bruh. Anyway, I guess this lil pretty mother fucking girl running around with y'all must be Candy? Damn, you a gorgeous black mother fucker too. It's about time we all met. As y'all probably already know, I'm the patriarch of my family."

"What fucking family is you talking about?"

"Come on Ski, don't play stupid nigga. They probably don't get it cause they aint from Jersey, but you ran these streets more than enough to know about the Green family."

"Aight, we know who your family is but we aint got shit to do with y'all."

"That's where you're wrong, Du. You don't mind if I call you that, right? It's just that I know somebody else with a similar name, and I don't ever wanna get y'all confused." He said as a statement more than a question. "Psycho regularly threw some chicken our way cause we been out here kicking up, putting in work in this war y'all got with them Neighborhood niggas after they blitzed y'all in Paterson."

"Well we don't know what type of arrangements you and Psycho had but we aint got shit to do with that."

"He wasn't supposed to have you or none of y'all family involved in nothing we was doing anyway."

"Well, whether he was supposed to or not aint important. We were involved. At the end of the mother fucking day, that nigga last name was Green. Even if we weren't involved before, we're here now because he's gone.

"What you trying to say?" Candy questioned, drawing her gun and pointing it at the man.

"Well aint you just a Puerto Rican ball of fire?" The man said, drawing a chuckle from his fellow gunmen as he tucked away one of his absurdly long four-four pythons.

"Cuban."

"And spunky too?" He smiled after she corrected him. Looking at Candy in her eyes, he disarmed her and reached around her back to tuck her small glock in the rear of her waistline. "It's crazy that both you tough ass niggas was slow on the draw, but this pretty mother fucker here was ready to go."

"So what's popping, you came to tell us that you was putting in work in this shit against Neighborhood?"

"Actually." He began resting the barrel of one of his twins under Candy's chin as his other hand slowly slid the strap of Candy's bag off her shoulders and down her arm. "I came to let you mother fuckers know that the Green's is morning."

"So you came to rob us?"

Quickly turning to Ski with Candy's bag in one hand and carelessly gesturing with the long revolver in his other, the man sounded offended. "Nigga aint nobody robbing your bitch ass." Young Du laughed, and the man waved the long gun in his direction. "Something funny?"

Drawing silence, the man turned back to Candy.

"Hold this mother fucking bag." When she complied, he dug in with his free hand and pulled out two wads of the money they'd just got. "I'm Blood just like you is nigga, I aint out here robbing no mother fucking homies. I am gon take what's mine, though. You niggas paying for services and funerals and shit for homies who died while they was rocking with y'all but aint no checks come over to the Greens and we lost three relatives behind this shit." The man completed his diatribe walking back towards his van as the seven gunmen accompanying him followed.

"What the fuck was that?"

"We just got robbed." Ski sarcastically shot at Young Du. "Fuck you thought it was?" In Ski's mind, he harbored crazy feelings of anger, anxiety, and angst. As the gunmen pulled away, he imagined different ways that the shakedown could have turned into a blessing for him and ended with Young Du's death. He was stuck in this trance until he heard Candy's voice.

"I don't know, I been robbed before and that shit aint feel like a regular robbery."

"I aint say it was regular, it was a shakedown. Only the fucking Greens can take shit from you and have you appreciate that they aint take every fucking thing. It's extortion. Crazy shit is this nigga was smiling the whole time, they came thru like cops in uniforms and shit talking about we homies while he got his hand in our pocket."

"So what the fuck is we doing?"

"I'm going with the plans for today and doing all the same shit we talked about. We got places to be and money to make. This shit just a bump in the road. Whatever gon happen between us and the Green family is gon happen, but I gotta stick to the script and get this bag. Aint shit change."

Minutes later, the man known as Young Du was pulling out of his parking spot, trying to clear his mind of what had just happened. Ski had said he believed the man who took the money from Candy's bag was, in fact, Psycho's older cousin, Itchy-Ru. Because there was so much going on, and they all had places to be after Ski spoke his peace, they didn't even go into what they were doing in response.

Trying to get back into the right headspace for the debriefing, he headed to Omar to shed his Young Du role. During the ride, he reflected on how, for the first time, he'd begun to have serious questions about whether or not his stepfather Du-Wrong was as foul as he'd been led to believe.

Thinking about some of his interactions with the man and some of the things he'd done, Omar saw wisdom in some of his ways. Even some of the things about Abdul that Omar still disagreed with, after knowing the man and being a man himself, Omar could at least rationalize and understand why Abdul thought certain things were right to do.

Slowly, Omar began to admit to himself that he didn't remember Abdul being some evil villain. He hadn't thought about the man since he was a kid, so it was completely possible that, based on childhood experiences, from a child's perspective, he had rashly judged the man and too quickly accepted his childish opinion about him without ever re-challenging it as an adult.

When Omar's mother and baby sister died in their apartment when he was only eight years old, it was a whole lot for him to take in. But now, as an adult, her felt like he'd been swindled into hating the man. Even worse, he knew that hate had been used to get an eleven-year-old to testify against Du-Wrong, and that had destroyed the relationship Omar and his brother should have had. They hadn't seen each other since back then, and while nothing could be done to change any of that now, Omar wanted to fix their relationship and help his lil brother.

Be it his grandmother's biased opinions about Du-Wrong, the FBI's insistence that he was a big-time gang leader on the East Coast, or a mixture of the two, that led him to believe the man was evil, Omar wasn't okay just accepting that today. Hindsight was twenty-twenty, and a different perspective now allowed him to see things completely different than he did when he was manipulated into taking the stand against the one man who'd ever really been a father figure to him.

To be clear, Omar knew that if Abdul hadn't got in a gunfight with the cops, his mother and sister would still be alive, and he'd have the family he should have had. But because of the gunfight, these things had been taken away. Now grown, having had a foot in the game himself and considering what he was currently doing to stay out of prison, Omar could at least appreciate, if not agree with, why Du-Wrong did some of the things he did.

Chapter Thirty-Three

As he pulled into the parking garage of a Jersey mall and drove to the top level, Omar realized for the first time that aside from being mad with Du-Wrong because of his mother and sisters deaths, he'd never had any legitimate negative feelings toward the man. Of course, when he took the stand against Abdul at trial, it was about him repeating the prosecution's story that Du-Wrong had started the gunfight that led to his mother and sisters' death and not his personal feelings about Abdul. Looking back though, Omar knew he never would've took the stand against the man he called dad if he wasn't brain fucked into hating him.

All these things weighed on Omar's mind because after not knowing his brother half his life, they'd now been in regular communication since they ran into each other at the Vagina Diner. Omar felt guilty for the fact that they didn't know each other, and he knew that his actions, more than anything else, had destroyed their relationship. He was committed to what he was doing now because he saw it as his only means of staying out of prison, but he didn't want to lose his brother again in the process.

Leading up to the day he was scheduled to testify against Abdul, all those years ago, Omar had rethought his position and even told his grandmother that he wanted to retract the original statement he'd been coerced into giving. But his father's family and the FBI had completely turned him against the man and indoctrinated him with so much bull shit that he began to believe that Omar was sole to blame for everything wrong in his eleven year old life.

Bringing his vehicle to a stop in the empty lot, Omar watched Helen Holmes exit her own vehicle while speaking on the phone, approaching his passenger side, and getting in.

"I understand your concerns, and we've directed some Marshals and other aid to help your office, but we just don't have the resources you're looking for." She said, ending the phone call.

"What's that about?"

"Somebody executed a state witness right in front of the Jersey City courthouse. State officials are nervous; everybody's going crazy, and they want to conduct a manhunt. Still, they don't understand that federal resources are tied up in this case, so we can't just stop what we're doing and redirect manpower. She paused, shifting in her seat. "Now, what's going on with you? Tell me something good."

"That's hard to do, aint shit good going on." He began by recapping the meeting with the G-Shine homies and the events that followed.

"The Greens is a dangerous family in Jersey. Both of Psycho's brothers are in federal custody for violent crimes. But why did they show up as cops?"

"All I know is every time I hear the name Green, back when Psycho first came in the picture and when I went to meet up with Wee-Wee, that fucking just sound familiar."

"That's not surprising. They are probably one of the biggest families in the state. You might have even gone to school with a few of them or something. She paused before redirecting the conversation. "Do we know if any of them are leaders of any sets?"

"I don't know. Besides Psycho, Wee-Wee and the lil interaction I just had with the nigga Itchy-Ru I don't know none of them mother fuckers. What I do know is this mother fucker Itchy was talking like he knew I wasn't Young Du?"

"I understand your concern about the threat they may present to you and the investigation. And I appreciate the importance of your identity remaining concealed. I know how important that is. However, you must trust the process. Let me dig through some intel and speak with some informants and see what I come up with. In the meantime, we need more deals, meetings, and transactions to be made with leaders of these sets because we're on a ticking clock now."

"I'm working, but I can't force niggas to buy shit."

Shifting in her seat to face him, Helen took a second to respond in a softer voice.

"I hate to say this, but you need to remember your deal with the government is contingent on you bringing us indictable and convictable evidence for street crimes of the highest degree on leaders of the top six Blood sets in the state."

"I know that but..."

"As of today, we have G-Shine, Murder, Teck, and Piru. Through your dealings with Hak and the arrangements you've made with his homies, we'll be able to secure their leadership. Due to Rollack's conversations, we got everything on his Murder homies. Through Ski, we have Teck, and as far as Piru goes, we can take Beefy, Prince-Ru, and a bunch of their homegirls who've made trips with Candy. Someone'll squell on Novella and the rest of their leadership."

"Aight?"

"I know with things being the way they are, you'll never be able to get close enough to Neighborhood. Samantha would spot you a mile away, and Ski can't even try because of this war. I can feed this to my superiors, and they'll accept it. Even though Neighborhood was one of the original six sets mandated in the terms of the deal, I know my superiors will understand. State prosecutors already have informants cooperating against Neighborhood in an ongoing investigation that I am aware of. But they won't understand why we didn't bring them Brims leadership."

"What you mean?"

Brim is probably the most dangerous set in the state. We have you masquerading under cover as one of them, and you have access to any street-level substance or contraband that we possess, but you can't conduct a few transactions with any of their leaders?

"Them niggas aint trying to do nothing with me. If I push too hard, it'll look crazy, and I might wind up somewhere with a hole in my head."

I'm not asking you to do anything stupid, and we're not letting anyone put any holes in you. Don't even talk like that. I'm only saying we need to get some of their leaders to the table because my superiors won't honor the deal if we only bring them four out of the original six sets."

"You keep saying that shit. I know I aint get shit on Neighborhood or Brim niggas. But you act like I aint give you shit on a bunch of other mother fuckers. I done sold shit or did some type of transaction with niggas that got status under damn near every fucking Blood set in Jersey. I did shit with niggas that's Crip, the Spanish gangs and neutral mother fuckers and y'all still saying it aint enough."

"I'm sorry, Omar." She spoke slowly to comfort him. "Evidence on people who weren't targeted in the deal doesn't necessarily help you satisfy the terms of the deal. Remember, the objective mandate of Operation Street Sweeper is to debacle the leadership of the top six Blood sets in the state."

"So if it ended right now, I'd still go to jail?"

If you focused on the mission instead of whether or not you were going to jail, the possibility of you going to jail wouldn't be on the table.

"You think I aint out here trying? This shit aint easy. You got me trying to make deals with niggas who aint trying to hear from me. They might even want my head. For all I know that could of been Brim niggas that shot my shit up before Psycho funeral."

"That's not the case. Of course, there are guys on street corners mourning over Talibans loss. But because his body was found with Psycho's, people think the same enemy slew them together. Our intel suggests that Run may like the fact that Taliban is gone for good."

Just hearing her reference intel pained Young Du and reminded him that he had something else he needed to get off his chest.

"What you mean?"

"The state was Talibans. Run acted content playing second fiddle cause there was nothing he could do about it. With Taliban gone, Run can consolidate all the power; the state is now his."

"More of the reason he would want me out the fucking way. If he thinks I'm Young Du, then he thinks I have a name that could challenge him for the state, regardless of his status.

"I think you're just paranoid." She dismissed his concerns. "Our intel..."

"You could miss me with the intel shit." he cut in before dropping his bomb. "What if the only way to get any Brim leadership is through the real

Young Du?"

"You mean your brother?"

"Yeah, he's home," Omar said, recanting the story of how he'd run into his brother.

After Helen had predictably acted like she was concerned with Omar's safety and suggested pulling him from the field, Omar assured her that he'd considered all that and that he wasn't trying to die or go to prison. He told her he'd to stay in and finish the mission or he'd wind up right back in cuffs, just like he was when they'd marched him into her office.

The vehicle fell momentarily silent after Omar made his argument, and Helen appeared to be coming to terms with everything that had been said.

Just like the Donnie Brasco case, this operation was controversial from day one. Knowing your brother's home and allowing you to stay in the field is extremely dangerous, completely unorthodox, and unethical. Additionally, it seems you're suggesting we use him to..."

"I aint saying we use him." Omar interrupted. "My lil brother been locked up for years, he couldn't of been too involved in running Brim from prison otherwise a couple of these Brim niggas out here would of been knew enough about him to know I wasn't him when I first came on the scene."

"Intel suggested he wasn't hands-on, which is why we suggested the use of his identity."

"I know that. I'm just lost as to how he was even thought to be involved in the leadership if he wasn't active."

"Investigations targeting leadership go after all leadership wherever it may be. You don't get a pass just because you're out of the loop or less active than somebody else."

"But I'm telling you he don't even want nothing to do with this gang shit no more."

"I find that hard to believe. I've reviewed his files and record enough to know that your brother isn't you. He prescribes to some extreme ideology."

"Fuck what it say on paper." Omar hit his steering wheel as he spoke. I'm telling you that's my brother... His emotion began to show through cracks in his voice. "I chopped it up with him at the Vagina Diner and I been talking to him since. I feel the vibes when I talk to him, we done had lil emotional moments and shit and I'm telling you he aint with none of this gang shit no more."

"I hear you..."

"His Aunt Samantha raised him when my mom's died. That bitch got shot, shit was looking crazy, she could of died and he aint even go see her in the hospital or nothing cause she still gang banging and he done with that dumb shit."

"You believe that?" Helen asked.

"I know that."

"Being done with gang banging and giving up the lifestyle is one thing. But being willing to help someone inform the government or helping send someone to prison is different. How do you think your brother will feel when he finds out you're an informant? That you've been running the streets using his identity, acting like him to get close to people he called his homies so you could send them to prison." Helen scolded him as her voice began to crack.

"All I know is he done with that gang shit."

"I remember both of you as kids; you two always looked just alike. Your families case was like the most traumatic shit I've seen. I didn't want your family to lose either of you to the streets. I've always looked back at your brother as the one I couldn't save. There's nothing I would like more than to help you, but I think he's too far gone.

"I'm telling you, you're wrong. You trust my judgment with these other mother fuckers, but you ignore me when I'm telling you about a mother fucker I know."

I think you're wrong, but if you believe he'll help you get close to Brims' leadership, then go ahead and prove me wrong. I won't get in your way. In fact, you should already know I'll do all I can to help, but you can't try to save your brother when you're not entirely out of your situation."

"He might be the only mother fucker that can get me close to Brim leadership."

"And the government would be happy for it. You, your brother, and Ski could all walk away from this, but I believe you're playing with fire."

Chapter Thirty-Four

After his debriefing with Helen, Omar had been thinking about how he would now tell Young Du the truth about everything. Omar hadn't exactly lied to Helen about his opinion on his brother's disposition. He believed Young Du was done with gang banging, just as he thought everything else he'd said about his brother, who appeared to be done with the streets in general.

The problem was that Omar had sold his plan to Helen as if he already knew Young Du would not only excuse all he'd done but also as if he knew Young Du would be willing to help him bring people to the law. The truth was Omar didn't have a clue how his brother would respond to what he had to tell him.

Leaving a sports bar where the brothers had spent most of the day watching football, Omar had no real idea how to start the conversation he desperately needed to have with Young Du. But getting in the passenger seat of Young Du's Cherokee with a lil alcohol in their system Omar just went along with the flow believing the opportunity for them to have the exchange he needed them to would come at the right time.

"Look at this shit." Young Du said, handing Omar his cell phone as a news video covering the story of a serial killer played on its screen. "They saying it's a nigga out here running around killing mother fuckers who told on somebody."

"Sound like some movie shit."

"Oh naw, that shit real. The news calling this nigga the Rat Hunter, they think he might have a lil camp of niggas following his lead that they calling the pest patrol and everything.

"So he started like a lil movement..."

"Facts, bruh. They saying this nigga done killed five or six mother fuckers already."

"What he supposed to just have a vengeance against mother fuckers who done told or something?"

"I don't know, but whoever it is that nigga a fool. It's entertaining and shit but it's way too much money and pussy out here to be tripping on some moral shit like you trying to save the streets or something."

The brothers continued watching the story of the Rat Hunter play out until Omar broke the silence.

"Now they saying he been posting live feeds on social media, so the cops think they got a way of tracking him?"

"Yeah, he fucked up. They got him now."

"What if that was one of your homies?"

"I aint got no mother fucking homies. I don't know if I told you, but when I first came home pops family flew me out to Cali, and they had a lil party for me and everything on some welcome home shit cause they think I'm like his heir on some gang banging shit. Everybody there celebrating on some stupid gang shit like that's what I wanted till I told them my position on everything. I just came home, I wanna live my mother fucking life. I don't care about no dumb ass red or blue flag and I aint heard from none of them since."

"Really?"

"Yeah. I mean I don't do the social media shit so they can't follow me on none of them platforms and I aint out here moving in the streets or nothing for nobody to be seeing me. If I do see mother fuckers in the streets in the midst of my travels I just curb them."

"Curb them?"

"Yeah. Bruh I'm done with that gang shit, the street shit and all that dumb shit in general. I'm out this mother fucker to live. You see this shit right here?" The real Young Du asked, grabbing a small dice-sized box that was attached to the bottom of his rearview mirror and twisting it around. "This the shit you see on TV, it's a camera and mic in this bitch. I got this shit cause all the cops out here killing niggas at traffic stops and shit. Remember I got bagged as a kid so it aint a million mother fuckers out here in Jersey that know me. But I done ran into a couple mother fuckers I met while I was locked up or something just in passing who asked me for a ride or something or just wanted to bust it up with me or something but as soon as I tell them about this mirror they don't want nothing to do with me."

"So that's how you keep them out of your car?"

"Absolutely. I tell mother fuckers it's a camera and mic in here. If they on some street shit and I get pulled over I'm stopping so if they get in here and drop something illegal this lil device is part of me proving my innocence."

"Never thought I'd hear some shit like that come out your mouth. I can't imagine how that would sound to your pops."

"He know my position on all that shit. He might not like it, but it doesn't stop me from being his son. Young Du paused before finishing as an afterthought. "That shit you did don't stop you from being his son either."

"Really?" Omar sounded relieved.

"Bruh, I don't know exactly what was said or what happened, but I do know you got on the stand and said some crazy shit. I can't front like I've always been good with it either. We might have had problems if we had run into each other a couple of years ago cause I had a lot of pain in me. I lost my mother fucking moms, pops and lil sister all at the same time. My pops told me the shit I'm saying now, at the end of the fucking day you my brother nigga. Only sibling I got. I could lose all of y'all, or I could still have a brother. I'm telling you pops don't hold none of that shit against you bruh. He know we was mother fucking kids, I don't even think he remember how all that shit happened."

"I don't know either," Omar mumbled after an awkward moment of silence.

"I'm saying of course you don't remember it now, we loss mommy and lil sis damn near twenty years ago."

"Nah, I aint remember that shit back then either."

"Yeah, you drunk nigga...

I'm saucy, but I ain't drunk. I know exactly what I'm saying. When the police kicked in that door all that shit happened so fast aint no way I ever had an idea of who shot first or any of that shit."

"You serious?"

"Absolutely. Them mother fuckers just gave me the story of how the police said it all happened, and they turned on the tape recorder and coached me through the shit. Right before trail I was having second thoughts cause I knew all that shit was bogus. Them people sat me down again and brain fucked me some more before going over the story with me and putting me on the stand."

The two continued speaking in a similar fashion, and the topics shifted until Omar finally saw an opportunity to segue into telling Young Du what had been happening. He told his brother everything that had happened to him, including Twizzy Rollack's and Black and Dough's arrest a year ago, his encounter with Helen Holmes, and his agreement to cooperate with the FBI.

He even told Young Du that to cooperate with the Feds, he'd have to run the streets under Young Du's identity, helping the government infiltrate different Blood sets.

Chapter Thirty-Five

Before spending the day with Young Du, Omar hadn't put some things in perspective. While focusing on increasing the work he could do so he could get on the Brim homies' radar, some of Omar's thoughts were still consumed with retaliation against the Neighborhood homies and vengeance against the Green family.   On some basic level this mother fucker was still thinking like he was some regular nigga in the streets. However, something about being debriefed and then spending the day with his brother helped him put things into perspective.

After seeing that Young Du wasn't only done with gang banging and the streets but had also understood Omar's position and reasons for cooperating with the Feds, Omar felt unbothered by everything that was going on. He was thinking about life after this case was over, so he didn't have time to think about responding to petty beefs. He wasn't a gang banger or even a gang member anymore. The base politics of the streets and all the things from that world didn't matter.

Responding to any of those problems wasn't only not important. At this point, Omar believed that occupying any of his time with anything that wasn't helping to close the case was a waste of time. The game clock was ticking, and he knew the only way him, Young Du and Ski wouldn't wind up in prison was if he got something on Brims leadership. This meant Omar had to adopt an all-hands-on-deck approach.

They needed to execute some type of transaction with some of Brim's leadership. But nobody over there was budging. Other than the unsuccessful sit down Omar'd had with a couple of Stacks' lieutenants a few months ago, he hadn't crossed paths with any of their big homies. Ski had tried but wasn't able to make anything happen, and because the real Young Du had been completely out of the loop, Omar knew he wouldn't be able to help either without exposing his true identity.

At this point, Omar was so desperate to get close to the big homies under Brim that he put the word out to everybody who trapped for them and to the hired muscle they still had that they would pay commission to anybody who could make deals with Brim homies. Omar, under the identity of Young Du, essentially told anyone who would listen that if they brought any Brim homies to the table for business, they'd be paid a finder's fee.

He knew this would sound crazy, thirsty and suspicious as fuck to anybody who actually thought about it. But the way Omar saw it, none of that mattered.

Coins were promised to anybody who brought some Brim homies to the table, so Omar was betting on somebody's greed to cloud their judgment. He figured somebody would line up some meetings so he could make some transactions with Brim homies before anybody stopped to think it all through. By the time anybody did, he figured he'd already have what was needed to wrap up Operation Street Sweeper.

Omar knew it was a gamble, but he also knew that the alternative was something he didn't even wanna imagine. If he couldn't get any Brim leadership and fulfill his end of the deal he'd made with the FBI, it was likely that he'd end up dead or in protective custody in federal prison for the rest of his life. That also meant, of course, that his brother, rehabilitated and reformed or not, would be one of the targets of a subsequent investigation into Brims' leadership.

While just about everything of substance had been discussed between the brothers, this last detail was something Omar had neglected to tell Young Du. He couldn't bring himself to tell his brother about the possibility of being a target because he didn't want to worry him if it wasn't necessary.

As luck would have it, it seemed like Omar wouldn't have to tell his brother that the FBI had him in their crosshairs after all. On the night of Twizzy Hoffa's funeral, just as Omar got off the phone with Candy, who was headed back from out west with a slew of Piru homegirls, Prince Ru called with good news. He told Omar, who he thought was Young Du, that he was with some Brim homies that wanted to buy over a hundred thousand in fake bills and a whole lot of pills.

Omar, acting like Young Du, called Ski's lil homie Blood Money, who'd been handling the pills, and arranged to meet him and Ski at the storage room. Grabbing a couple of bags, Young Du, Ski, and Blood Money hit the road and pulled up at a laundromat a little after midnight.

Ducking under a gate, the trio walked through the doors and past two homies sitting on the washer and dryer machines inside a laundromat that appeared to be under renovation. Crossing the tarp-covered floor, they approached Prince-Ru, who stood with two other homies on the opposite side of a folding table covered with wads of money.

To Young Du's surprise, the homies standing with Prince were Stacks Brim lil homies that he'd met with while Ski was still in the hospital. But without formal greetings and before Blood Money could even drop the bags, Prince-Ru got straight to the point.

"I'm gon tell you niggas straight up, the homies that's here with me came to spend money. But before any of that get discussed some other shit just hit my ears that need to be ironed out."

"What's good?" Ski asked as the homies they'd walked past crept up behind them.

Picking up twin revolvers from the table, Prince-Ru pointed them at the trio and spoke as the homies behind them patted their waists, disarming them.

"You niggas gotta answer for some shit that's going on." One of the lil homies said plainly as the two behind the trio now held them at gunpoint. "One of you mother fuckers is telling."

"What!"

"These some crazy ass accusations."

"If you aint got no mother fucking proof you might wanna watch your next words lil bruh." Ski thought about whether this was his chance and shot back at the lil homie after Blood Money and Young Du.

"I aint gotta prove shit when I'm telling you to your fucking face what the fuck niggas is saying about you. You fuck boy!"

"Dig, Bro." Prince-Ru interrupted, directing the convo. "You niggas got the best shit on the streets, that's facts. Anybody question that or how you do business I can speak out against it and vouch for y'all. But even though I done heard you mother fuckers names before we did anything together you niggas is still new to me. I can't speak up for you when I hear some bullshit. All I can do is line up some shit like this so you mother fuckers can clear the air." He ended.

"Exactly what the fuck need to be cleared up?"

"Which one of you mother fuckers went to meet with my nigga Taliban in the park and rocked him and that nigga Psycho to sleep?"

"What?" Blood Money was surprised by the lil homies' question.

"One of y'all know what the fuck he talking about. It's the same one of y'all that was at y'all trap in Newark when it got shot the fuck up."

"What the fuck any of that got to do with this?" Ski asked, remembering the events, but lost as to how it all went together.

"Come on Ski, you aint slow nigga. Regardless who it was that blitzed Taliban and Psycho in the park, niggas saying whoever the fuck you sent to meet up with them had to be the one to flip the script and lie to the police saying Mill did the shit."

"What?"

"What the fuck that got to do with the trap house shooting?"

"It gotta be the same mother fucker from y'all trap house cause they got the homie charged with that shit too." The homie said, giving a lil insight to their logic.

Ski instantly remembered everybody on social media mistakenly saying that it was his lil homie Blood Money instead of Nickels that got shot in the trap house shooting. If the streets thought the survivor told the cops that the shooter was Mill, Ski understood why they got blitzed in Jersey City, and Nickels was shot dead in the backseat of his truck. Believing what they did, their actions made sense.

"So what you niggas saying, we can't leave or something?" Blood Money outburst.

"Fuck all these mother fucking questions."

"You niggas need to start coming with some answers." Prince Ru de-

244

manded cocking his weapon.

"Hold up Prince, you niggas really called for some work and shit so you could set us up for an ambush?"

"Don't trip, bruh, I get chicken. I aint into no jack moves. I got you niggas here cause I rock with y'all a lil but I'm hearing some foul..."

"Fuck what you hearing bruh."

"Cool the fuck out." Ski scolded Blood Money.

"From your end, if you aint the one running your mouth I know this shit look crazy. But I'm the nigga copping from y'all so I'm in the middle of the shit. I make money with you mother fuckers, but I rock with the homies that's questioning shit about you niggas."

"So what you saying?"

"I'm saying shit gotta be answered. Work gotta be put in." He paused, sitting one gun on the table before the trio. "Either that or fuck doing business, fuck you niggas walking out of here or anything else. At this point, we passed all that. We done did all types of transactions and shit together and one of you niggas is suspect. If aint nobody answering these questions I can't let none of you mother fuckers just walk out of here like nothing happened cause somebody in your camp got a question mark on they head."

"If it aint one of y'all, it's all of y'all."

"After making moves with niggas you can't see through that gossip shit?"

"I aint trying to hear none of that shit. You niggas is still strangers to me. Fuck I look like trying to vouch for you niggas bruh." Prince-Ru shot back at Young Du. "No bull shit, I like the business but you niggas is still new to me. If aint no questions getting answered..."

"This the new nigga!" Blood Money barked, grabbing Prince's second gun from the table and turning to throw its barrel in Young Du's face before Prince continued speaking.

"We got action!"

"Go ahead." The lil homies taunted.

"Whack that nigga!"

"Blood Money," Ski called from behind. "Give me that shit bruh."

"This the new nigga right here! All this shit started popping off back to back soon as we started fucking with this weird ass nigga."

"Ski, you know me."

"Shut the fuck up!" He barked at Young Du. "Blood Money, I brought that nigga in our circle. It's my work to put in."

Grabbing the revolver from his lil homie, Ski knew it was the moment he'd been waiting for. Since this rat mother fucker told him who he was and that he was working for the fucking cops Ski knew it would come to this. Fuck what they wanted from him and what was expected of him he was gon do what the fuck he wanted to do.

Stepping between the two men, Ski turned to throw the barrel in Blood Money's face and pulled the trigger all in one motion before his lil homie could even say anything.

The room fell silent until Young Du spoke up, explaining that Ski was Blood Money's big homie. He said Blood Money was trapping for them at the Newark trap house when it got shot up. Young Du also explained that him and Ski were together halfway across the state when Psycho had hit Ski, telling him about the meeting in Audubon Park. Since Blood Money had been shot in the trap house, Young Du said they had him making lil deliveries and handling meetings, so when they didn't think they'd be able to make the meeting, Ski sent Blood Money to meet with Psycho and Taliban instead.

Ski chimed in telling them Blood Money had hit him a lil while later on some hysterical shit saying Psycho and Taliban was dead when he got there. Ski couldn't believe what he'd just done and the way he was standing there lying. As much as he wanted to kill Young Du, something about the timing didn't feel right.He lied telling Prince and the lil homies that a lot of shit Blood Money had been telling him wasn't making sense but he aint ever really suspect his lil homie of doing no bullshit like this. He told them it'd been so much shit going on that he never got the chance to put all the pieces together and connect the dots from the park shooting, the ambush at their trap house and the arrest of the Neighborhood homie Mill like they had.

Everything didn't add up, but them hearing an explanation with even a semblance of logic was far better than nothing. Ski and Young Du knew they benefited from the assumption that neither of them could have been the cop if Ski had just killed Blood Money point-blank.

With the questions answered, the lil homies who'd disarmed the trio immediately folded the tarp around the body and cleared the bulk of the mess away while Prince-Ru and Stacks' lil homies spoke with Young Du about the purchase of pills and fraudulent money.

Chapter Thirty-Six

Omar or Ski hadn't said shit to each other during the ride back to Ski's car after Blood Money was killed. Knowing it was all type of shit that Ski was being forced to deal with Omar'd just dropped him off. He knew he was going through all type of fucked up emotions, so he never expected to get a call from him less than an hour later.

Ski said Psycho's lil homie, Slugs, had hit him, saying he had some of Run Brim's lil homies looking for half a million in fake money. Omar, knowing that Ski had just been forced to kill his lil homie and hadn't even had time to digest it, asked Ski what he thought.

Ski dismissed his concerns stressing to him that they needed to get with them Brim niggas by any means necessary. He told Omar they had to work through or go through whomever they had to, to get to the Brim homies. Otherwise, he said, it'd be like everything done to get this far was in vain.

While the dealing they'd arranged with Stacks' lil homies earlier that night was good Ski and Omar knew them niggas was lieutenants. That said, it was no telling how long it could take for them to get them in direct negotiations with double OG Run or any of their big homies who were directly under him.

Because of that, this opportunity Slugs was calling about was extremely attractive both because the amount of money they was talking about spending wasn't the kind of figures lil homies negotiated and because Slugs specifically said one of the Brim niggas he'd spoke with was directly under Run Brim.

When the talking was done, Omar approached Slug's car and got into the backseat. Seated behind the driver and next to A.K., Omar reached across the center console to give Ski a firm handshake after noticing that Slugs and A.K. were wearing gloves when he greeted them. The four made small talk as Slugs and A.K. passed a blunt of angel dust back and forth, but Ski and Omar didn't want any of that, so the moment the dust was gone, A.K. lit up a blunt of weed.

"Damn, that's the good shit." He said, coughing up smoke before passing the blunt to Omar.

The conversation shifted from one current event to another until Omar reached around the front seat, passing Slugs the blunt, and noticed that the ignition was missing from the neck of the steering wheel.

"What's up, I see the ignition missing, you mother fuckers wearing gloves and shit, you niggas stole this g-ride or something?"

"Bruh, you niggas get money selling drugs and shit, we get paid for action."

"So we always ready for action!" Slugs chimed in, handing the blunt to Ski, and after a brief moment of laughter, Omar continued.

"What's popping with them Brim niggas y'all talking about trying to get some work?"

"I'm saying, they aint far. But we don't know all the details and shit. We leave that to y'all. Thats why we just came to get y'all so y'all can bust it up with them and see what it is." A.K. tried to calm the concerns.

"You do know who the niggas is though right?"

"Damn bruh, you just gon keep asking questions and shit?" Slugs asked with a laugh, and A.K., ready to tag team the man, followed up, sounding direct and extremely serious.

"Let me ask you some mother fucking questions for a change bruh."

"What's up?"

"Is you the only Brim nigga in Jersey named Young Du?"

"What?"

"You heard what the fuck he said!" Slugs demanded as A.K. drew two revolvers, pointing the one in his right hand at the back of Ski's head and putting the other in Omar's face.

Omar's heart immediately dropped, knowing exactly where things were headed.

"Fuck is you niggas doing?"

"Answer the fucking question nigga!"

"Slugs, what the fuck is you niggas..."

"Shut the fuck up!" The driver interrupted Ski, leaning over to take the weapon from his waistline as A.K. reached forward to rest one of the barrels on Ski's head.

It almost felt like this was the moment Ski had been waiting for but how the fuck could he play it. There was no way he could tell Psycho's trigger-happy lil homies anything true about everything that had happened and walk away. The truth would definitely get him killed.

After Ski was disarmed, A.K. dropped one of his guns in his lap, freeing the hand to disarm Omar as Slugs continued.

"One of you mother fuckers is gon open y'all mouth and tell us what the fuck is going on."

"We seeing a lot of weird shit that aint adding up." A.K. chimed in, holding the two at gunpoint. "Months ago, my nigga M-Dot started asking questions about this nigga sitting next to me and putting shit together, cause something aint add up. Next thing you know, he got his shit knocked off. Big bruh Psycho aint like this nigga Young Du right here then somehow his shit wind up getting blew off."

"That dust got you niggas high on some paranoid shit sounding just like Psycho."

"Shut the fuck up!" Slugs demanded backhanding Ski.

"Meanwhile, I'm trying to figure out who the fuck this nigga Young Du is cause you been on the scene moving and shaking since like right after new year's."

"But it's real right niggas I did time with who know Young Du pops and his family, and they been getting at me like the nigga Young Du just came home top of the summer," Slugs added, looking at Omar in his mirror as Omar realized the car was now being navigated through dark back roads. "To put it real simple, if y'all aint got no explanation for this shit my mother

249

fucking homie gon blow both you niggas shit off."

"What you mean, y'all?"

"Bitch, you running with this nigga!" Slugs barked on Ski.

"Fuck you been out here damn near a year when niggas out west who know your whole family saying you just came home?"

Silence answered the question, and out the corner of his eye, Slugs caught Ski fidgeting with the door lock, trying to open it.

"Fuck you think you going!" He backslapped the man he'd once called Big Bruh. "That shit aint opening from the inside, bitch ass nigga."

"Slugs, I don't know what the fuck you think going on but..."

"I told you shut the fuck up!" He barked, throwing the man's gun in his face. "A.K., whenever you ready, you know what time it is, bruh."

"I wanna hear what they got to say first."

"They aint got shit to say! We already talked about this, aint no good explanation for whatever weird shit these niggas got going on. You minds well go ahead and bang these niggas."

"I don't think you wanna do that," Omar warned, his voice almost sounding like a whisper.

"What!"

"I don't think you wanna do that unless you wanna go to jail forever."

"Fuck is your man talking about!" A.K. demanded, banging the but of his gun against Ski's head.

"I'm an informant for the Feds."

"Oh shit." A.K.'s eyes opened as wide as doughnuts as he put both barrels in Omar's face.

Slowly, Omar pulled out his smartphone and held it up.

"Everything that was said since I got in this car was recorded, and they are listening, so they already know what's going on."

Still driving, Slugs menacingly looked back and forth from Ski to the road with disgust in his eyes as he smirked.

"You hear this shit! You running around with a rat. Hoe ass nigga! You been with this mother fucker all this time, you can't tell me you aint know he was cop!"

"It aint what you think. I just found out, I was waiting for the right time to... "

"Shut the fuck up! You bitch ass nigga!"

"Give me that shit," A.K. said sitting one gun on his lap as he took Omar's phone.

Now, with one gun trained on Omar and the other two sitting on his lap, A.K. scrolled through the phone. "I don't see shit in here."

"I'm telling you the truth."

"The nigga phone aint gon say 'I'm a fucking rat' right on the screen bruh." Slugs told A.K. "Let me see that shit."

As Slugs took a handoff the wheel to reach for the phone and A.K. moved to hand it to him, Omar swung his right hand up, knocking A.K.'s gun out his face, and the two began to tussle for the weapon.

"Fuck." Slugs groaned, dropping the phone as Ski punched him in the face and went for the gun.

Releasing the steering wheel, he swung back, and they began to wrestle across the center-council for the weapon.

With one hand, Omar had the wrist and back of A.K.'s gun hand pinned up flat against the ceiling as A.K. desperately fought against his strength and tried to point the weapon down at his head. Grabbing the man's neck with his other hand, A.K. squeezed until he felt Omar's grip on his wrist begin to weaken. Then, just as he was able to point the gun down a lil, an unexpected shot went off, sending a projectile up through A.K.'s chin and lodging itself in his head.

With no hands on the steering wheel, the car deviated left and collided with something, jerking its occupants forward as it crashed to a halt.

"Aww," Ski grunted, coming to his senses and looking around moments after the impact.

Instinctively reaching for the door handle, he tried to open it before re-membering Slugs had said it wouldn't open from the inside. Stretching his arm out the passenger side window, Ski braced his palm on the top of the car and lifted his body up through the window.

"Aww shit." He moaned as his body fell hard on the glass-sprinkled pavement.

Struggling to stand, Ski looked down at the blood all over his jeans and realized he'd been shot in the leg just as he realized that he was still holding a gun and had probably shot himself sometime during the tussle for the gun and the collision. Looking into the vehicle, he watched Omar moving around, apparently trying to open his door, and without thinking, Ski began to raise his gun, hand pointing the weapon at Omar.

This was the chance he was waiting for. The idea of just pulling the trigger and killing this rat ass nigga he knew as Young Du flashed through his mind as the cobwebs from the accident began to clear from his head and he heard sirens wailing in the distance. Tapping the rear passenger side window with his barrel, he got Omar's attention before shattering the window with the but of his gun.

Chapter Thirty-Seven

Before they could process what had just happened, U.S. Marshals and state police arrived, grabbing Omar and Ski and throwing them into the back of a large Mercedes Sprinter van. That SUV was followed by another one, and the two government vehicles were led away from the accident by a slew of state police cars.

Ski was dumbfounded by everything that was happening and how quickly things were unfolding. He knew Omar was a rat bastard, but everything that had just happened, and the pace at which things were moving, almost made Ski dizzy.

On one side of Ski Omar sat casually telling the agents everything that had just happened, and on his other side, a Marshal propped up his leg, injecting him with something for pain before verifying that the bullet had come out the other end and stitching him up. He felt like he had been thrown into the weirdest situation as he listened to Omar sit right next to him, freely talking to the agents.

From the day Omar told him that he was working with the FBI and Ski came to the realization that he wasn't going to kill this rat ass nigga he had come to terms with the reality of the situation and gradually thought of some of the weird shit that could happen due to his affiliation with Omar. He'd long ago considered the crazy shit that'd be said about him and all the bizarre situations he'd find himself in as an accomplice to a rat, but this was just different.

Ski didn't think he was fooling himself. He knew that the code of everything he'd once stood for said that helping Omar, vouching for him, and even just remaining silent about him being a rat made him a rat or at least akin to one himself. Call it naiveté or whatever else, but Ski thought he was better than the man seated next to him. As if they were that much different or one was worse than the other.

Omar was a rat running the streets under somebody else's identity to fool gang members into accepting him as one of their own, so they'd engage in all kinds of illegal activities with him. He did this so he could help the Feds send all these gang members to prison. Somehow though Ski'd tricked himself into thinking he wasn't doing the exact same shit.

He conveniently ignored the fact that he was literally helping spy on people and infiltrate mother fuckers he called his homies. Sitting right next to the man, Ski actually looked down on Omar for what he was doing and almost saw himself as a victim of circumstance.

Despite all this, Ski thought he had come to grips with all these things and was ready to face his new reality but listening to Omar shamelessly telling the agents the gory details of everything that had happened tonight made him feel out of place and awkward as fuck. Ski hated himself for winding up in this situation.

With his elbows on his kneecaps trying to drown out their conversation Ski leaned forward burying his face in his hands wondering how the fuck all those cops had even got to them so fast. Omar had told him they were always listening but damn. It was like they had crashed one minute and the very next minute mother fuckers in suits with wires hanging out their ears was pulling them away from the accident and throwing them in a government sprinter van. This and other questions Ski had were answered when one of the agents handed Omar a tablet with a female on the screen.

"Mrs. Jones.

"I need you to listen." The female spoke clearly and directly. "About an hour ago was the last time I spoke with Candy. Our conversation ended abruptly when the call was dropped on her end. I called back and got no answer. We monitor what's happening with you in real time via the audio feed from the microphone in your phone. Her feed ended when the call did, which means the battery was removed. At the same time, we lost her phone's GPS signature. The signal just disappeared. They were in Mississippi at the time, so I spoke with my liaison out there. He deployed units, and a strike team located the cars a short while ago.

"What you mean they found the cars?" Omar asked, looking over to Ski.

"It was eight females with her who were members of the Piru set. They were in three vehicles, with three to a car so they could alternate driving. Through intel, we had all their cell phone information as well. The problem is that all their phones are now going to voicemail, and a GPS tracking of their last coordinates shows they were all together."

Until something happened to their phones.

"Exactly."

"So you think they dead or something?"

"Well, we're not going that far. No bodies have been found, and beyond what I told you, there's no sign of distress. At this point, there's just so much going on that I have to bring you in."

"What you mean, what's going on?"

Helen went on to remind Omar of their last conversation. She told him since then they'd found out that the witness killed outside the Jersey City courthouse was the witness in a separate ongoing case against Neighborhood homies. Even crazier, she reminded him of the comments her coworkers had made about a serial killer. Helen told Omar that they now believed that he was a serial killer and that he was responsible for the murder outside of the courthouse.

She said he'd embraced the name the Rat Hunter that the media had given him, and he was stupid enough to post videos all over social media about the killings. The Rat Hunter was smart enough that they couldn't pinpoint the exact I.P. address he was posting from.

But he wasn't as sharp as he thought he was. Helen said they knew just enough to narrow down his location to a couple of possible places. It all sounded as if they had enough to know that he was in one of a few spots and that they were waiting for him to post another video so they could track him and take him down.

"Now, on another note, I don't want you to go crazy or overreact, but

I have to tell you there was a soft threat made against your grandmother."

"What?"

"Listen, your grandmother is okay. There's a detail outside her house. However, she was approached yesterday by a strange older man as she was leaving church. He told her something like, 'I know your grandson, he's a good guy, and he never forgets to take care of his grandmother or his family. I hope he doesn't forget to take care of my family, too."

"Where this come from?"

"I'm as puzzled as you are. Considering the potential threat to the principals of the case, i.e., you, Candy, and now Ski, I must remove you from the field. As of now, Operation Street Sweeper is concluded. You two are going to a safe house. In the following days, you'll be debriefed, and you and your families will be relocated to witpro. In the meantime, over forty arrest warrants for high-risk targets have already been executed. Throughout the night and in the coming days, over two hundred more will be executed."

Ski just listened in as the conversation between the rat and his handler went on and on. He was shocked to hear about the number of warrants in the case. He'd known about different instances where twenty or thirty homies got caught up in a case, but he'd never heard of anything even close to this. As surprising as that was, he almost had to bite his tongue to keep his mouth closed when he heard Candy's name come up.

Omar had told Ski that he was the only one who knew about what was going on. That being the case, he had never known about Candy being involved. At first, he'd considered it for a moment but dismissed the possibility due to all that had happened between them and the nature of Candy and Omar's relationship. Ski hearing about her involvement in the case the way he just had, considering their sexual relationship, made him hate that bitch.

After Omar told Ski what was going on back in the hospitals parking lot and he gradually got to a place where he reluctantly went along with things there were a few times when he almost threw caution to the wind, said fuck keeping this rat nigga a secret and told Candy everything. This, of course, included his ideas about killing the man. It was fucked up that Candy could be involved in something like this and Ski felt stupid and played for not putting two and two together.

Just over a mile away from the FBI headquarters where Omar and his codefendants were brought for interrogation, and he was turned was a police department. Directly across the street from this downtown Newark precinct was a duplex brownstone that was dubbed as an FBI safe house.

Omar turned up the volume on the tablet, and Helen Jones gave him and Ski the layout of the do's and don'ts of witness protection as one of the Marshals escorted them into the brownstone. As far as they could tell, everything about the building was normal. They couldn't see any extreme security measures in place. Inside, the actual safe house was the same. Everything looked like a typical apartment. Aside from the Marshals sitting outside the brownstone and it being directly across the street from a precinct, there appeared to be no other security.

Immediately after they arrived at the apartment, the U.S. Marshals left, and a few minutes later, Helen told them she had a call she needed to take. Alone in the apartment, Omar and Ski talked about everything, and it didn't take long before emotions and concerns came pouring out.

Omar was dumbfounded about what was going on with Candy. Ski was surprised about it too, but after hearing about her involvement in the case, he had no sympathy for he. That bitch was just as much a rat as Omar was. Though he felt like he needed to act concerned about her well-being to hide his true feelings from Omar, Ski honestly couldn't have cared less about that bitch. She was a rat.

After they had recapped what had happened in the car with Slugs and A.K., Ski got quiet. For a second, he believed that Omar knew he'd been thinking about whether or not he could kill him all along. But the very next second Omar broke the silence telling him he understood that he had to say the shit he did.

Still trying to wrap his mind around everything that was happening, Ski changed the subject to something he actually was worried about—his newborn baby and his baby's mother, Amy.

Helen had told them that to protect the integrity and security of their location, everything concerning them needed to be done with great care. This meant they couldn't communicate with anyone, and due to the circumstances at that moment, the agency wouldn't be able to transport their loved ones securely to them tonight without potentially compromising the integrity of their location.

Checking his pockets for his phone Ski didn't care about none of the security shit that bitch was talking about. His cell phone was missing, though, and he chalked up its loss to it being dropped during the accident until he vaguely remembered being grabbed up by the Marshals, still in a haze on the heels of the accident, and he considered that their hands might have run through his pockets in a quick frisk.

Helen told them their families were safe and that no threats existed because, to everybody else, everything was still normal. The bureau had monitored the telecommunications of everybody who had done any transaction with Omar, Ski, or Candy. That said, it was highly unlikely that they had been labeled food, or a green light had been approved on their lives, because the FBI hadn't heard anything about it.

Helen said, despite the seriousness of the attempt that had already taken place, intel suggested that Slugs and A.K. had gone rogue and acted alone entirely on their own volition. She reminded them that the mission was covert, so nobody could know what was going on with them. She said the only way something could go wrong now was if they panicked and did something stupid.

Ski interpreted all of this to mean that either there wasn't a real serious reason for them to be hauled up in this tight ass apartment like they were hiding from the world. Or, it was a legitimate threat, and because the cops didn't care about their lives, they didn't take the threat seriously enough to make real arrangements to protect them. In his mind, it was likely the latter alternative that explained the lack of security measures they saw.

Ski told Omar that he'd heard everything Helen had said, but he was still worried about his baby's mother. Omar shared these concerns, and even though he wanted to trust Helen's wisdom and not reach out to anyone, he thought about what she'd told him had happened to his grandmother, and a million "what if" questions about his son and his baby mother's safety popped into his head.

Omar didn't have his phone either, but he did have the US Marshal's tablet. Even though he didn't remember anybody's number, it didn't take long before he'd accessed his account on a social media platform and in-boxed Tiffany. In minutes, she responded with the number, and he was calling her.

From the moment Tiffany picked up the phone, she scolded Omar about how he's always doing something without thinking about its effects on her and the baby. She went on and on, and he couldn't even get a word in until he cut her off when she mentioned how it took his brother a long time to think about getting her and the baby to ensure nothing could happen to them.

"Whoa. What the fuck you talking about?" Omar interrupted. "My brother came to get you?"

"What up, bruh?" Omar heard Young Du's voice on the phone. "I don't know if I was out of line or overreacting or whatever, but I had to go get your family. It's some crazy shit going on out here, niggas pulled up on me gripping, with all type of iron out on display looking for you and coming crazy talking about you owing them and being in debt to they family."

"What!"

"Yeah, I know it sounds crazy. It's facts, though, bruh." Young Du said with a nervous chuckle. "Imagine what I was thinking. I knew they had me mistaken for somebody else or something, and when one of them said something about me acting stupid, as if they hadn't had this talk with me before, I thought about what you told me about using my name to do what you've been doing out here. By the time they left, it seemed like they knew I wasn't whoever they thought I was."

"Really?"

"Yeah, I blew your phone up and everything I could do to get in touch with you but..."

"Just like always, you wasn't answering your damn phone." Tiffany chimed in.

"Naturally, I'm thinking about you and what could have happened to you. Then, I'm like, 'oh shit, Tiffany and the baby.'"

"All the shit you don't be thinking about." Tiffany cut in to scold Omar..

Shocked by everything Young Du and Tiffany were saying, Omar was speechless for a second, just listening to the story of his lil brother's encounter with the gunmen. Then, Omar remembered the threat against his grandmother that Helen had told him about, and he made the connection. The threats came from the same people that had blitzed him, Ski and Candy, coming out of the chicken shack in Trenton. It was Psycho's family. The Green family.

Despite all the bad news, Young Du did tell his brother something he was happy to hear about. He said that before he was ambushed, he had just come from the gym where he worked. Today, just by coincidence, he'd had a chance conversation with Run Brim.

Young Du said he was a Runs trainer at the gym, and apparently, after seeing his trainer check a bill someone had given him for its authenticity, the two began chopping it up about fake bills. Young Du, whom Run had known as Trainer Ab, then let it slip that his brother, Young Du, had sold fraudulent bills to Omar. Let Young Du tell it, that was all it took for Run to jump on the phone and arrange a sit down for Young Du with a few of his lil homies at a store that Run owned.

This was music to Omar's ears. Of course, he had wanted to get close to the Brim homies to help his own case, but now, since him and his brother had been in tune with each other, he knew he also needed to fulfill his obligation to the Feds to prove to them that his brother had severed his gang ties.

Omar's mind was all over the place. Getting close to the Brim leadership was exactly what he needed. The timing was completely off, though.

They were in a safe house across the street from a precinct. How the fuck was he supposed to get to a meeting with anybody? If Helen wasn't willing to move things around so their families could be brought to them, he knew she wouldn't be willing to do what was necessary to let them return to the field.

"Why the fuck is we sitting around getting babysat like we need permission to go outside or something?" Ski challenged. "I been in the streets all my mother fucking life. I've never needed a cop to watch my back before, and I don't need them now.

"So what you saying?"

"Your bro already got your baby mother with him so if he came to get us we could grab some money from the storage room and go to the nigga Run spot to bust it up with them niggas. When we're done, I can go get Amy and my daughter, and we can all come back here."

Chapter Thirty-Eight

Omar was ecstatic to escape the safe house and finally be able to end things on his terms. He knew Helen had said she officially ended the investigation, but having things end abruptly without everything being done made him uneasy.

He'd agreed to infiltrate and help the Feds bring down the leadership of the state's biggest Blood sets. And anytime things appeared to be getting rough, or he seemed to be thinking about pulling out, Helen would occasionally remind him that bringing down the leadership of Brim was part of his mandate. Ending it now, as he did, without fulfilling his obligation to the Feds made him feel unsure whether his plea deal would even be honored under these circumstances.

For that reason alone, he didn't feel comfortable ending things without doing all he could to infiltrate Brim. At least if he could make a deal with some of Run's lil homies while Omar believed it would help the Feds get close to Run and the rest of Brims leaders.

Agreeing with Ski was one thing, but Omar and Ski getting out of the safe house and slipping past the detail vehicle outside was something else. Omar wrecked his mind considering the confrontation they'd have with the

Marshals as they tried to slip past them and get in the vehicle with Young Du.

That said, when they finally did get outside, Omar was appalled and even insulted to see that there was no security outside at all. He was already feeling some way about Helen since she'd slipped up and mentioned that they'd executed forty arrest warrants. Why the fuck would they jeopardize his safety and do that with him still running the streets and not even give him a heads up.

That slap in the face, along with the Feds not even knowing that his brother had come home, and this lapse of security made him mad as hell. He realized in that moment that they didn't give a fuck about him and that them catching their man was all they cared about.

The first few minutes inside the vehicle, Omar barely greeted Tiffany and his son because as Young Du pulled away from the curb with him in the passenger seat, he was too busy looking around in sheer surprise. It was hard for him to believe that after everything the FBI had invested in him and the operation, they'd be so careless with his security.

"These mother fuckers aint even out here trying to protect us." Ski's words validated Omar's thoughts and helped snap him out of his trance.

"Don't even worry about that shit bae." Tiffany's comforting voice came from behind the driver seat. "Y'all about to end all this shit tonight, so we don't have to think about these mother fuckers no more."

Pulling out the tablet, Omar called Helen and spoke his mind.

"You know it aint no Marshals or no security or nothing sitting outside that mother fucking safe house?"

Yes, I do know that there are no Marshals. They had to be deployed somewhere else. However, the location is directly across from a precinct; nothing is likely to happen.

"Well, I aint sitting around to find out."

"What do you mean?"

"I mean I aint staying in that lil ass apartment waiting to see if somebody who might wanna kill me is gon be bold enough to find me and come get me."

Are you saying you're not in the safe house?

"Hell no. I seen enough gangster movies and shit to know that's the spot they send the killers to get you. I aint sitting in that dumb ass safe house just waiting to get whacked."

"Omar, listen to me, you don't wanna..."

"You don't even know what I'm doing." He interrupted her. "I'm going to meet some homies that's directly under the Brim nigga Run. They wanna buy some..."

"What? Wait, what are you talking about? Omar, exactly where are you, and who are you even with?"

"I aint getting into all that right now." He answered plainly.

Omar, you have to know that this is not safe. This is not the way to do this..." Helen managed to say before he hung up on her.

"Can't they track them phones or something, bruh?" Young Du asked.

They see where we are; she's gon to send those people to get us before we make it to the deal and long before I get a chance to get Amy and my son.

"If you holding onto that tablet cause you need something to record whatever's said at the meeting you could use my shit."
Young Du offered while buckling his seat belt, but Omar barely paid attention because he was already moved by the worry he heard in Ski's voice.

Without really thinking it through, Omar tossed the tablet out the window as Ski unbuckled his bugged wristwatch and did the same.

"They know everything about this shit dangerous so why the fuck wouldn't they have security outside the house they bring y'all to?"

"Them crackers don't give a fuck about us," Ski answered the driver.

"I'm saying, earlier she was saying something to me about all they lil agents trying to chase down a serial killer or something."

"Serial killer?" Tiffany asked, leaning forward to hand the baby to Omar as the vehicle abruptly accelerated forward, quickly picking up speed.

Then, just as Omar grabbed his son and began swinging him over the center of the jeep, Young Du slammed down on the brakes, abruptly stopping the jeep. Inertia pinned everyone's body back in their seats before they were rammed hard from the back by a van and jerked forward.

Clutching the baby for dear life, Omar's body rocked forward. As his face was pulled toward the dashboard, it seemed as if time stood still, and he could see everything that'd ever happened to him.

In an instant, Omar remembered being a kid and seeing his mother smile for the very first time. He remembered how it'd felt knowing he'd upset her.

He remembered all the times he'd played with his brother and baby sister, as well as all the interactions with their father, Abdul. He remembered all the contempt he'd felt for the man who tried to be his stepfather. As he saw their encounters flash before his eyes, he recalled the anger and animosity that his grandmother and Helen had instilled in him, which ultimately led him to take a stand against Abdul.

Omar seen the day him and Black drove to Jersey City selling guns before they all got arrested. He saw himself speaking with Helen and remembered knowing that he couldn't go to prison, or he'd die. He had seen all the moves and deals he'd made in Northern state prison to prove to the Feds that he was serious and could handle a covert operation. He'd seen everything he'd done on the streets and everybody he'd met with to infiltrate different groups and further the investigation.

He even saw the day he and his brother spoke about Abdul senior, and the last thing he remembered was the feeling he'd had when his brother told him that his father, Abdul, wasn't mad at him. That was the last memory he had before the collision; everything then went black.

Losing consciousness, and Omar had no real distinguishable concept of time. But after a while, he felt his body being pulled from the vehicle, and he began to come to.

"Take these fucking clothes off!"

"Cop ass nigga!" Somebody barked on him pulling the clothes from his body.

Looking up at his assailant's face, Omar was surprised when he realized it was Itchy-Ru. Before he could even think about resisting, another man walked up and stood over him. But just as the familiar face began to register as Taliban's brother Charley, the man struck him across the face with the butt of a gun knocking him back out.

At this point, from Omar's perspective, everything was happening in flashes. It was almost as if he were seeing through the lens of a camera. The shudder would open, and he'd see a few seconds before blanking out again until the figurative shutter opened again.

A minute later, Omar opened his eyes just in time to see the jeep they'd rode in go up in flames. Somewhere along the line, Omar had been thrown into a van, and he briefly came to again as his naked, hog-tied body slid back and forth across the floor of a van as it swerved in and out of traffic.

When Omar fully awoke, he was naked and tied down to a chair. The room was dark, but he immediately knew he was in the living room of Tiffany's apartment. In a chair next to him, Omar saw Ski tied down just like him, but he was still knocked out. On the floor in front of him, he saw what looked like a man with his back turned to him squatting over something. For a second, he thought it might be his brother Young Du, but as his eyes began to adjust to the darkness, he made out a naked body on the floor in front of the hunched-over man. It was a female's body.

"Tiffany!" He yelled before Charley stepped from behind him and punched him in the face.

"Long time no see. What's it been, about a year now?"

"What the fuck is you niggas doing?"

"What the fuck is going on?" Ski grunted, waking up.

"If you niggas think you in a position to ask questions you aint paying attention."

"What the fuck is he over there doing to my baby mother?"

"Don't worry about your bitch bruh." Wee-Wee stood up and turned around holding a syringe "I'm a good nigga dawg, I aint no creep. I'm just making sure she relaxed, helping her enjoy her mother fucking self."

"I know you aint shoot no dope in my baby mother!"

"Why the fuck wouldn't I? Nobody wanna put up with all that crying shit. Like I said, I gave her something to help her enjoy herself."

"Why the fuck am I tied down naked!" Ski yelled

"Shhhh." Itchy-Ru quieted the room as he walked in, carrying Omar's baby. "If you niggas wasn't running around wearing wires and shit trying to record every mother fucking thing so you could send niggas to jail you probably could of had your clothes on while we have this talk. But I aint trust shit you niggas had with y'all. Aint no telling where you hoe ass niggas let the law put a mic at to record something."

"So what the fuck you niggas want, why y'all got..."

"I aint here to be answering your questions, going back and forth or none of that goffy shit." Itchy cut off Omar, silencing the room as he pulled out a revolver. "We aint got time to be in here playing with you mother fuckers and I'm zero tolerance for bull shit. I'ma say all this shit one time and if you mother fuckers wanna make it out of here you gon shut the fuck up and listen."

"But what the fuck is..." Omar began, and Itchy quieted him, sitting the barrel of the four-four python in his mouth.

"You don't need to ask no questions, just shut the fuck up and listen."

"Aight, but y'all got us in here naked and tied the fuck up so why you gotta keep waving guns around and shit?" Ski asked, and Itchy calmly swung the gun in his direction and put a bullet in his forehead.

The room erupted as Tiffany screamed out loud in fear, regaining consciousness, and Omar began to cry.

"You and your baby mother can still make it out of here with your mother fucking son. Y'all can be a lil family, live happily ever after and all that good shit. You might even see your mother fucking brother again but only if you shut the fuck up and don't make the same mistake he did. Aight?" Itchy-Ru demanded.

Slowly, Tiffany's wails became whimpers, and Omar sniffled dry blood from his nose, quieting his cries. With the barrel of Itchy's gun back in his mouth, Omar looked up at Itchy and slowly shook his head up and down.

"Aight then." He said, tucking the weapon away.

Handing the crying baby to Charley, Itchy pulled out a cell phone and wireless ear pods and approached Omar.

"We about to stream you live on Facebook 'cause I got a public announcement for you to make. You only got one chance to get it right so I'ma put this in your ear and you gon be told exactly what the fuck to say. But I'm telling you now, if you slip up and say the wrong shit or if you look too nervous on camera like you scared or being pressured or if you do anything else even by accident not to sell my mother fucking message exactly the way I want it I aint gon hesitate, try to correct you or give you another chance. I'm pulling this trigger and putting every bullet from this four-four in your mother fucking head."

"Get up bitch!" Wee-Wee barked, reaching down to grab Tiffany's bare breast. "You coming with me?" He demanded, pulling her out of the room by her hair as she whined in protest.

With a wet wipe, Charley wiped Omar's face clean to get him camera-ready as Itchy pulled up a chair and sat right in Omar's face. Resting the barrel of his gun under Omar's chin, Itchy looked into the man's eyes and spoke plainly.

"I see the way you looked at your baby mother when she got dragged out the room. I know you worried about her and what the fuck Wee-Wee doing to her in the room, but you don't need to think about them right now. If you think about your baby mother and your son that shit gon show on your face or you gon fuck up and I don't need none of that to happen. You don't need it to happen. I want y'all to walk out of here but if you think about your son or baby mother while we live, and any bull shit happen you already know I'm knocking your fucking head off and they gon get the same shit if not worse. This shit could end happily ever after, or it could be a massacre in this mother fucker. Just clear your mind, say exactly what the fuck you told and all this shit gon be over."

Minutes later, Charley walked out with the baby, and the room fell silent. Itchy put the phone's camera in Omar's face, and the live streaming began.

"What's up, world? What's going on? This gon be a lil confessional session." Omar slowly began repeating what Charley told him in his ear. "A year ago, I was recruited by the Feds to help them in an investigation called Operation Street Sweeper. They wanted me to infiltrate the Bloods, and they gave me drugs, guns, and fake money. They set up fake truck heists for me to use to make transactions with members of different Blood sets, and they even allowed me to get away with murder. They did all this so I could help them entrap mother fuckers and I went along with it like a coward. I was lower than a coward. A bitch. To do this, I lied to mother fuckers who called me they homie and I even lied to the Feds and manufactured evidence against some of the mother fuckers they wanted so that I could help them end this operation. I betrayed every mother fucker who called me they homie, every mother fucker who deserved my loyalty and everything any real mother fucker stand for. I'm disgusted with myself. I did all kinds of hoe shit and every type of dishonorable deed that could be done. No man for any reason should ever do any of the fuck boy shit I did. For this I'm a rat, lower than scum and I don't deserve to live."

Just as Omar finished the last word, Itchy tapped the phone's screen, muting the sound of the video stream.

"Call yourself my mother fucking brother." Omar heard a familiar voice come from behind Itchy-Ru and was dumbfounded when Young Du stepped forward, waving a gun around as he spoke. "I don't give a fuck about you coming out my mother's pussy, you took the stand against my mother fucking father nigga. Then you ran the streets telling mother fuckers you was me. Nigga you a bitch! You a rat! You the opposite of me! You doing all type of hoe shit to send niggas to jail and I'm out this bitch exterminating niggas like you."

As recognition and fear washed over Omar's face, the real Young Du pointed his gun down at his brother and pulled the trigger.

"I'm the rat hunter bitch!"

<u>THE END</u>

-

Extra

You can find Street Sweeper Chronicles Dishonorable Deeds
and other titles from Top of the Line Publishing @
Facebook: facebook.com/totlp2020
Instagram: topofthelinepublishing
Snapchat: topofthelinepub
TikTok: topofthelinepublishing
Goodreads: Top of the line Publishing